BILLY HOUSTON

RAGS TO RICHES

BY
GREG HOLMAN

DISCLAIMER

COPYRIGHT

Also by Greg Holman

BILLY HOUSTON
FALL FROM GRACE

CHAPTER 1

IT WAS THE middle of July, and yet another hot day in Bangkok.

For the last couple of months, my life had consisted of a seemingly continual progression of trips—from the island of Koh Samui, where I was living, to Bangkok for meetings with my Thai lawyers and accountants.

I was embarking on yet another business venture—but this time, I'd already told myself it would be my final one.

Just four more years of hard work and I could have it up and running, ready to sell for a tidy sum. I'd be fifty-five years old by then—and then it would finally be time to slow down and smell the roses.

My new business idea was to conquer the world of fitness, diet, and gym apparel in Southeast Asia—a market of over 600 million people, with one of the highest uptakes of new Internet connections on the planet.

The digital revolution was about to hit the area hard, and I'd seen an opportunity to combine mobile apps with the fitness revolution I believed would soon sweep across Southeast Asia. With the enormous growth of the middle class in that region, I saw an opportunity to make some serious money.

That's the kind of opportunity I've always got an eye for—I'm a serial entrepreneur.

The press in New York described me as a "Business Builder", but I think it's more that I have a knack for being able to see what consumers want in advance of everybody else—well, most of the time, at least.

My focus in the past had been the world of tax and financial services. That might sound boring to most people, but believe me—there was a truckload of money to be made in those two industries.

My first business started as a tax and accounting refront in Santa Monica, California, with just one employee—me. Within eight years, I'd franchised my ble brand to over two-hundred-and-eighty fronts across America—and made a bucketload of y along the way.

My next venture was inspired by the saying: "It's where life can take you." That morphed into an when I realized that many people in America had a of where to invest their surplus savings. I built a ss out of that – and soon, I had over eight- ed licensed advisors across America all working my umbrella; known as Future Wealth.

ture Wealth has since been acknowledged as one leading providers of financial planning advice for -class Americans – and along the way, I gifted equity in the business to key staff—about fifty in total. Everyone made a nice amount of money. Just over fifteen months ago, Future Wealth was listed on the New York Stock Exchange. The share price has continued to rise since listing and has made a lot of people very wealthy.

Future Wealth was my retirement package. The lure of Choeng Mon, on the island of Koh Samui—the second largest island in Thailand—became a reality for me as a result; after many, many years of hard work and a lot of stress.

After spending a couple of months lying on the beach in Koh Samui, the creative juices came flowing back. Many close friends thought I should write a book and share my experiences. We all have a story to tell, perhaps some more interesting than others.

I should also mention that my entrepreneurial creative juices started flowing again, too – and I started another business, which turned out to be an absolute disaster. I started Future Wealth inspired by an old saying, but there's another one I should have remembered, too: "Stick to what you know, and you'll make lots of money."

Well, as smart as many people think I am, I'd failed to follow my own advice—and so *lost* a lot of money, instead. A bit more about that later.

Throughout my business career, my best friend, Pat Gabriel, has always partnered with me. We first met as fourteen-year-old boys at Santa Monica High School. Pat's now a lawyer, incredibly smart and an expert in franchising – which has proven to be an invaluable skill in building our businesses. We've shared many high and lows together over the years. We've become more like brothers than friends, and we trust each other completely.

Along the way, I've also had three divorces. Yep, each business cost me a wife – and they've cost me a lot of money. The problem is that in addition to being an entrepreneur, I'm also a workaholic – and when I'm building a business, I tend to develop tunnel vision and focus on the business instead of on the wife.

In addition to the three ex-wives, I also forgot to mention my Thai girlfriend. That didn't last too long either – which leads me to wonder: Given all the failed relationships I've had, perhaps *I'm* the problem, not them.

• • •

I ARRIVED IN the foyer of the new, state-of-the-art Bangkok Central Building – home to most of the leading lawyers and accountants in Bangkok. As I arrived, I grumbled to the concierge that it was too bloody hot outside. I was covered in perspiration, so the concierge passed me a cold, damp towel to wipe my face and neck with.

My phone rang as I stood in the foyer. It was Cynthia Fleming, from World Focus Publishing. I'd promised Cynthia I'd call her the previous week, and this was the third time she'd tried to call me since then. I knew she wasn't happy with me.

I answered the phone, apologizing profusely.

"Hi, Cynthia. Listen, I'm sorry I didn't get back to you earlier – *really* sorry. I've just been swamped with some family matters." That was a lie. I'd been devoting all my recent energy to my new business venture.

"Billy, we really need to see the manuscript of your book now," Cynthia demanded. "We need to be published by the end of October to launch the book in time for the Christmas sales. World Focus took a big, big punt on you, Billy. We agreed to publish you based on your life story, even though you'd never written a book before. That's a big gamble. We also advanced you $500,000, which is unheard of for a guy who's never written a book before. We did all that based on who you are, and the successes you've had in corporate America – but we need this manuscript *now*. You promised me I'd have it by the end of July. That's only fourteen days away. That was our contractual agreement, Billy."

"I've nearly finished it, Cynthia," I lied. "I just need a couple more weeks."

"Billy, my directors at World Focus are starting to get nervous," she warned me. "They're starting to doubt my judgment, given how I went out on a limb for you after hearing your story and undertaking all that research on you. I told them you could be the next big-time author – that we'd be missing an opportunity if we didn't back you. Now, you're making me nervous. If my judgment proves wrong, I might be out of a job at World Focus Publishing – and perhaps forced out of publishing forever."

"I appreciate you backing me, Cynthia. I'll have the final draft to you within the next two weeks, I promise. I've just got to rush off to a meeting now." I made my excuses and hung up, rushing into the elevator for my 2pm meeting with my Thai lawyers and accountants.

As the lift carried me upward, I thought about what an eventful day it had already been.

Earlier that morning, I'd taken a phone call from Tom Carroll. Tom was the previous chairman of Future Wealth – but I'd had no personal contact with Tom since our eventful meeting two days before the stock exchange listing of Future Wealth went live, some fifteen months earlier.

I hadn't been going to answer the phone when Tom's name came up on the screen, but instinct got the better of me. I found that I'd automatically picked up before I'd properly registered that I'd be taking his call.

"Why would you ever bother calling me, Tom?" I answered the phone tersely. My disdain for the man was obvious. "Pat and I both told you we never wanted to have anything to do with you ever again."

"Billy," Tom replied, "I need to ask you for a favor."

"A favor?" I shook my head. "Leave me alone, Tom. Don't ever call me again."

I'd hung up on him while rushing to the terminal to catch the early morning flight from Koh Samui to Bangkok. I couldn't believe Tom Carroll had the audacity to ask me for a favor after what had transpired between the two of us.

No thanks to Tom Carroll, I was still a major shareholder in Future Wealth – having cashed out only about half of my stock over the course of the last twelve months. It was a smart bet to stay invested. When Future Wealth had been initially listed on the New

York Stock Exchange, we'd over eight hundred advisors across America. Under the chairmanship of Pat Gabriel, the business now had over a thousand.

Pat and I had spent eight years building Future Wealth. The first five years had been an absolute joy. The last three had been a nightmare.

I'm a big believer in karma, though – and it all worked out in the end. The only downside was that it had nearly killed me along the way. My brain had been fried, and I'd suffered a major mental breakdown. It wasn't diagnosed at the time, but my breakdown resulted from the stress of too much hard work, three failed marriages, the failure of one of my businesses, and – of course – the problems at Future Wealth Ltd.

More about that later.

• • •

EVERY STORY BEGINS somewhere, and the foyer of the Bangkok Central Building is as good a place as any to start telling this one. However, before I begin, I should also mention that I'm an Australian by birth. In fact, I'd spent my first thirteen years growing up in Melbourne – barracking for the mighty Essendon Football Club, commonly known as the Bombers.

It wasn't until I was thirteen that I first arrived in the mighty USA, where I spent the first year living in Washington D.C. My father was a diplomat there, based at the Australian Embassy. As the son of a diplomat, I attended a school in Washington for twelve months – one which catered exclusively to the children of the Australian and British diplomats and their staff in

America's capital city. It was a somewhat sheltered introduction into the American way of life.

That changed when Mum and Dad broke up – after Mum met a B-list, budding Hollywood actor who lived in Los Angeles. At the age of fourteen, I moved with Mum to Santa Monica and started at Santa Monica High, which was a great school. I was the only Aussie kid – but I soon became Americanized. I still had the laid-back, Australian sense of humor, but I quickly came to love the USA. To me, it was the land of dreams, ambition, and reward – and remains so to this day.

Yep, I've packed a lot into my life – a lot of good things, and some bad things. For better or for worse, this is my story – and as important as that day in the Bangkok Central Building was, perhaps I should start it even earlier – at Santa Monica High.

It was there that I displayed the first signs of my entrepreneurial spirit – and experienced the first of many mishaps in my life.

CHAPTER 2

FOR A SHY, young Aussie kid, coming to Santa Monica to attend high school was an experience I'd never forget. At fourteen years old, I was different to all the other kids. I spoke differently, dressed differently, and was the typical Aussie kid from Melbourne – who'd grew up with two dreams: To play cricket for Australia, and football for the mighty Bombers in the Victorian Football League.

At Santa Monica High, like all high schools across America, the preferred sports were gridiron football, baseball, and basketball. Try and explain to an American kid that Australia's national summer sport was cricket – and that a game could go on for five days straight, still with the possibility of there being no winner! The typical response I'd got was: "Fuck me. You Aussies are weird."

There was a lot more freedom for students at Santa Monica High than I'd ever experienced back in Australia. The kids there seemed much more advanced in all aspects of life compared to me – but one thing I did have going for me was my laid-back Aussie attitude and humor.

Soon, the students in my classes warmed up to me. They loved my accent and loved hearing about my experiences growing up in a country of only twenty million people. I was something different – something novel. I was the kid from the Land Down Under.

It didn't take too long for me to acquire a close group of American friends. There was Chook Burns, a long-haired and fun-loving surfer. He taught me how to surf – and before long, we'd spend every weekend down in Malibu catching waves and hanging out with young, hot American chicks.

Chook's real name was Ben Burns. He never told anyone where the name Chook came from, aside from claiming it was a family secret. He could have been a professional surfer, but unfortunately got messed up with drugs later in life. In fact, we both eventually got expelled from Santa Monica High – although I'm sure we weren't the first students to ever be expelled, and we certainly weren't the last, either. Chook and I have remained close friends for the rest of our lives.

Roger "the Dodger" Freeman was also part of our crew. He was one of those guys who always had a story or joke to tell, and the sort of guy everyone warmed to at a party. He wasn't too gifted academically, and he came from a family who lived on the poverty line, but we liked him. Seven years later, Roger would be behind the wheel of the car in which one of our best friends died.

The final member of our little crew was Pat Gabriel. Pat was a quiet, unassuming guy who was the smartest of all of us. He was a gifted student and was always at the top of his class. Later in life, he'd become involved in all but one of my business ventures.

So, Chook, Roger the Dodger, Pat, and I used to hang out at school, after school, and on weekends. Of course, there were other kids we hung out with—both male and female, and black, white, Hispanic, or Asian. They were all part of the scene at one point or another – and would drop in and out of the group as the years went by. Skin color and race weren't an issue with our group of friends. Everyone was treated as an equal.

Freshman, Sophomore and Junior years at Santa Monica High rushed past. While I wasn't the smartest kid in class, I nevertheless found school easy – managing to get above-average grades without putting in too much effort. I'd become assimilated into the American way of life and loved the lifestyle and attitude of my American friends. Australia soon became a distant memory – and after four years living in America, I felt as American as any other kid at Santa Monica High. That being said – according to my American friends, I still had the funny Australian accent—which is an accent I still have today. When I walk into most business meetings, the first thing a person asks me while shaking my hand is still: "Are you Australian?"

In my Senior year at Santa Monica High, I first displayed my entrepreneurial talent. A family had moved into the same condo block that my mother and I shared with her B-list actor boyfriend. The oldest son in this family was Benny – a somewhat-troubled, twenty-one-year-old who'd lived in various foster homes for wayward kids growing up. Benny was unemployed and broke – and despite he and I being very different, we hit it off right away. Once or twice a week, we'd sit in the park across the road from our houses and just chew the fat.

Benny would share his life problems with me—the fact he had no money, no girlfriend, and – in his eyes – no future. I guess I became a sounding board for him.

In California, the legal drinking age is twenty-one – and I had a small business opportunity for Benny.

"Benny – do you want to make some money doing me and Chook Burns a favor?"

"Yeah, man – providing it doesn't require too much work." One of the reasons Benny had no job, and subsequently no money, was because he was averse to doing too much actual work.

"Mate," I told him – an Australian term for someone who's a friend, "I'm thinking of running a little side business at school, selling raffle tickets. The winners get a supply of alcohol. As you know, Benny – we all like to party down at the beach on Friday and Saturday nights, but the problem is we can't get alcohol. I was thinking you could buy the alcohol for me, and the winners of my raffle could pop around to your condo after school and pick their winnings up from you. I'll pay you a small retainer – fifty bucks per week – to get the alcohol and distribute it for me. It'll be the easiest money you'll ever make."

So, before long, Chook Burns and I were selling raffle tickets to more than fifty kids at Santa Monica High each week – and with some forward planning, we expanded this little racket until we had kids in neighboring schools also buying tickets. Within four months, we were making five hundred dollars in profit every week, just between the two of us. Our only costs were the alcohol itself, and Benny's fee. Benny wasn't too smart and he never asked for an increase in his fee, even though the amount of weekly alcohol he was buying went up tenfold over the next few months. We soon had a network of kids in the Santa Monica neighborhood selling tickets for us, and we just gave them free alcohol in exchange.

Through this little venture, I first learned about leverage, processes, and distribution— all things that would serve me well in my future business ventures. These were tricks of the trade I'd never have learned by attending business classes at school. Chook and I soon realized that the more kids we had selling raffle tickets for us, the more money we could make. We also discovered that we needed the seller of each book of raffle tickets to work off a script to ensure the sale. We needed a consistent approach across our ticket sales team – which soon numbered more than thirty kids; twenty-eight boys and a handful of girls.

We knew that as this racket expanded, so did the risk of getting caught – and the entire money-making venture would come crashing down if that happened.

And that's exactly what *did* happen. After eight months of making really good money each and every week, in addition to mastering the concepts of leveraging, distribution, and process, it all came crashing down. One of our ticket sellers had sold raffle tickets to some fourteen-year-old girls from the neighboring Fleetwood High – despite being explicitly instructed that only high school seniors could buy tickets. As a further measure on our part, when the winners of each weekly draw went to Benny's to collect the alcohol they'd won, they needed to produce ID to show they were at least seventeen years of age.

Well, these girls knew Benny would never give them the alcohol because they were too young, so they organized for one of the girl's sisters – who was eighteen – to pick up the alcohol from Benny using their winning ticket.

Long story short – these girls, five of them in total, took their winnings down to Santa Monica Beach on Friday night and got absolutely wasted. I'm assuming it was the first time they'd ever sampled alcohol, because two of the girls drank so much they passed out and an ambulance had to be called.

The sister who'd collected the alcohol for them confessed to her parents what she'd done – and how she'd picked up the alcohol from Benny. The concerned parents had then phoned the Santa Monica Police Department.

I'd been sitting at home the following Saturday when I'd first heard the sound of police sirens getting louder. Then, I'd heard the screech of brakes – followed by pounding on Benny's front door. The police were screaming: "Santa Monica Police! Open up before we break down the door."

Understandably, Benny opened the door – and quickly told the police about the whole scheme, along with the fact that Chook Burns and I were the two masterminds behind it. Within twenty minutes of the police knocking on Benny's door, they were knocking on mine.

Chook and I got into a lot of trouble. The police had initially planned to press formal charges and take us to court. Thankfully, due to some parental pressure – not to mention Chook's family having some sway with the authorities – they decided not to press charges. However, that all hinged on Chook and I both being expelled from Santa Monica High.

Both Roger the Dodger and Pat remained to graduate from Santa Monica High, and they both got accepted into UCLA. Roger studied marketing, while Pat started a business degree.

Much to both our parents' disdain, Chook and I embraced our expulsion by dedicating our lives to surfing and partying. One thing neither the police or the staff at Santa Monica High realized was just how big our raffle selling business had become – or how much money we'd made over the last eight months—all cash, and completely tax free. So, we each had a nice little stash to last us at least six months and allow us to have a lot of fun in the meantime.

• • •

"HEY, BILLY," CHOOK had suggested one night after we'd been expelled. "Let's get Roger the Dodger and Pat together and head down to Tommy's for a wild night.

His parents are still overseas, so we could get a couple of those senior girls from Fleetwood High to join us."

"Yeah man, count me in."

Billy was the name Chook Burns had given me. My real name was William, but only my mother called me that – and only when I was in some kind of trouble. The name I went by with everybody else was Bill – but Chook told everyone that Billy rolled off the tongue far easier.

For the six months following our expulsion from Santa Monica High, life became one big party fueled by a lot of marijuana and alcohol. With the occasional girl thrown in, plus a lot of surfing, life was stress free and easy. The two biggest decisions I had to make each day were what time I should go out surfing, and what time I should have my first drink or joint afterwards.

There were a lot of hangovers and arguments with my mum and her B-list actor boyfriend—who I despised—about getting a job or going back to school. I had no intention of doing either.

That day at Tommy's, Pat said to me: "Billy, what the fuck you are doing with your life? Out of all of us— Roger the Dodger, Chook, and myself – you were always the guy full of ideas; always saying how you'd make your first million by the age of thirty. Now, you're always drunk and stoned. You're fucking up your life – and I know Chook is dabbling in hard drugs now. Tell me you're not doing the same, Billy?"

"No, Pat, I'm not doing hard drugs – but I am struggling, mate. Struggling to find my purpose in life. I'm not stupid enough to do hard drugs. I've warned Chook it'll only be a downward spiral for him if he keeps it up. Before he knows it, he'll be hooked on them."

I leaned in closer to Pat to explain further:

"Chook had some bad news six weeks ago," I told him. "You know his passion has always been surfing? With the goal of getting on the professional tour? Well, Mike Jedinak, the head of Star Surf, just told Chook they were going to take his sponsorship away. Jedinak said there were younger kids on the circuit now, who had more promise. That's why Chook's been on a bit of a bender the last few weeks. He's been hanging out with Benny and starting to mix with a pretty bad crowd."

I saw the anxious expression on Pat's face.

"Anyway," I reassured him. "I understand what you're saying, Pat. I do need to turn my life around – just not yet."

The truth was, I still had a bit more money left in the bank to enjoy myself with, left over from my high school business venture. When that was gone, then I'd worry about the future.

• • •

TWO MONTHS EARLIER, with the help of my mum – who I loved and adored, but constantly argued with - I'd been accepted to attend a local GED program, so I could graduate and meet the requirements to attend college. I'd showed up on the Monday to enroll and there were literally hundreds of other kids all doing the same. By the time I'd gone from the back of the queue to the front, the first question I'd asked was how to defer. I was having too much fun partying – and I'd decided I wasn't ready to attend college yet, not for at least another six months.

During the months that followed, there were plenty more hangovers and arguments with my mum and her B-list actor boyfriend about what the fuck I was doing with my life.

I was smart enough to know that when the time was right, I'd stop the partying and go to college. I still had the burning goal of making my first million by the time I was thirty.

However, I couldn't possibly have known – and nor could anyone else – about the two major events that would take place in just a couple of years' time; and send me completely off the rails.

CHAPTER 3

FLASH FORWARD A few years. Pat, Roger the Dodger, and I were sitting in the courtyard at UCLA, chewing the fat.

I turned to Pat:

"Hey, remember our conversation about three years ago – when you'd asked me what the fuck I was doing with my life?"

"Yeah, Billy, I remember," Pat snorted. "I'm proud of you, man, for sorting things out and joining me and Roger at UCLA. I'm just sad Chook got messed up in hard drugs for all those years."

I shook my head. "Mate, it's something I think about every day. If only he hadn't lost that surf sponsorship. That devastated him. Chook had been dreaming about being a professional surfer since he was six."

"You know, guys," Roger said, "he and I have known each other since we were toddlers, always living around the corner from each other. When I'd be out playing basketball in the park with the other kids, he'd always been down at the beach with his older brothers, surfing all day long. He'd tell us all how he'd make it to the pros one day."

Sadly, that hadn't gone as planned for Chook.

Many of our plans had changed over the last few years. Pat was in the final year of his bachelor's degree, with plans to complete a law degree afterward. He was a smart guy, and I always knew he'd have a distinguished legal career if he pursued that path.

Roger the Dodger, meanwhile, had failed the first year of three different degree courses. We all felt like he'd end up a full-time student for the rest of his life – until the powers that be eventually kicked him out of the California College system entirely for failing one too many times.

As for me? I was in my third year at UCLA, about to complete a major in Business Studies. Yep, I'd got my GED, been accepted into UCLA, and slowed down on the partying just like I'd said I would.

Life had been toughest for poor Chook Burns. He was still partying hard and picking up casual work wherever and whenever he could. The good news was a couple of weeks earlier, he told me he'd been clean from hard drugs for the last three months. We all hoped and prayed it would stay that way.

• • •

CHOOK BURNS, PAT, Roger the Dodger and a couple of old mates – Tommy Jones and Leroy Smith – were all meeting up for a few drinks at my house. It was the first time in about six months the old crew had all been back together.

I was still living at home with Mum at the time, while I studied full time at UCLA. She'd broken up with her longtime boyfriend by then, who still hadn't cracked it for a major gig in any movies. She was in Vegas for the week, recovering from the breakup – so tonight had promised to be a big night of drinking for my old mates from Santa Monica High.

Yep, the boys were drinking hard – and by 10pm, a couple of the girls who'd been with us had decided to head home, as they had to work the next day. Aside from Chook, the rest of us we were all college students – and none of us had any classes the next day.

By midnight, we'd run out of grog – another Australian term, meaning alcohol.

Tommy mentioned that Charlie Wright, an old friend of ours who lived fifteen minutes away, was having a party that night as well. One quick call to Charlie confirmed he had plenty of both grog and women – so it was a no brainer to hop into a car and get to Charlie's for more drinking and partying.

Roger the Dodger offered to drive. "I haven't had that much to drink, and my car is right out front anyway."

"Count me out, boys," Leroy said. "I need to get home. I've got an assignment due tomorrow."

So, it was just five of us – Pat, Chook, Tommy, Roger the Dodger, and I – who'd piled into Roger's car.

Chook sat in the front, I sat in the back behind Roger, while Pat was in the middle and Tommy sat next to Pat.

The drive to Charlie's house should have taken us fifteen minutes – but we never made it. On the way, a car heading toward us crossed the white line onto our side of the road. Roger was forced to veer off the road, causing us to hit a telephone pole full on.

This was California, back in 1988. There were generally no seat belts in the back of cars at that time, and if there were – nobody wore them. If we'd have known what was going to happen that night, we'd have changed our minds.

Our car was a complete write-off. Roger managed to get out of the car via the driver's door, somehow relatively unscathed. Chook was hemmed into the front passenger seat. Later, he'd have to be cut out of the wreckage by the fire department. The fact that he'd been wearing a seat belt saved his life.

Pat had bounced right between the two bucket seats up front and broke both his hip and his leg, also cutting his head badly. I managed to free myself from the wreckage, blood pouring from my face. I was in a state of complete shock. Tommy appeared unconscious.

The car that forced us off the road had sped straight off. The driver was never found.

Ambulances and police arrived within a matter of minutes. Except for Chook, the four of us were laid down on stretchers and rushed to the hospital. Chook joined us there once the fire department had cut him from the wreckage.

Unfortunately, Tommy never regained consciousness. Our friend died in the hospital less than twenty-four hours later.

Roger was discharged the next day, but was in a state of shock so severe, it lasted for many months. As the driver of the car, he'd carry a scar on his heart for the rest of his life. While the accident wasn't his fault – and despite being under the legal blood alcohol limit – he'd never overcome the remorse he felt for the loss of Tommy's life.

Pat was discharged from the hospital after a week. He made a full recovery.

Chook had his head and face stitched up. After about six months, the massive headaches he'd experienced after the crash finally ceased. As for me? Well, I had to spend about three weeks in the hospital. As I'd mentioned, the rear of the car had no seat belts – and on impact, my face had hit the back of the driver's seat full on. The windscreen of the car had shattered and I'd caught most of the glass right in my face. Every bone in my face was broken, and most of my teeth were shattered or shorn in half.

Mum rushed back from Vegas as soon as she'd heard about the accident. She arrived at the hospital at around 3pm, less than fifteen hours after the crash. I was in a room with one other patient. When Mum arrived, the nurse told her I was in Room 3C – but when Mum walked into the room, she immediately left; telling the nurse she must have the wrong room as she didn't see me in there.

The nurse had taken my mum's arm, pointed in my direction, and whispered: "That's your son – over there, in that bed."

I was completely unrecognizable.

Since I'd suffered massive facial injuries, my face had ballooned to the size of a basketball and was black and blue, and heavily bandaged. Mum became distraught at the sight of me and fainted in front of the nurse.

Initially, they couldn't operate on my face as I had internal bleeding behind my left eye, and they were concerned I'd lose the sight in that eye. Because the bones around my left eye socket were so badly broken, they'd later remove some bone from my right hip to rebuild it.

My nose had been hanging off my face, and because of the deep cuts on the rest of my face, I'd later be required to have plastic surgery – with hundreds of stiches patching my face back together. To aid the healing process, I also had to wear a steel frame attached to my face, screwed directly to my forehead.

My jaw had been so badly broken they'd had to use a new form of technology which involved them inserting a wire below my chin, which they passed an electric current through. This wire was powered by a small transistor -sized package, which I'd had to carry in the top pocket of my shirt once I was discharged from the hospital. I'm not sure if the new technology actually worked or not, but it would leave a scar under my chin I'd have for the rest of my life – right where the wire had been embedded.

My teeth would take over ten months to be fully repaired, requiring a couple of bridges and extensive dental work. I now have an adverse reaction whenever I visit the dentist.

Because of the severe nature of my facial injuries, I actually became something of an exhibit for the surgeons – who'd use me to demonstrate to their medical students which techniques they'd pioneered to repair my face. No doubt I'm lucky to be alive – and I'm certainly grateful for the staff at Los Angeles Hospital for repairing my face.

In the end, I was incredibly fortunate I didn't lose my sight. I was just lucky they'd managed to control the internal bleeding behind my left eye.

However, the most painful part of my injuries were my exposed teeth. There was no painkiller strong enough to reduce that pain. After being discharged from the hospital, I spent the next three months at home in recovery. My jaw was wired shut, and I spent weeks eating via a syringe through the gaps in my mouth where my missing teeth were supposed to be. Because of the bone graft from my right hip, I had to use a cane for about a month.

Unfortunately, Pat, Chook, and I were unable to attend Tommy's funeral to give him a proper farewell, as none of us were in a fit state to be discharged from the hospital at that point. Roger did attend – but was distraught throughout, at one point on the verge of collapsing.

Even after being released from hospital, I still had to go back for weekly checkups. It was at one of these checkups that they discovered I still had glass from the windscreen buried in my upper right arm. They suggested I have it removed – but also mentioned there wouldn't be any future repercussions if I chose not to, since the glass would be covered by scar tissue in any case.

Today, at fifty-one years of age, I still have a lump at the top of my right arm where the glass remains buried.

A few scars on my face remain, too – and my left eye socket sags. I jokingly tell everyone that I could have been an attractive soul if it wasn't for the car accident.

There's a saying: Everything happens for a reason. Well, I'm not sure what the reason was for our car accident – or the tragic loss of Tommy, at the age of just twenty-one – but a couple of years after the accident, Chook, Pat, Roger, and I agreed that every twelve months we'd get together to honor Tommy's life.

Some thirty years later, this get-together still takes place. However, due to the sad and recent death of Roger, from cancer, only Pat, Chook, and I get together now.

CHAPTER 4

GIVEN THE AMOUNT of time I'd spent in hospital, and then recovering from my injuries at home, I was forced to defer the final year of my studies at UCLA and took a twelve-month leave of absence instead.

Over the previous two years, while studying, I'd been working at Billy Brown's Bar in downtown Los Angeles. Billy Brown's Bar was a happening place for the horde of Los Angeles office workers, who'd pour into the bar after knocking off time. They were a bit of a young, yuppie crowd – at least in my eyes, as a part-time cleaner, dishwasher, and jack-of-all-trades.

Of course, I'd also had to take a leave of absence from my part-time work at Billy Brown's Bar while I recuperated from my injuries. Fortunately, Joe Engle – the owner of the bar – was understanding about it. He and I had always got on well – he'd always give me lip about being the young college student with the funny Aussie accent.

By the time eight months had passed since the accident, though, I'd made a good recovery. My body was feeling fine, and the patchwork of plastic surgery on my face had become far less noticeable. I could now walk freely without the use of a cane, and most of my damaged teeth had also been repaired or – in some cases – completely replaced. As a result, I phoned Joe to see if I could come back to work – and before too long, I was working thirty to forty hours a week at Billy Brown's Bar with plans to resume my studies once the new semester at UCLA started in a few months.

After a few months of working at the bar, I asked Joe if I could take a couple of weeks off before I started back at UCLA, to get some sun and have a quick break by the beach. I told him I was thinking of heading down to Mexico.

"No worries, man," Joe told me. "A break will do you good, given what you've been through. Tell you what – I own a little villa in Koh Samui at Choeng Mon Beach. Catch a plane to Koh Samui via Bangkok, and you can stay at my villa for free."

Within a week, I was stepping foot onto the beautiful beach at Choeng Mon, Koh Samui, for the first time. Back then, it was just for a two-week vacation. Little did I know that I'd return to that same beach some thirty years later.

• • •

IT WAS MY first day back at Billy Brown's Bar after two relaxing weeks of soaking up the sun and swimming in the warm, crystal-clear waters of Choeng Mon, Koh Samui. I was feeling really good.

There'd been a special function the previous night at Billy Brown's, with over five hundred attendees – all part of a conference group from England.

Joe was there when I walked into the bar at 7am to start my shift.

"Billy! How was the villa in Choeng Mon? I bet you loved it! You're looking nice and tanned, man."

"What a beautiful part of the world," I told Joe. "I can see why they call it the 'Land of Smiles.' Two weeks of lying on the beach in the beautiful, warm sunshine was just what the doctor ordered. I'm nice and relaxed and ready to go back to UCLA and finish my studies next semester."

"Listen, Billy," Joe warned me. "We had a big night here last night. A large English crew spent lots of money and made a big mess. I'd arranged for Pete to come in and do a special clean at 1am this morning – but between you and me, I've just about had enough of Pete's cleaning work. There were cigarette butts left on the floor in the men's room in the lounge bar. He's due back here at any moment, and I'm going to have a serious talk with him about his sloppy cleaning efforts."

Pete was the cleaning contractor who normally did the late night clean and then came back first thing in the morning to get the restaurant set up for the lunch crowd. He'd recently had a couple of serious run-ins with Joe about his sloppy work – and it appeared that during my absence, there'd been no improvement in their relationship.

"Get over here, Pete, and come the fuck with me," yelled Joe, the moment Pete walked through the front door shortly just after seven.

I deliberately kept my head down, unstacking chairs in the main bar area – pretending to be oblivious to their exchange as they marched off together to the bathroom in the lounge bar.

Five minutes later, the door to the bar area suddenly flew open, and a man wearing a balaclava waved a shotgun at me – bellowing: "Get your fucking hands in the air, blondie – or I'll fucking shoot you!"

Startled, I looked up. In front of me stood Joe and Pete, both with their hands held high in the air. The man in the balaclava stood behind them with the shotgun pointed directly at me.

I froze. I couldn't believe this was happening. Three days ago, I'd been lying on a beach in Koh Samui without a care in the world. Now, I was staring down the barrel of a shotgun. This was surreal – I must be dreaming.

Then, I heard his booming voice again: "Get your fucking hands in the air, or I'll shoot you."

"Billy, this guy is serious," Joe warned.

The three of us marched in single file to the main office, our hands held high and the shotgun pointed at our heads.

"Look at the floor," the gunman growled. "No one look at me or I'll shoot you all."

He turned the gun to me and Pete.

"You two! Get down on your elbows and lie on the floor. Keep your heads down! If you move, I'll shoot you both." Then he turned to Joe. "Open the fucking safe and put all the money in this bag." He threw a bag to Joe.

In a matter of minutes, Joe nervously emptied the safe of the previous night's busy haul. I was lying on the hard, concrete floor, not daring to raise my head. My elbows hurt and my heart was pounding.

Terrifyingly calmly, the gunman then told us to get up and walk in single file to the men's bathroom in the main bar area.

Only five or six minutes had elapsed since the gunman had first confronted Joe and Pete. We'd later learn that the cigarette butts Joe had discovered were those of the gunman, who'd been waiting in the toilets for Joe to arrive. They'd never been a result of Pete's sloppy cleaning – and my arrival at 7am had forced the gunman to delay his robbery plans until all three of us were at work.

Once we entered the toilets, the gunman produced some rope and told Joe to tie us up. Pete and I – with that sawn-off shotgun pointed at our heads – were then told to lie down. We were warned that if anyone made a wrong move, we'd all be shot.

After we've been tied up, the gunman demanded that Joe take him to his car.

Nobody knows how they'll react during an armed holdup – not until they're the victim of one themselves. There are so many questions you keep asking yourself – like was it worth trying to tackle the gunman? Even though he was carrying a sawn-off shotgun?

As much as I liked Joe - was my life worth risking for the daily takings of the business?

Obviously not – and that's why I was lying on the floor, tied up.

So, what was I thinking as I lay there, tied up?

Well, I thought that if I survived this and didn't get shot dead, I was going to stop smoking dope, stop partying, cut my long hair, stop arguing with my mum – and become the model UCLA student she'd always wanted me to be.

A sense of claustrophobia quickly set in. Here I was, confined in this tiny room, tied up, and not even sure whether the gunman was still in here. I suspected he was – but I wasn't entirely sure.

The claustrophobic feeling became overwhelming. Finally, I lifted my head slightly to peer around the small confines of the restroom. I then realized the gunman was gone – most likely getting away in Joe's car even as I lay there.

I wriggled my hands – and, to my surprise, discovered there was movement in the rope. Joe must have been a shitty Boy Scout, never learning to tie knots properly!

I turned and whispered to Pete, whose head was right next to mine on the bathroom floor: "That guy's gone – and my ropes are loose!"

With more wriggling of my wrists, I managed to free my hands. Pete's rope was as poorly tied as mine. We'd later learn that Joe had actually done that on purpose. I'd joked about him being a shitty Boy Scout – but in actuality he'd been a Boy Scout leader, no less – and was an expert in ropes.

We both got up and shook the ropes from around our wrists. Our hearts were thumping—we couldn't believe this was happening.

We were about to open the door to make our escape when we heard some muffled voices approaching. It sounded like the voice of the gunman. What was he still doing here? We'd expected him to have taken Joe's car to escape.

Unbeknown to us, though, our colleague Robbie Bryant had arrived at work while the gunman was in the middle of escorting Joe through the bar room to his car. The gunman had coolly and calmly confronted Robbie - and was in the process of escorting both Robbie and Joe back to the men's room.

Fuck! He was going to kill us all for sure when he saw that both Pete and I had untied ourselves.

At this point, I thought my short and eventful life was about to end – killed by a gunman with a sawn-off shotgun, along with the others.

But despite being under stress, I was able to think logically and strategically, and I didn't lose my cool. This was actually a trait of mine – one that would eventually become an important tool in my business dealings. Believe me – I've seen plenty of people lose their cool during meetings and lose a business deal as a result.

I calmly told Pete to lie back down on the ground and quickly wrap the ropes back around his wrists. I thought if the gunman saw us in roughly the same positions he'd left us in, he might not look too closely or check if the ropes were still properly tied.

The door to the men's room swung open and Robbie and Joe walked in, the gunman close behind them. Pete and I were lying back down on the floor, and we kept our heads down. My heart was pounding, and I prayed the gunman wouldn't notice we weren't tied up properly. I literally thought my life would end, right then and there.

Looming over us, the gunman threw some rope at Joe and told him to tie Robbie up.

After what seemed like an eternity, the gunman and Joe left. For the next few minutes, there was no noise or movement from any of us. Robbie, Pete and I lay there, frozen in shock and disbelief.

It was only when we finally heard the police sirens approaching that we were game enough to take the ropes back off our wrists and get up from the floor.

The gunman was never caught. Joe's car – which became the gunman's getaway vehicle – was found abandoned five miles away just a few hours later.

We were lucky that the gunman appeared to be a professional, who'd dealt calmly with Robbie when he'd interrupted the robbery. If he'd been a crazed junkie, I believe he'd have shot us all, right then and there.

While Robbie, Pete and I were lying in the men's room, the gunman had tied up Joe in the bar, before taking his car. As he'd sped off, Joe had managed to untie the ropes and run down to the police station, which was only a couple hundred yards or so from the bar.

Once the police had surveyed the crime scene, they'd interviewed each of us separately. Unbelievably, within just a matter of hours, Pete, Robbie, Joe, and I were back at work – getting the bar set up for the busy Monday despite it haven't been robbed at gunpoint that same morning.

Back in 1989, there was no such thing as counseling, or stress leave for workers – nor was there any discussion about possible compensation for the distress we'd endured.

The whole event had shaken me up, though. I had my own set of keys to the bar and was used to getting to work early to get the bar set up for the day. This set up normally only took a few hours, and before the robbery, I'd figured that the quicker I set up the bar, the quicker I could be back out surfing. Some mornings, I'd be there as early as 4am to set up – before heading out to the beach for a surf.

Now, though, I found myself jumping at shadows when I turned up at the bar. In the early mornings, I was often the only employee there – and so I'd wonder if the gunman was going to come back, and I'd jump whenever I heard a strange sound. What made it worse was that the bar was in an old building with constantly creaking floors.

Even today, some thirty years later, I still get nervous if I enter a bank – or any other business that would be tempting to armed thieves – and find I'm the only customer there.

The robbery was the culmination of a tough period in my life. In the span of twelve months, I'd lost one of my best mates in a car accident, had my face completely rebuilt, and had then been tied up by a guy in a balaclava, armed with a sawn-off shotgun.

That was why, at the tender age of twenty-one, I decided there was more to life than getting my degree and making my first million by the age of thirty.

I didn't want to keep working at Billy Brown's Bar.

I realized that a life with little or no stress was what I was after. My old days of hanging out with Chook Burns, drinking to excess, and smoking too much pot sounded so appealing right then. That's why I quit college and also quit working at Billy Brown's Bar.

CHAPTER 5

"YOU KNOW WHAT?" I said to Chook, while we were sharing a joint in his parked car alongside Santa Monica Pier one day. "Life's about doing what you want when you want, on your own terms and no one else's."

"Totally agree, man," Chook nodded. "It's how I've been living my life ever since we got kicked out of school. Billy, I'm glad you've finally come to your senses after wasting those two years at UCLA."

"It was the armed robbery that got me, man," I shook my head. "I mean, shit mate, the accident was bad enough – losing Tommy and all that – but once we'd all got fixed up after our injuries, we'd started to get on with life. That gunman at Billy Brown's, though – I thought he was going to shoot me and the others, right then and there."

Chook nodded sagely, and then asked: "So, what do you plan to do for money?"

With the effects of the second joint setting in, I said: "I'm going to start a lawn mowing business in town. How's this for a slogan? 'Sit on your arse and let Billy mow your grass.'"

We both burst out laughing.

"Mowing grass, smoking grass," Chook joked. We both pissed ourselves in fits of laughter.

"I'll tell you what, Chook," I nodded along. "That's not a bad marketing angle of mine. 'Sit on your arse and let Billy mow your grass.' It kind of flows off the tongue, nice and easy."

Believe it or not, that was actually the beginning of my real-life lawn mowing business in LA. My advertising slogan certainly upset some people – but I'll tell you what: It also got people's attention. It also got me a lot of lawns to mow—and a lot of cash in a short space of time.

I contacted my long-lost father, who was living back in Melbourne and about ready to retire, about my new business venture. I was hoping he'd give me fifteen thousand dollars to buy a pickup truck, along with some lawn mowers and sundry tools.

He and I had kept in contact only sporadically – talking on the phone maybe three to four times a year. Nevertheless, he reluctantly agreed to *lend* – not give – the fifteen thousand dollars I needed. As a result, within two weeks of my brainstorming smoking session with Chook, my new business 'Sit On Your Arse and Let Billy Mow Your Grass' was up and running.

I designed some nice pamphlets with my slogan plastered across the top, and then used a couple of local schoolkids to hand-deliver thousands of brochures to the mailboxes of local homes. After a couple of months, I'd picked up enough business from local residents and condominium blocks to have more than enough work to keep me busy.

There were a couple of business principals I quickly learned about the mowing business – principles I imagine applied no matter which city or country you operated in.

Firstly, the barriers of entry were low. Anyone could buy a pickup truck and a couple of lawnmowers and become a competitor. No apprenticeship or certificate was required.

Secondly, in addition to not requiring certification, there was actually very little skill required in mowing a lawn – which further increased the number of potential competitors.

Thirdly, unless you could differentiate your product and service from all the others, the average household simply shopped around based on price. No matter what price I charged, there was always going to be some mug who'd mow the lawn for cheaper.

I soon realized that to make a reasonable amount of money lawn mowing in LA, the principals I'd learned by selling raffle tickets at Santa Monica High would become critical. I needed to apply the same three guiding business principles – rules that would later continue to guide my business endeavors.

Leverage, process, and distribution.

I was never going to make any real money if I was mowing lawns on my own. So, with another twenty-thousand pamphlets printed and handed out by a bunch of schoolkids, work started to stream in – more than I could possibly complete on my own.

I soon recruited Chook Burns to work for me, along with another three contractors. They were all paid eighty percent of the fee for mowing a lawn. They provided their own transportation and trailer, while I provided the mowers and other required tools. I soon became known as "Mr. Twenty Percent" to them.

Now with four contractors mowing lawns, I needed to ensure the consistency and reliability of the services I was offering. To that end, I developed the *Billy Houston Lawn Mowing Process* – a simple manual listing the expectations I had of the contractors who worked for me.

This Do's and Don'ts of Working With Billy became the process of my business – and because some of my contractors could hardly read and write, the manual was written to be a really simple document to follow.

The more lawns I had to mow, the more money I made from my twenty percent cut. Therefore, I needed distribution to get as much business as possible. Often the simplest ideas work the best, and I'd found that the more pamphlets I delivered to local mailboxes, the more work I picked up.

So, I just did that – and before too long, Billy's lawn mowing business was cutting over one hundred and sixty lawns a week in LA. It was making a nice little profit.

However, I shouldn't take all the credit for the success of my lawn mowing venture. Back when I was eighteen – shortly after I was expelled from Santa

Monica High – Mum had shipped me out to stay with my dad in Melbourne for a while.

The idea had been that a new environment – along with the discipline of my stern, diplomat father – would sort out my life. Well, that didn't work out as my parents had planned, and within a couple of weeks I'd been back in Santa Monica.

While I was in Melbourne, though, Dad had seen an advertisement for lawn mowing contractors in the local paper. A guy called Steve Reece had been after contractors to mow lawns in the southeastern suburbs of Melbourne.

Early one Monday morning, I'd met with Steve— an unassuming chap whose office was his lounge room in suburban Melbourne. Steve had started mowing lawns in Melbourne a couple of years earlier, but he had a big problem because he had too many lawns to mow and couldn't keep up with demand.

He'd shared his vision of starting one of the first lawnmowing franchises in Melbourne with me – in the hopes of eventually expanding it throughout Australia. He was working on developing an operations plan for the *Steve Reece Way of Servicing Your Lawnmowing Customer*. For a franchise fee, he'd allocate a territory or area for you to work in – and with his marketing efforts, he'd provide you with an endless supply of lawns to mow.

In his shabby lounge room, he'd drawn all this on a whiteboard in front of me. To him, it was exciting. To me, it was all too far-fetched and unachievable – but I'd been just an eighteen-year-old kid back then, one who'd just been expelled from high school in America.

At the time, the whole idea had sounded fanciful. I remember telling my dad the idea would never take off – and there was no way I'd work with that guy. I thought he was crazy.

But over the next three years, Dad had been forever giving me updates about the success of Steve Reece during our sporadic phone calls, and how he'd now got over fifty franchises up and running across the country since my initial meeting with him three years earlier.

Today, some thirty-three years after that initial meeting, Steve Reece now has over three hundred franchisees in Australia – and has expanded from lawn mowing into house cleaning, window cleaning, car detailing, and installing TV antennas. You name it, he does it.

This was another important lesson I'd learn for the future – never discount a person's idea. If a somebody has the passion, the drive, and the vision – they can turn their dreams into reality.

So, I guess that chance encounter with Steve Reece unwittingly became the catalyst for my own lawn mowing business venture.

Over the following three years, business went well, and I was making a steady income. It was never going to make me rich, but for a guy in his early twenties, it provided me with a good living. The hardest part was finding reliable contractors who'd stay with the business. Other than Chook, most of my contractors didn't stick around longer than six months. They either got sick of the industry, couldn't make enough money, or simply found the work too hard.

During this time, I met Julie Longman. Julie had just qualified as a pharmacist after attending San Diego University. Her father, Jim Longman, owned a large accounting firm in Hollywood. He managed the accounts of many leading actors and actresses in Tinsel Town.

Jim had a beautiful house in Bel Air. He'd seen my pamphlet and was quite taken with my bold advertising slogan, so he contacted me and asked for a quote to mow his lawns.

I travelled to his house – and after ringing the doorbell, a tanned, well-built man in his fifties had opened the door.

"You must be Billy – the man behind the slogan 'Sit On Your Arse and Let Billy Mow Your Grass .'" He was chuckling, clearly taken with this slogan.

"Yes, I am, sir," I replied. "Billy Houston – owner of the business." We shook hands to introduce ourselves.

"I admire people with some get-up-and-go," Jim grinned. "I liked your pamphlet. It shows innovation." He opened the door wider. "Come on in and I'll show you around the yard, so you can give me a quote. I'm looking for you to maintain my lawn on a weekly basis".

Jim had a large property – the size of two regular city blocks. I could tell Jim was a successful man, although at this stage, I didn't know exactly what line of business he was in. He took me around the back, and I noticed a group of young girls sunbathing by the pool as we walked past it.

"Billy, this is Julie – my daughter – and some of her friends. They recently graduated from college."

43

He introduced me to the lovely young lady. "Julie – this is Billy, the lawn mowing guy. You gave me his pamphlet, remember?"

"Sit On Your Arse and Let Billy Mow Your Grass," Julie laughed, followed by her friends. I just stared at her, dumbstruck. Julie was stunning.

If I get this contract, I decided, there is no *way* Chook Burns or anyone else was mowing this lawn. This would be the one and only lawn I looked after myself.

I then realized there was one way I could guarantee acceptance of my quote – do it for half price. So, for a job that should have cost sixty dollars a week, I quoted only thirty. As a result, for the next six months, I mowed Jim's lawn every week – and got to know both Julie and Jim in the process.

In fact, Jim would occasionally even ask me in for a beer – and so, over time, I got to share my story with him. From being expelled from high school, to the car accident, the armed robbery, and my false starts at college – even my earlier life in Australia. Jim took a liking to me and admired my entrepreneurial spirit. I myself could sense that Jim was an opinionated person who liked to have things his own way – something I'd experience first-hand a few years later.

Late one afternoon – the day before I was scheduled to mow Jim's lawn – I received a phone call from him.

"Billy! Would you be able to stay back and have a beer with me tomorrow after you're done mowing the lawn? I want to discuss something with you."

I was a bit concerned about what he wanted to talk to me about – because over the course of the previous fortnight, I'd started dating his daughter Julie. But I'd always been a proper gentleman with Julie – and, heck, Jim seemed to like me; so surely there'd be no problems.

Perhaps he didn't like my lawn mowing – but, bugger me, he was paying less than half of the normal price, so he had no reason to complain.

After mowing Jim's lawn that Friday afternoon, I nervously packed away the mower in the trailer before being invited inside for the beer and chat with Jim.

• • •

"BILLY, PLEASE SIT down," Jim gestured to his chairs. "I've got to know you over the last six months. You've been through a lot in your short life so far." He sat down opposite me, beer in hand. "I can pick out talent when I see it. Billy – and I see you have an entrepreneurial flair; something you appear to have displayed since your high school days. Most people don't have that flair. It's why most of them are caught up in the nine-to-five, mundane routine of life."

He leaned back in his chair.

"Don't get me wrong, Billy – for some people, that's the right thing to do. But you? You're wasting your time mowing lawns and running this small band of contractors."

"Sorry?" I looked at him uncertainly. "I don't understand where this conversation is going. Do you want me to stop seeing Julie because I mow lawns?"

"No, Bill! Not at all! Please – continue to see Julie, and whatever develops between you and her is your business, not mine."

Phew.

Jim sat up a little, and continued.

"I was speaking to Jim Bartlett at UCLA last week. Do you remember him?"

"You mean the professor of accounting?"

"Yes."

"Yeah," I nodded. "He was my accounting professor for a couple of courses I completed. I used to love his tax law class."

"Jim tells me you were one of his top students. He said it was a shame you never came back and finished college after your car accident." Jim's tone deepened. "Billy – I'm looking to retire in the next five years. I've got two other accounting partners who'll be looking to retire in the next ten years or so, too. That means we need some young blood in the firm – people with the ability to grow the firm once we retire."

He paused, studying me as I listened, before asking:

"Why don't you consider selling this lawn mowing business to your friend Chook and come work with me? Full time in my accounting firm. You can go back to college part time while you work – and Jim Bartlett checked your records and confirmed that you could finish your Business Degree in just two years, part-time, with all the credits you've already earned."

My mind reeled as he kept talking.

"For sure, you'd be starting right at the bottom in our accounting firm – but with your drive and abilities, it'd lead to a fast-track career development. I think within five years, if you tick all the boxes, it's entirely feasible that you could end up as partnership material."

"Wow!" I said to Jim. "I'd really need time to think about this. This wasn't the conversation I'd been expecting to have with you – not that I'm not happy about it." Everything Jim had told me started racing through my mind. "Besides, Chook Burns has no money. He couldn't afford to buy the business as it is."

"Well, what's the value of your business, Billy?" Jim asked. "Ten thousand for your customer list and contracts? Plus, equipment worth another twenty thousand?"

"Yep," I nodded, impressed with his math. "I reckon thirty thousand, all up."

Jim nodded.

"Well, as part of your thought process, why don't you consider this? I could lend Chook thirty thousand – interest free – with monthly payments of principal over five years."

I couldn't believe the opportunity that was being offered to me – and I knew I'd be dumb not to jump at it.

So, within the next three months, I'd sold the lawn mowing business to Chook and started working at Longman, Delix, Norris & Associates in Hollywood – more commonly known as LDN. Meanwhile, I re-enrolled at UCLA and busied myself completing my Business Degree.

Things went more or less according to plan – so much so that just two years later, Julie Longman became Julie Houston as we celebrated our marriage.

Over many dinners and drinks, Jim enjoyed constantly mocking me – telling everyone how he'd screwed me down and got his lawns mown at half the asking price. I'd respond that I did it on purpose – just so I could eventually marry his lovely daughter. While this was true, I'm not sure Jim believed me – but it made for a good story.

It was a good time in my life – one of the best. Little did I know, however, that in five years, Jim and I would have a major falling out and would never talk again – a falling out that divided me and his family forever.

CHAPTER 6

"WELL LOOK AT you, man. Wouldn't recognize you with that short hair and cool suit." Pat shook my hand when we met up.

At age twenty-four, I'd just begun my second week working as an associate accountant at Longman, Delix, Norris & Associates.

Accepting Jim's offer had meant I'd had to get a haircut, unfortunately – and had to ditch the board shorts and t-shirts that had been my wardrobe for years. After having shoulder-length hair for the best part of a decade, getting all those golden locks cut off was something I'd only reluctantly done.

"Tell me about LDN, Billy," Pat demanded.

"Well, it's only been two weeks, Pat – so I'm still learning the ropes about who's who in the business, and how they do things." I was cagey with my answers. "It's a bit of an eye-opener for me, given that just three weeks ago, I was in board shorts and short sleeves, supervising lawn mowing contractors."

"Don't worry about it." Pat, of course, had earned his law degree and gone professional a lot earlier than I had – so I listened to his wisdom. "The first three months are always the most difficult, Billy – but you'll be surprised how quickly you pick things up and fit into the flow."

As a qualified lawyer, now, Pat had spent the last year working in the downtown Los Angeles office of McIntosh & McIntosh – a mega-sized firm of lawyers with offices in LA, New York, Boston, and Chicago. The firm comprised over fifty partners, and more than four hundred associates.

I answered his question: "Well, LDN is a large accounting firm – with three partners, Longman, Delix, and Norris, hence the name. There are more than seventy staff, and the company specializes in tax, accounting, and business advisory services. We've got the one office in Hollywood – and while the company predominantly works with clients in Los Angeles, Stuart Delix and some of his team travel on a bi-monthly basis to New York to look after some wealthy business clients over there. It's not as big as McIntosh & McIntosh, but it's the biggest accounting firm in Hollywood."

Pat used to go on and on when he'd first started with McIntosh& McIntosh about how big and impressive the firm was – but now he'd come to the realization that working for a smaller firm of lawyers might have been far more enjoyable than working at a mega-sized one.

"How did the business start?" Pat asked.

"Well, Jim and Stuart Delix worked together for three years or so in a small accounting firm in Santa Barbara. Jim then decided to set up his own CPA firm, some thirty years ago, and he convinced Stuart to come on board with him – on the basis that he'd make Stuart a partner within three years of starting the business. Jim purchased some of the clients he was looking after from his previous employer and started with about a hundred clients in downtown LA."

"What about the Norris part?" asked Pat.

"Brian Norris started as their first hired accountant when he was fresh out of college. He became a partner after seven years or so. The three of them have remained together ever since. Brian and Jim are great. I haven't met Stuart Delix yet, as he's in New York right now and not back until next week."

I continued: "Jim is planning to retire in the next five years or so, and he's told me confidentially that both Stuart and Brian would like to retire themselves within the next decade. Jim is senior partner, and so he has the largest equity in the business."

"And that's an opportunity for you to buy in, right Billy?" Pat snorted. "I mean you're taking out the boss's daughter – so with that pull, the firm might be called Delix, Norris, and Houston in the next five years."

"I'm not sure about that, Pat," I laughed. "It's only my third week in." I started wishing I hadn't mentioned anything about the retirement plans of Jim or the other partners. "Besides, I still have to finish my degree first. I've been accepted back into UCLA on a part-time basis, but it's going to take me two years to complete it."

For the next couple of months, Pat and I would try and catch up every week for a coffee or a bite to eat during our lunch breaks. We only worked ten minutes away from each other via cab.

• • •

"WELL, PAT – I just had my initial three-month probationary review. Looks like I'll be calling Chook to see if I can get a gig with him mowing lawns," I joked.

"Very funny, Billy. So, all good? No doubts?"

"Yeah it went great," I told my friend. "Brian Norris and his manager, Curtis Handly, undertook the review. All good. They said I'm picking things up well and progressing faster than they thought I would. I'm now a permanent part of Brian's team, and I'm looking after the small IRS returns, given the busy season from January to April is about to start. Thereafter, I'll be trained on providing business consulting services to larger clients." It wasn't all smooth sailing, though. "I'll tell you what, Pat – I'm just amazed how inefficient and out-of-date some of the things they do are."

"Like what?" asked Pat.

"For example, I've now discovered that we only sell two things – time and so-called expertise. I guess, as a lawyer, you do the same. I'm required to have ninety-percent productivity – or, in other words, ninety percent of my time each day must be charged to a client."

"Tell me about it, Billy," Pat snorted. "I work fifty to sixty hours a week just to meet my target, and that's even before I enter any bonus territory. I'm told the harder I work, the more chance I have of becoming a partner one day. All the lawyers at the firm do the same – working fifty to sixty hours per week just to meet target. They all have the same goal, too – to become a partner. But you know what the scary thing is, Billy? There are sixty people, all qualified lawyers, all doing similar work to me. McIntosh & McIntosh has a partner-to-lawyer ratio of roughly one to eight. That means, of the sixty of us, only about eight will ever become partners. What happens to the other fifty-two? Do we keep working fifty to sixty hours a week just to keep on being a salaried lawyer?" Pat shook his head.

"I get it Pat, believe me," I nodded. "So, at LDN, our productivity is monitored every day by a manager and reviewed by a partner each week. At the monthly partners' meeting, a report is provided to the partners of our overall productivity and billings by each employee. So, basically, the more inefficient we are, the more the client pays. As you know Pat, I've always joked about how I was going to make that first million focusing on three things: Leverage, processes, and distribution."

"Don't remind me, Billy. You used to drum the importance of that into Chook's head with that little raffle business during our high school days."

I grinned at the memory.

"At LDN," I continued, "the more inefficient I am, the more I charge the client – and the more efficient I am, the less I charge the client. What a weird way to charge people – no matter what product or service you're selling. We never even quote for the job. We just tell our client our hourly rates from the partner level right down to the receptionist level, and then the time everyone allocates to complete the job will determine the final fee. I mean, of course we tell the client our services are of the highest quality, and our staff are among the highest trained in the State of California – but that's something I'm sure all our competitors say, too."

"Don't worry, Billy," Pat lamented. "The exact same thing happens in my law firm, too. It's all about billable hours and charging time to the client – just to make the partners a nice little profit."

For the next twenty minutes, I vented my frustrations about the inefficiency of the accounting profession – in which we were expected to charge as many hours as possible to a client to ensure we met our individual productivity targets – and, of course, that the firm reached its cumulative target to ensure the partners made their big, fat profit. Then, everyone was happy – except the poor, old client, of course, who had no idea how they were being charged, or what for.

"Billy, I hear loud and clear what you're saying," Pat agreed with me. "I don't mean to laugh at you, it's just everything you complain about at LDN goes on at McIntosh & McIntosh, too. It's part of the flawed system that most accounting and legal firms use – and the scary thing is that clients aren't even aware of it. One in thirty clients might complain about the fee – but it's how loud they complain that determines whether or not they get a discount."

I pursed my lips. "You know, Pat? I'm inexperienced in this accounting firm – but if LDN is typical of accounting firms in America, then I see a great opportunity for someone to shake this profession up;

and make some serious money in the process. Someone who can disrupt the old, stale accounting industry."

"How would you do that, Billy?"

"As I said – I'm inexperienced in this profession, but it's often an outsider looking in who sees the opportunity to make change. First, I'd ditch this whole notion of charging by time. It only rewards inefficiency and penalizes efficiency. Second, I'd standardize every workflow process, so everyone does things the same way. Third, I'd tell the clients up front what their fee was going to be before we even started the work. Finally, I'd offer a menu of services."

Pat listened intently.

I snorted, shaking my head.

"Tell you what – talk to me about it in three more years, after I've got some more experience. I'll probably have a better idea then about what changes are required to the dour, traditional accounting model."

Then, I asked Pat: "Enough about LDN. How's the world at McIntosh & McIntosh?"

"Same old, same old, Billy. Simply head down, ass up – getting there at seven every morning and leaving at seven each night to ensure I meet my chargeable hours. I mean, I get on well with Steve, the partner I report to. He started at the firm ten years ago, and he's gone through exactly what I do. He keeps telling me that if I keep working the hours I do, and keep the quality of my work up, I could be a partner in six or seven years."

"That's great, mate," I said.

Pat frowned.

"No, it's not great, Billy. I'm not sure if I want to be a partner at McIntosh & McIntosh – to slave my guts out for the next forty years just to get a nice retirement package at sixty-five. Steve works even longer hours than I do. He's got to make sure our team meets its billing targets. The fifty partners meet every three months, and to remain a partner for the long term, you have to consistently make sure your division meets its budget, so all the partners get their profit share. It's a dog-eat-dog world, Billy – believe me."

I did believe him – and in the following five years, Pat would come to leave McIntosh & McIntosh and work with me.

CHAPTER 7

FIVE YEARS PASSED since I'd joined LDN as a junior accountant, and a lot happened during that time.

Three years earlier, at the age of twenty-six, I'd finally graduated with a Business Degree from UCLA. I'd celebrated my achievement with Chook Burns, Pat Gabriel, and Roger the Dodger – my old crew – with a few too many drinks after work at Billy Brown's Bar.

Joe Engle was still running the place, and he was always pleased to see me. After a few too many drinks, he'd always recall the story of the armed robbery in front of everyone. He'd recount every minute detail and have people on the edge of their seats as he went through a blow-by-blow description of the ordeal.

Roger the Dodger had been kindly asked to leave the California College system after failing to pass the first year of five different degree programs. He was now working for Chook, mowing lawns, and was in a discussion about buying into Chook's business. I was somewhat amused that these discussions only appeared to take place after he and Chook had both consumed far too much alcohol – so, I was somewhat doubtful whether there was any real intention there from either of them.

In my mind, I believed Roger was still suffering from the guilt and trauma of Tommy's death – and while I wasn't an expert in psychology, I believed that Roger's failure at school was largely due to the emotional stress he was still carrying.

Nevertheless, Roger seemed happy enough working with Chook, and he could be found in a bar on most nights – having a few quiet drinks with Chook after a long day of mowing lawns.

Julie Longman and I had been married for a while now. My mum adored Julie, and Julie's parents – Jim and Adele – seemed to like me. I was madly in love with Julie, but I'd become slightly concerned that she'd inherited her father's temper – and often demanded things her own way.

We'd had a big wedding—all paid for by Jim and Adele. Both Jim and Adele came from large families, so with all of Julie's uncles, aunts, and cousins, a lot of her extended family had been in attendance. My mum was there, too, of course – along with my old mates from Santa Monica High School and some of my college buddies. Even Dad made the trip from Australia with his new wife, who he'd been married to for five years at that point. She was a fellow diplomat with whom he'd previously worked with in Melbourne.

Of course, Jim asked most of the staff at LDN to attend, so the number of guests soon rose to nearly two-hundred – but I couldn't blame Jim and Adele for asking so many people. It was a special occasion, seeing their one and only daughter getting married.

● ● ●

TO THE OUTSIDER, I probably appeared to be in a happy place – but in reality, nothing could be farther from the truth.

Pat and I were still catching up most weeks, for either coffee or lunch, and chewing the fat together. Pat wasn't happy at McIntosh & McIntosh. He enjoyed law, but didn't like the dog-eat-dog nature of large legal firms. Part of him was urging him to leave – while the other part insisted he stay, as Pat had a strong sense of loyalty to the partner he reported to.

I'd been putting in similarly long hours at LDN to fast track my progression to partner, and it was paying rewards. I was now a senior manager and looking after fifteen other accountants. That had also meant a big pay increase. However, I'd come to the conclusion that being a partner at LDN wasn't for me. I'd told nobody about this – not even Julie – because I didn't want Jim to be aware of my dissatisfaction.

At our regular family dinners, at the home of Julie's parents, Jim would always take me aside and discuss LDN with me.

Eight months earlier, at a family catch up, he'd said to me: "Billy – I just want to give you an update. Brian, Stuart, and I are really pleased with your development.

To become a senior manager within four years of joining our firm – especially without any previous accounting experience – is a testimony to your hard work and talent. If you remember our initial discussion, over four years ago now, I'd said you had partnership potential. Well, Billy – I've never spoken a truer word. Over the next twelve months, I think you and I need to start the process of you buying me out and becoming a full partner of LDN."

I stared at Jim as he continued – aware that he probably thought I had as much enthusiasm about this as he did.

"I've had initial discussions with both Stuart and Brian about this, and they're fully supportive of the idea."

I asked: "How would this buyout work, Jim?"

"Well, I own forty percent of the shares in the business, and Stuart and Brian each own thirty percent. We did have Brian Rafferty marked as partnership potential, and we'd been having ongoing discussions with him over the last eighteen months about his buying in. Then, he upped and left and started his own accounting firm three blocks away. He's taken some of our clients, too. Between you and me, Billy – Brian is about to be served with a lawsuit for damages. We're suing him for breach of his employment contract. He'd signed the standard employment contract, same as you, and you can't just take clients of LDN from the firm when you leave. We'll spend whatever it takes in legal fees to nail him for it."

"How much are you suing him for?" I asked.

"Half-a-million dollars, plus whatever our legal costs are."

"That's a lot of money."

"Well," Jim shrugged, "he's taken $250,000 worth of client fees off our books. Based on our profit margin, those fees are worth about $500,000 of capital value."

"It all seems such a shame. I mean, Brian had been with you guys for over ten years."

"Yep, so true. We'd made him an attractive offer to buy in, too – which would have set him up for life. We'd even organized a bank finance for the full purchase price of the partnership."

Jim sighed.

"For whatever reason – after months and months of negotiation – he told us late one Friday night that he'd decided to decline our partnership offer. That was his decision, and we accepted it – until a week later, he resigned and told us he needed a break from accounting."

Jim shook his head.

"Anyway, Billy – that's nothing you need to worry about."

He leaned in closer.

"Now, as far as you're concerned, the plan is for both Stuart and Brian to buy half of my share of the business, and then offer you the opportunity to buy the other half – which equates to twenty-percent of LDN."

"What's that twenty-percent share worth?"

"Well, after the partners' salaries, the business makes a profit of $1.5 million. Based on five times profit, we put the value of the business at $7.5 million."

"So, my twenty-percent stake would cost me $1.5 million, then?"

"Correct - plus, you'd receive the base partners' salary of $200,000 a year. So, your total package would be $500,000 made up of $300,000 in profit share, plus your partner's salary of $200,000. There's also a partners' bonus system, based on fees and profit produced by your team, but we can discuss that later."

I leaned back in my seat, frowning.

"Well, Jim – that seems like a lot of money. I mean, I'm twenty-eight-years-old, and you're asking me to give you $1.5 million for twenty-percent of the firm. The problem is: I have no assets other than some cash Julie and I have saved over the last couple of years. I don't think a bank would lend me that sort of money."

"Billy, it's all sorted," Jim reassured me. "LDN is a big client of Standard Mutual Bank, so finance won't be a problem, believe me. The bank will simply take a charge over your equity in the business, equal to the amount of money they lend you. That, of course, would require the approval of Stuart and Brian – but I've already discussed it with them, so that won't be a problem."

"Back to Brian Rafferty," I said. "It seems pretty tough suing him for half-a-million dollars. I mean, he's got a young family and a mortgage. His wife is expecting their third child in six months."

"Billy," Jim frowned, "one thing you need to learn when you become a partner is that business is tough. We work hard getting new clients – and equally hard keeping the old clients happy enough to stay with the firm. The major asset of our business is the client.

Without clients, we *have* no business – and, hence, no value. Not to mention, to encourage staff to remain with LDN, we invest in developing each staff member's competencies and skillset over time. This costs the firm a lot of money. As part of that growth, we give you and the other accountants a lot of client contact. In your case – and Brian's, for that matter – you manage other staff and have your own client base. By the point you're at, the partner you report to has practically no direct contact with the clients – because we've trained you so well that you've become fully competent in servicing all their needs, without any input from a partner."

I nodded in agreement.

"But, Billy – you've got to remember that the clients belong to LDN, not the employee. Employees can come and go at their own free will, but the client *must* remain with LDN. You can't poach the client, like Brian's done. If every employee who left took their clients with them, we wouldn't have a business – LDN wouldn't exist."

I interrupted Jim. "I understand."

He raised his hand.

"Let me finish, Billy. I'm a big believer in karma. If you do the right thing by people, I believe it'll come back in spades of good karma. Thirty years ago, when I decided to start my own firm, I approached my bosses about my plans. We were living in Santa Barbara back then, and Adele wanted to return to Los Angeles and be closer to our families. So, I had an idea about starting my own business, and I had a group of clients I was looking after in LA. So, I approached the partners and told them Adele and I wanted to return to LA.

I negotiated a price with them to purchase the hundred or so clients based in LA that I'd been looking after. I figured it was all about karma, Billy. I did the right thing by my previous employer."

He shook his head sadly.

"Brian could have approached us and paid fair market value for his clients, too – and we'd have agreed to it. Instead, he's effectively stolen assets worth close to half-a-million dollars from LDN. That's not acceptable behavior. I practice what I preach, Billy. Nothing more, nothing less."

• • •

AT OUR MOST next weekly catch-up, Pat said to me: "What the fuck's wrong with you, Billy? The last few weeks you haven't been the chirpy guy I've known ever since high school. Married life not agreeing with you?"

"It's nothing to do with married life, mate. The problem is her father – and Longman, Delix, and Norris."

"What's the problem there? I thought you enjoyed life as an accountant. You're now making good money, and you're a manager at the firm. You've got your own clients and staff reporting to you – what's there to be unhappy about?"

I sighed.

"I haven't told you this before, Pat. In fact, I haven't told anyone."

I leaned in closer.

"Jim Longman had a heart-to-heart discussion with me about eight months ago. He wants me to become a partner – to buy twenty percent of LDN for $1.5 million dollars."

"Fuck! That's a lot of money, Billy."

"Yeah, it is – but it's not the money that scares me. I'll be making $500,000 in salary and profit share, plus the potential of a further $50,000 in partner bonuses. I've done the math, and it all stacks up."

I then shared with Pat the discussion Jim and I had, eight months earlier – along with the ongoing discussions Jim was still having with me. He was starting to put real pressure on me to agree to the buy-in – even down to starting to draft the agreements.

Stuart and Brian were also putting pressure on me to buy in and become a partner. They both shared their vision of the future with me – which was to dramatically grow the firm in the coming years. Stuart had plans to double the size of the firm over the next five years by opening an office in New York, to service the growing number of East Coast clients he and his team were picking up during their regular visits to New York.

I'd recently asked Jim, Stuart, and Brian if they could hold off any further discussion for another four months. I said I was newly married and needed to get five years under my belt at LDN first – to ensure I felt like I was partnership material.

But that was only that I'd told them.

"Pat, what I'm about to say is completely confidential. Even Julie knows nothing about what I'm about to tell you."

"My word is my honor, Billy. I'll tell no one."

I sighed.

"Mate, the truth is – I don't want to become a partner at LDN. It's been a good firm for me to get experience at – I mean, in four months, I'll have five years of experience as an accountant. My skill set is up there with the best of the seventy or so employees there. In fact, I have better client relationship skills than either Stuart or Brian, and I'm above Stuart on a technical level – and at least equal to Brian."

I leaned in closer as I continued:

"The firm is old school and set in its ways. They use outdated systems and processes, and are horribly inefficient. LDN is the way of the past, not the future."

"Well, that's simple Billy – just tell them you don't want to be a partner." He paused. "But if you do that, I can't see you remaining there as an employee."

"That's part of the problem, Pat. You've always known I felt the firm was out-of-date in their systems, processes, and technology. I've decided I want to start my own accounting firm in Santa Monica – and I have plans to grow the business across America over the next ten years."

Pat snorted. "Well, to most people, I'd say: 'You're dreaming, man.' But, knowing you and the way your mind functions, I don't doubt for a second you can do it – and be extremely successful."

"I've been secretly working on a business plan," I confessed. "It's a franchise system working with the low-level tax returns during January to April. In my own time, I've built the systems and processes to automate the whole tax return process – so even the least-qualified person in the office could complete a Form 1040 tax return in half the time it currently takes a qualified accountant at LDN. The Form 1040 is the most common type of tax return in the country. Close to eighty million of these forms are filed with the IRS every year – and fifty million of them by accounting firms. I even convened a special meeting with Jim, Stuart, and Brian a few months ago to show them what I was working on, and the benefits in efficiency, cost savings and profit it could bring LDN."

"What did they say, Billy?"

"They basically sat there, stone-faced, during my entire presentation – and then Stuart said: 'Billy, we've seen stuff like this before. It just doesn't work.'"

Pat's eyes widened.

I continued: "Jim told me: 'Billy, we've been in this game for thirty years. We know accounting inside and out. It's why we've been successful. Please don't take this the wrong way, but you've only got four-and-a-half years of experience in this industry. Across the table, the three of us have a collective *eighty* years of experience. I think it's fair to say that we know best what works and what doesn't.'"

Pat shifted in his seat.

"What about Brian? What did he say?"

"Brian was quiet during the entire presentation. He said nothing. He came to my office afterward and basically admitted that he saw the merits in what I was proposing – but that I needed to understand that Jim and Stuart owned seventy-percent of the business, and were too set in their ways to shift things up like I'd suggested."

I sipped my drink. "You know what my real problem is, though, Pat?"

"No."

"Jim gave me a start in the accounting industry nearly five years ago. He shared with me his plans for retirement, and he took a gamble on me – thinking I had the aptitude, skillset, and motivation to become a partner in LDN. Hell, he even saw me as part of his exit strategy. What makes it even more complicated is that I'm married to his one and only daughter. Not a week goes by when Julie doesn't remind me of how lucky we both are that her father gave me a shot to be part of the family business."

I shook my head.

"Once a week, we have dinner at the Longmans – and I'm reminded by both Jim and Adele of how lucky Julie and I are with the start they've given us both. Jim always brings up the partnership option with a wink. The more red wine he drinks, the bigger the wink." I laughed bitterly.

"Yeah, I can understand your predicament, Billy," Pat commiserated.

I sighed.

"You know, after that initial meeting with the three partners, I managed to get them together again a month later to show them in full the prototype I'd developed. Guess what they said, Pat?"

"Let me guess," he snorted. "They told you it looks good, but that they've seen it all before – and believed that the way they've always done things was far superior."

"Exactly," I nodded. "Over the last two weeks, I've had Cindy – one of my team's administrative staff – complete thirty simple tax returns using my process.

Cindy isn't a qualified accountant and has never completed a tax return on her own – until now."

Pat's eyes widened. I continued.

"I've then had Heck and Bob, two of my junior accountants—both qualified, with one year of experience at LDN—complete fifteen similar tax returns each, *not* using my method. Heck and Bob are two good, young accountants – but you know what the results were?"

I didn't give Pat a chance to answer.

"Cindy completed all thirty returns in half the time it took Heck and Bob to complete their fifteen. All of Cindy's tax returns were spot on and needed no corrections. She simply followed the system I prepared to complete a Form 1040. Twenty percent of the tax returns prepared by Heck and Bob required reworks because they had an inadequate and out-of-date system to follow – the LDN system. I shared the results with Bob and Heck, and I showed them how Cindy had completed the Form 1040 returns far quicker than them, and with zero mistakes. They didn't believe me – so I showed them the system I'd built that Cindy had followed. Both Heck and Bob asked if there was any way they could start using my system and process rather than the existing LDN one. They both think my system runs rings around the antiquated LDN system."

Pat smiled. "Well, you know what you should do, Billy?"

"I know what I should do," I nodded, "but let's hear your suggestion first."

"You should convene a meeting with the partners with two items on the agenda – the first being your

Form 1040 Preparation System, and the second being your future partnership. You should explain to them what you've just told me about LDN's outdated and inefficient systems, and how they represent the past and not the future. On that basis, you don't want to buy in as a partner – but, if they change and become a firm of the future and not the past, you'd be happy to reconsider and buy in at $1.5 million. Part of that change would require they use your tax preparation system. Share the results of what you've achieved with Cindy, Heck, and Bob – or, better still, have all three of those accountants present their own conclusion about your system; and how it could reengineer the preparation of Form 1040 returns, cut costs, and grow the profits of LDN."

"Mate, you hit the nail on the head," I grinned. "That's exactly what I plan to do – and there are over two thousand Form 1040 returns in that firm. The potential increase in profit using my system is massive – absolutely massive, Pat."

CHAPTER 8

I'D MANAGED TO convene a meeting with the firm's three partners, sending a memo with a simple agenda listed that contained just two points for discussion. The first was my partnership buy-in, and the second was my completed Form 1040 Tax Preparation System.

Over the previous week, Heck, Bob, and Cindy had been telling all the accountants at LDN about the incredible, systemized tax preparation system I'd built. Many of those accountants had then been to see me for a firsthand look – and were all equally in awe of what I'd developed. No one had ever seen anything like it before. To all the accountants who were open to the idea, it was a game changer in how things were potentially done at LDN. I knew this positive feedback had been shared with all three of the LDN partners – Jim, Stuart, and Brian.

So, based off that, I was expecting a positive meeting with the three partners when I entered the boardroom. I smiled as I saw all three partners already seated on one side of the table as I opened the boardroom door.

"Billy, take a seat over there," said Jim. I noticed his voice was stern as he pointed to the seat directly opposite them.

As I sat down, Stuart spoke:

"We're not at all happy with you, Billy. We'd already told you we weren't going to look into your tax preparation system any further. We've seen these kinds of systems before, and they don't work. Despite that, you blatantly ignored our earlier decision and deliberately undermined us by having Cindy, Heck, and Bob undertake a meaningless test of your system. Then, you had the audacity to show most of the accountants at LDN."

I could see Stuart was visibly shaking with anger as he muttered those words. He was leaning forward over the table, his face was all scrunched up. I could just about see smoke coming out of his ears.

The study of body language is an interesting subject – and one I'd come to master in future years. In eighteen years, I'd see similar personality traits in Steve Roberts, the CEO of Future Wealth.

My father-in-law, Jim, was glaring at me with similar disdain – his cheeks flushed red. Brian made no eye contact with me at all, instead staring down at the piece of paper in front of him.

Stuart went on to say: "As far as I'm concerned, Billy, you've openly and blatantly disrespected our instructions." He stood up as he continued, shaking his clenched fist at me. His face was wrinkled with anger.

Awkwardly, Brian tugged Stuart's shirt to try and get him to sit back down, but Stuart ignored him.

"As far as I'm concerned, Billy," Stuart continued, "I don't want you to become a partner in this firm any longer."

Jim spoke next, saying: "I can't believe what you've done, Billy. Roughly five years ago, I offered you a career path at LDN, and over the last eight months, we've been having detailed discussions about your buy-in. Hell, we even had your finance all approved, and I had plans to retire any day now. Yet, you ignored all of that and instead undermined the wealth of knowledge and expertise the three of us have – over eighty years of experience in all. We explicitly told you we weren't interested in your tax system – and look what you did anyway?"

He sighed.

"Accepting a new partner is something all three of us have to agree on, and with Stuart now against the idea, we can no longer offer you a partnership." Jim shook his head.

Brian then uttered his first words he'd spoke that day – finally making eye contact with me.

"Stuart? Jim? I think Billy was just looking to improve things. He's younger than all of us, and has a fresh set of eyes. We do need to encourage new ideas." Brian turned to his partners. "Stuart – if Billy agrees to cease all work on this system, and commits to doing things the LDN way, will you then allow Billy to buy Jim's share and become a partner with us?"

Stuart didn't hesitate.

"Yes, I would – on the basis that Billy gives us his word he'll immediately cease all further discussion about a 'better' way to do things, and simply continue operating the LDN way – as we've done successfully for the past thirty years."

The three partners nodded, and then turned back to me.

"Well, gentleman," Jim said, looking very happy and smug. "I believe we can now move onto the second point on the agenda – the partnership discussions."

"I'm afraid not, guys," I countered – noticing the look of astonishment on all three of their faces as I spoke. "I respect the business you guys have built over the last thirty years – but while it's profitable now, I believe that if LDN doesn't change, it won't be anywhere near as profitable in five years."

I met the gaze of each partner in turn.

"I'll be frank in what I'm about to say. Jim, as my father-in-law, please don't take this personally. LDN is the way of the past, not the future. You use an antiquated charging system, which rewards inefficiency and penalizes efficiency. You reward staff with the highest productivity, not efficiency. Such a reward leads to staff abusing the system and charging time to clients for work that was never done in the first place. One in three of the accountants in your firm are guilty of this, and I'm sure you know which ones they are."

The three men stared at me, open-mouthed.

I continued: "You have a lack of systems in place to prevent this – and in Stuart's case, he and his team use no systems at all." I could see Stuart glare at me as I spoke. "I've spent countless hours of my own time over the last twelve months designing a far better workflow management system to complete Form 1040 returns. Under my system, I could halve the amount of time it takes to complete a Form 1040 return. Furthermore, the office administration staff – who are paid a fraction of the salary of an accountant – can fully complete a Form 1040 return with no mistakes. You don't need to be a qualified accountant to use my system."

"Bullshit!" Stuart screamed.

"No, it's not," I hissed. "You haven't – and won't – even take the time to look at the system, so how could you claim to be making an informed decision about it?"

I replied in a calm and measured voice, which seemed to infuriate Stuart even more.

"LDN completes roughly two thousand Form 1040 returns a year," I continued. "You don't need to be an accountant to work out the extra profits LDN could make by using my system. I'm talking *massive* profits."

"Well, how much training would the office staff require to use your system?" Brian asked diplomatically.

"If they have no knowledge of the tax system, they'd require three weeks of training to give them sufficient skills. I've already designed the complete training system."

Three pairs of eyes stared at me.

"If they're qualified accountants like Heck and Bob," I continued, "it would take only one day to train them."

"I find that absolutely staggering – I can't believe it," Stuart retorted.

"I agree with Stuart," Jim nodded. "It's a load of bullshit."

"Neither of you two have even taken the time to look at my system," I countered. "Furthermore, I've developed a possible franchise model for Form 1040 returns, which we could roll out across America—all owned by LDN. I'm happy to share that model with you now, if you're interested."

"Pie in the sky stuff," Stuart snorted, as he slumped back in his chair and turned sideways to face his partners with a chuckle of laughter.

"You've accused me of undermining you all by having Bob, Heck, and Cindy prepare those Form 1040 returns," I said coldly, "first by using my system, and then by showing it to the rest of the staff. I want to clarify that first, I developed this system to improve how LDN does things and to improve the quality of work – and therefore the profits of this business. Second, I wanted some real data to show you, hence why I got Cindy, Heck, and Bob involved. I didn't tell the other accountants – they all came to me after hearing about the results. They were astonished that a novice like Cindy could use my system and outperform some of the qualified accountants at LDN."

"Cut it there, Billy," Jim interrupted me. "No more discussion about franchises, systems, or Cindy, Bob, and Heck. Stuart has very graciously agreed to allow you to become a partner in LDN – but only on the condition that you follow the LDN way and cease all work on your tax system. I agree with Stuart – it's not negotiable."

"Can I at least introduce the system to my team if I become a partner of LDN?" I asked.

"Absolutely not," both Stuart and Jim said in unison.

"Brian?" I asked.

"I'll have to go with the majority, Billy – so, no."

I sighed. "Well, then – I'm afraid I don't wish to become a partner of LDN. I formally resign from the business, effective forthwith. I'll be starting my own business – which will become a franchise business for Form 1040 returns, all across America."

Both Stuart and Jim feigned chuckles of laughter when I uttered those words, but I was determined not to let their childish approach get the better of me. I continued without raising my voice or losing my temper.

"For future reference, please remember that I offered my system to LDN and agreed to become a partner of LDN if you at least allowed my team to use my system – just *my* team. You refused my request, which I acknowledge is your right. Similarly, I will not be taking any clients or any LDN staff with me to my new business."

I then stood up and went to shake their hands – but only Brian accepted the gesture.

As I turned to exit the boardroom, Jim lost his cool. He called me every name under the sun, and I thought for a moment he was actually going to cross the room and try and punch me. In fact, he had to be restrained by Brian so he wouldn't do so.

Stuart was also muttering expletives at me, although with the volume of Jim's ranting, it was hard to hear exactly what Stuart was saying.

Not that it mattered. I wasn't going to let it get to me. Another important business trait I'd learned was to never lose your temper in front of other people. That showed a complete weakness in your personality and business acumen – giving them the upper hand in all negotiations. The first person to get angry always loses.

• • •

WHILE JIM WAS the one to get angry, I felt like I was the loser at first. I was immediately banned from all future get-togethers at the Longman residence, and was further told by Jim that I was never welcome at their home again.

Julie couldn't believe that I'd declined the partnership offer. She was fuming when I returned home from work that afternoon. She didn't want to hear my version of events, telling me she'd heard a blow-by-blow description of what had happened from her father, and reiterating what an ungrateful son of a bitch I was.

Within one day, Julie and I were sleeping in separate beds. Within one week, she had moved back to her parents' home. Within two months, she filed for divorce. For months, her father continued to tell her what a horrible person I was. Stuart Delix even contacted her the same day I'd resigned to tell her that she deserved much better than being married to a person like me.

Their behavior confirmed how glad I was never to have become a partner at LDN.

Later, Adele Longman contacted me to apologize for Jim's rage. She'd secretly met with Brian Norris to gain a clearer understanding of what had transpired during that eventful boardroom meeting – and Brian had told her I'd been professional and civil during the meeting, and had outlined in a clear, concise, and rational manner why I'd declined the offer of partnership – and tendered my resignation.

Adele admitted that Jim would always fly off the handle when he didn't get his way – something I'd observed myself on many occasions, both in the office and at social functions. She'd also said that, unfortunately, Julie displayed similar traits to Jim – which was probably a result of being their only daughter, who Jim had spoiled growing up. That, too, was something I'd observed over the previous four or five years.

Adele then added that Jim had seen me as his retirement package. He'd been hell-bent on ensuring I bought his twenty percent share and had already been planning his life of retirement based off the back of it – his dream of playing golf with his buddies every day. My decision not to buy into the partnership had thrown a wrench into those plans, which had brought out the worst in his temper.

Adele wished me all the best for the future, and at least she fully understood what I'd done and why I'd done it. She told me she was sorry that my marriage to Julie had ended in such circumstances – but that she'd watch my future success with interest and pride, and that she had no doubt I'd be successful in whatever new venture I embarked on.

Some three months after the boardroom meeting, Brian Norris contacted me, and we met for a drink. He apologized for the behavior of both Jim and Stuart, and told me that I'd warranted far more respect from both of them. Since my departure, he'd heard more and more positive things from the other accountants about the system I'd developed – and that he believed I was onto something. It had great potential, but he wanted me to understand that he was bound to follow the decisions of Jim and Stuart, as they'd been the ones who'd given him his start at LDN. He felt a sense of loyalty to both of them.

I could respect that – and we shook hands, with Brian wishing me all the best on the launch of my new franchise accounting system. He wanted to know more details, but I told him I was bound by confidentiality agreements – nevertheless admitting that I'd been working feverishly on it since my departure from LDN. The launch of my business was only three weeks away – just in time for the busy January to April tax season.

I told Brian I understood his loyalty to both Jim and Stuart, and that I respected the decision he'd made. We parted on good terms.

CHAPTER 9

SINCE MY ABRUPT departure from LDN some three months earlier, I'd been working seven days a week getting ready for the launch of my new accounting business.

I called it The Tax Refund Shop, and I'd secured a storefront on Santa Monica's busy Main Street with a two-year lease, with options to extend the lease term.

With the breakup of my marriage to Julie Longman, the family home had been sold – and instead, I'd managed to rent a small, two-bedroom unit within walking distance of my new office. I figured I had at least twelve months of extremely hard work in front of me, burning the midnight oil in an attempt to grow The Tax Refund Shop.

The launch date of the business was January 7. I'd spent three weeks training my three new employees, Jenny Bower, Helen Stevens, and Jane Spencer, on how to use my automated tax preparation system.

These ladies were all in their late thirties and had reentered the workforce after raising their families. They were all available to work for my business between 9am and 3pm, Monday to Friday. These times worked well for them as it allowed them to get their kids ready for school in the morning and be back home before they returned from school. The job gave them some extra income, in addition to their husband's salary, and would supplement their respective family finances.

None of these ladies had ever worked in an accounting firm before, and none of them had ever completed any education beyond high school. They had, however, all previously worked in general duty office roles, even if they'd been out of the workforce for over eight years by then – raising their young families.

The three of them had answered an advertisement I'd placed in the local newspaper – looking for permanent, part-time office work during January to April each year. The three of them were the perfect group of people to come and work for me at my first Tax Refund Shop – if only to prove that my systems worked. If I could get people like these three ladies to make it work, I had a business model I could potentially franchise all across America.

That night, I was meeting up for dinner with Pat. I hadn't seen any of the old crew over the last three months, as my focus had been on completing all the preparatory work to launch my new business. I was looking forward to seeing a familiar face.

• • •

"HOWDY, STRANGER," SAID Pat, as I walked over to the table he was seated at, in Barry's Steak House.

"Hi, mate. Long time no see. I've been working so hard – believe me – on getting ready for the launch of this new business."

I sat down with Pat, and once we'd both shared the usual gossip – Pat giving me an update of what had been happening in the world of McIntosh & McIntosh, and with me sharing the details of my marriage breakup – it became time to share my business plans with Pat.

Pat spoke first, demanding: "Tell me all about this latest venture, Billy. You're twenty-nine years old, so you've only one year left to make that million dollars you kept talking about at school."

Over the last five years of weekly catch-ups, Pat had developed a detailed understanding of my frustrations with the operation of a typical accounting firm – along with how I felt about the whole profession in general. I'd explained to him how I thought it was an industry ripe for disruption and a new way of doing things.

That being said - he wasn't aware of the details of my planned franchise system.

"Well, mate. I've systemized the whole simple tax return process. I've had a coder working with me for the last three months, and the whole process is now completely automated on the PC. It's gone from the manual system to completely computer driven. The test of how effective it's going to be is my new business venture, which I've called The Tax Refund Shop."

"I like the name, Billy," said Pat, nodding.

"Thanks. I've seen the trademark lawyers and everything's been trademarked, including the logo."

I produced my new letterhead and showed Pat, who nodded with approval.

"I've got three ladies working for me on a permanent part-time basis. None are degree qualified, and they've never completed a tax return before – but they've each undertaken my three-week tax preparation course and are able to complete a Form 1040 tax return in twenty to twenty-five minutes, without errors." I say that with a big smile on my face.

"Wow!" Pat's eyes widen. "Three weeks training, without any previous experience? And they can complete a tax return?"

"Yes, mate. I've systemized the tax return process from start to finish. There are fifty million standard tax returns completed by accounting firms across America every year. Most firms undertake a first interview with the client, then the work is given to a young junior accountant – who normally makes a couple of mistakes, which means the work is then redone. It's all very inefficient and doubles the number of people doing the work. That's why the average fee charged by accountancy firms is between $200 and $250."

"What will you charge, Billy?"

"Well, my system is quite different. The ladies I've mentioned will undertake the interview process and complete the client's tax return, live and right in front of the client. We only charge $100, and the client must pay then and there. I therefore carry nil debtors and nil work-in-progress, and I can complete a tax return in a third of the time it takes a typical accounting firm.

Plus, I pay these ladies a fraction of the salary a typical accounting firm would pay a qualified accountant to do similar work."

"So, big profit margins then, Billy?"

"You bet, yeah!" I opened my laptop. "I'll show you my expected profit for the next four months. Because this accounting model of mine only needs to operate from January to the end of April each year, we only do the simple tax return—no business clients, no complex work."

"Wow," said Pat as he looked at my spreadsheet. "$140,000 in profit for four months of work?"

"Yep – that's based on The Tax Refund Shop completing 2,000 tax returns during January and April - or 125 returns a week during this period."

"That's good bloody income for four months of work! But how will you get 2,000 tax returns to process? I mean you have no clients at all."

"I've started this business with my life savings - $50,000, half from the sale of our house, and half from my remaining savings." I took a deep breath. "There is no Plan B, Pat. If this business doesn't work, I'm screwed – but I don't think like that. I only focus on the positive, and I know it will work out as long as I put the work in. Anyway, back to your question: How do I plan to get 2,000 tax returns? Well, look at this."

I pulled out a glossy, two-sided color brochure, which I handed to Pat. He flicked through it.

"Looks fantastic, Billy. I love the slogan: 'Half Price Tax Returns' and the fact they're done on the spot. Graphics are great, too – the colors really stand out."

"Well, mate, thirty thousand of these brochures are getting delivered to every household within a five-mile radius of the office in the first week of January. In the first week of February, I'll have twenty-five advertisements on local radio every day, running for eight weeks. I reached under the table and produced a CD player. "Listen to this, Pat."

For thirty seconds, Pat and I listened to the recording.

"Sensational – sounds fantastic. Love the jingle," said Pat, as I turned off the CD player. The guests in the restaurant were now looking over at us to see what all the noise was about.

"So, Billy," Pat leaned in closer, "you plan to make $140,000 in profit running a business from January to April. What are you going to do for the rest of the year? Head down to the beach in Mexico?"

"No, not at all," I grinned. "For the rest of the year, I'm going to travel all around California selling The Tax Refund Shop franchises – using the actual success I'll have had here in Santa Monica. This office is my testing ground to prove my system works, with just three housewives preparing and completing tax returns for me. I'll show you the numbers based on my five-year projections."

Pat read my projections – his eye widening.

"Fucking unbelievable, Billy. Six million bucks in revenue within five years? From operating an estimated hundred franchises?"

"That's conservative, Pat," I smiled. "In fact, this is where I have an opportunity for you. If this business works as planned, I'd like you to join it. I need franchise agreements prepared. I need someone on the road with me helping to sell the vision." I opened a soft copy of my business plan on my laptop. "Look at this, Pat. You don't need to be a qualified accountant to operate my franchise. You can be an ex-bank manager, an insurance salesman, or even a housewife. It makes no difference, as long as you follow the system I've built. You simply complete three weeks of intensive training. I'm pitching the one-off franchise fee at $50,000, plus I take fifteen percent of all revenue. For that, the franchisee receives the training manuals, along with both initial and ongoing training. I've finished all the training manuals, by the way. Plus, they'll get the software and the complete marketing kit with the brochures, radio jingles, and all the other new marketing initiatives I'll develop as we grow."

"And they make $140,000 in profit every tax season?"

"Yep – if they average 2,000 tax returns. Not a bad return on investment, Pat. Each franchisee needs to be in a catchment area of a hundred-thousand people, minimum, and they should aim to complete two thousand tax returns during January to April."

"So, if you have your three little ladies seeing the clients and completing the tax returns, what will you do between January and April?"

"I'm just there reviewing and tweaking the process to ensure it's working as planned. This first office of The Tax Refund Shop will be my testing ground." I looked around the restaurant, and then back at Pat. "I'll tell you what, mate – let's continue our discussion in May. This way, you can see the actual results I've achieved from January to the end of April. If you're happy with the figures I've achieved, you can buy one-third of the business for only $15,000."

Pat's eyes widened, so I answered his unspoken question:

"Why $15,000? Well, that's one-third of what it cost me to get everything set up. Of course, that doesn't include my time – but we're mates. We've known each other for over fifteen years."

"That's a very generous buy-in price, Billy."

"Of course, you and I don't receive any salary for the first twelve months. I get two-thirds of the profit for the first twelve months, and you one-third. After twelve months, we can each draw a salary of $150,000 and continue to split the profits based on shareholding. Remember what I always say are the three key ingredients for a successful business? Leverage, processes, and distribution. At a franchisee level, this business model has all three of those nailed. It doesn't rely on the business owner doing the work – it's completely process-driven and has distribution through marketing in the local community. Furthermore, from a franchisor level, it satisfies all three. It doesn't rely on you and me to produce the revenue – the franchisees produce the revenue for us. They follow the processes which we've built, and we have massive distribution potential because there are thousands and thousands of towns throughout America where more than a hundred-thousand people live."

"Billy, you have an outstanding mind," Pat whistled. "I love your enterprise and your vision, and I can see your passion for this project. Of course, I'd love the chance to be in business with you – so why wait until May? Let's join forces now."

"No, Pat," I shook my head. "You've a good-paying job with McIntosh & McIntosh – and if you stay, you could be a partner in twelve months. Let's wait until May so you can see what I've achieved over the next four months. If it doesn't work, I don't want to screw up your life as well as mine, so let's wait until then."

Pat nodded sagely, and as he did so, I leaned in and confessed:

"By the way, Pat – I don't have an outstanding mind. I'm just full of ideas—some good, and some bad. What I've realized is that great businesses are also built on two other key attributes. It's about having the right strategy, but it's equally important to implement your strategy. I reckon its only five percent having the right strategy and ninety-five percent about implementation. Unless you can implement your strategy, you'll never be successful."

With that, Pat and I resolved to have our next discussion – about him joining me as a business partner at The Tax Refund Shop – in just over four months. We also resolved to have no more discussions about The Tax Refund Shop until after my four-month pilot program. After all, I was more than likely going to be too busy over the next four months to be able to catch up with Pat, Chook Burns, or anyone else, for that matter.

Two weeks later – on January 7, 1997 at 9am CST, the launch of the first The Tax Refund Shop in the United States would take place, at 22 Main Street, Santa Monica.

CHAPTER 10

JANUARY 6 WAS the last training day for Jenny, Helen, and Jane, as the next day we'd be officially opening the doors of The Tax Refund Shop for our first day of business. I'd explained to them in detail the Key Performance Indicators (KPI) of The Tax Refund Shop.

It was all quite simple: Each lady had to complete eight tax returns during their six-hour working day, allowing for morning coffee and lunch breaks. Our target when operating at full capacity - which was expected to be by week five – would be 125 tax returns per week. If we achieved our targets, then I'd make close to $140,000 in profit during those four months.

At the end of the day, I gathered Jenny, Helen, and Jane together.

"Ladies – I'll see you all at nine o'clock sharp tomorrow, ready for day one. We're officially launching

The Tax Refund Shop. Make certain you have a good night's sleep."

• • •

AT NINE O'CLOCK the next morning, there were already thirty people lined up outside the front door of The Tax Refund Shop.

I let the first three people in and sat them down individually in front of Jenny, Helen, and Jane. With calendar in hand, I then went out the front and organized thirty-minute time frames for the rest of the people to meet the tax preparers.

The rush was repeated the following day, and grew even larger by the third. During our first week, the three ladies completed 165 tax returns, with me staying back till 9pm each night checking their work and reviewing and tweaking systems. By that third day of the first week, I was sitting down with clients and preparing tax returns myself, just to keep up with the demand.

For the next month, we'd continue to average 170 tax returns a week. I'd managed to get the ladies to stay until 5pm two days per week to cope with the workload. At my weekly staff meeting with them, they told me we needed extra staff to cope with the work. They were all feeling rushed. I told the ladies I'd place another advisement in the local paper and try to have two more tax preparers trained and on board by the end of February. That way, at least they could assist us during the busier months of March and April.

By April 30, we'd completed 3,200 tax returns, which was 1,200 above the target I'd initially set out. We'd also discovered a few flaws in our system, so I'd been forced to re-hire my coding expert on a permanent, part-time basis throughout the January to April period.

Understandably, I was over the moon with the results we'd achieved.

The profit was $180,000, even allowing for the extra costs involved with recoding the system. We had an error rate of less than five percent – and most of the errors were because of the system tweaks. As part of the pilot program, I reviewed twenty-five percent of all returns completed, which meant I was starting at seven o'clock most mornings and finishing at nine o'clock in the evening.

The four-month pilot program proved beyond doubt that I'd developed a robust accounting model that didn't require the services of qualified accountants. Five housewives had been recruited, and after just three weeks of training, they could each consistently and accurately complete a Form 1040 tax return. Given there were fifty million Form 1040 returns being lodged by accounting firms across America each year, I knew I was onto something big.

In the first week of May, I took the five ladies and their respective spouses out for a night of drinks and dinner as a way of saying thank you for all their hard work. They'd also received bonuses based on the number of tax returns they'd completed, as I'd developed an individual bonus system to reward performance. This was something all the staff appreciated and something that would become a cornerstone in the recruitment and retention of tax preparers in The Tax Refund Shop process in the years to come.

I needed a few days off in May to recharge my batteries. Pat and I were due to meet the following week to discuss the results of The Tax Refund Shop in detail. I'd deliberately stayed away from Pat since our initial meeting in late December, sticking to our agreement to catch up only after the initial four months of operations. I knew he'd be eager to see the results I'd achieved – but I needed to spend a couple of days compiling a detailed report to demonstrate to Pat the overwhelming success of The Tax Refund Shop pilot program.

$$\bullet\ \bullet\ \bullet$$

"BILLY, I'VE BEEN dying to hear the results of how The Tax Refund Shop has performed over the last four months," Pat grinned, munching on his bacon and eggs at Joe's Grill on Santa Monica Pier. "There were so many times I was going to call you and ask you how it was going – but no, we'd agreed to wait until May. I'm dying to hear all about it."

I gave him a huge smile.

"Pat, the results of The Tax Refund Shop…"

I paused as I sipped my coffee. Pat stared at me intently. I could see he was waiting nervously in anticipation. I was enjoying messing with him.

"…have been fucking incredible." I gave him a high five. "We actually *killed* our targets. Fifty percent more tax returns completed than budgeted, and I had to cancel the radio advertisements because we had too much work and just couldn't cope with it. Profit was thirty percent above budget, and I trained another two ladies in February to keep up with the demand."

I opened the detailed report I'd prepared for Pat on my laptop.

"I'll show you in detail what we've achieved."

For the next two hours, over many coffees, Pat and I excitedly poured through the numbers. I shared my vision for a national franchise of The Tax Refund Shop all across America.

"Who are the biggest competitors in this space?" Pat asked.

"Good question. I've been analyzing the market for the last twelve months. There are a lot of small players scattered across the country. I researched several of these groups. They tend to have four to five branch offices and don't do any proper marketing. They tend to have junior qualified accountants undertake the work, with none of them able to complete a Form 1040 return in front of the client within twenty minutes like The Tax Refund Shop can. Prices range from $100 – the same as us – to $250."

"So, no real competitors."

"There's one large group based in New York with close to five hundred offices in the eastern half of the country. They're called A & C Tax Refund, the biggest tax return preparers in the country, according to their web site. They appear to have an automated system similar to mine, and recruit and train unqualified tax preparers like I'm planning to do. The big difference is that they haven't automated the process like I have, and they don't appear to complete the returns in front of their clients."

I pursed my lips, before asking Pat: "Remember Amy Fox from school?"

"Yes, of course I do," he laughed. "Amy with the big boobs."

"Yep. Well, Amy is living in New Jersey now – she and I kept in contact. She's been working in sales for a large IT company. I phoned Amy two months ago and said I'd pay for her tax return to be completed if she went to one of the A & C Tax Refund offices in New Jersey. I explained why, and I gave her a list of questions to ask the tax preparer so I could further understand how they did things. I even had Amy secretly record the conversation."

"Probably highly illegal, Billy," Pat warned – ever the lawyer, "but carry on."

"Well, long story short, the young lady completing her tax return couldn't answer all of Amy's questions, and the return took three days to complete. When I reviewed the return, I discovered so many mistakes that Amy had to go back to A & C Tax Refund and get it fixed. Anyway, it ended up taking two weeks to complete correctly, and it cost $250. It could have been a one-off, but based on that experience, they certainly didn't appear to have an automated system like mine."

"Billy, what you've achieved is phenomenal – unbelievable. I'm ready to jump in and join you now. I've had enough of McIntosh & McIntosh and the dog-eat-dog world of big legal firms. I've had enough of working twelve-hour days to make the partners rich.

I've had enough of keeping time sheets and recording every hour of what I do. Beam me up Scotty!"

Pat burst out laughing, giving me a high five.

With that, Pat and I shook hands. I told him: "Welcome as a one-third shareholder in America's newest accounting franchise, The Tax Refund Shop. Let's remember Saturday, May 17, 1997 as something special. Our plans between now and August are to sell twenty of The Tax Refund Shop franchises, and that means we've got less than four months to do it. During the months of September, October, and November we'll need to deliver four three-week blocks of training to the owners and support staff." Then I told him more exciting news. "Based on the results I've achieved with the Santa Monica office, I've decided to increase the franchise fee to $60,000. Initially we'll focus on San Francisco and Los Angeles and all the major towns in between."

"When do you want me to start? I mean, I'll have to give four weeks' notice, but based on experience, once you resign from McIntosh & McIntosh, they're happy for you to go immediately. In fact, they normally march you out the front door then and there. Given today is Saturday and I plan to resign on Monday morning, I might be around to start by the middle of the week."

"Perfect! I'll need you to start drafting the franchise and operational agreements. I also need you to find us a web designer and graphic designer, so we can standardize the web page, stationary requirements, and all the legal guff. I'll focus on tweaking the training material, and I've got a marketing person I'm meeting with next week to complete a professional franchisee marketing kit – based on what I've already developed, plus a few other options incorporating the Internet and possible use of email marketing. I've been to a couple of sessions now on digital marketing and SEO. I can see great opportunities in it to gain new tax clients for the franchisees and make our business the industry leader in the accounting franchise market."

"I'm assuming we'll both work out of the store-front you have in town?"

"Yep – that'll be our base from now until the end of December. In January, the five ladies all come back for another busy tax season. Before then, we can lease a bigger office. We may have another five-office staff working for us, if all goes according to plan!" We both laughed with excitement at the potential of our new business.

Pat resigned from McIntosh & McIntosh on Monday. Steve Menzies, the partner he reported to, was away sick, so he met with the person in charge of HR instead. What Pat had told me was correct. Thirty minutes later, he was cleaning out his office, and by ten o'clock he'd been walked out of the front door of the offices of McIntosh & McIntosh for the very last time.

• • •

PAT AND I worked feverishly during May, June, and July – completing every detail of The Tax Refund Shop franchise kit. The marketing consultants I'd engaged proved to be a godsend. I thought the stuff I'd designed and originally used for the launch of the Santa Monica office had been good. Well, believe me, with the stuff these guys produced, they made me look like an amateur.

In collaboration with the web designers, they designed and produced a slick marketing kit, which included brochures, print advertisements, radio jingles, store displays, web pages, and some simple email campaigns. They'd also convinced me to spend a large amount of money on search engine optimization. They told me this was where the so-called 'digital marketing revolution' was headed. Everything was designed to attract tax return clients to The Tax Refund Shop franchisees.

Another important lesson I'd learned in business was that whatever you budgeted to spend on something, double it. I'd budgeted to spend $25,000 with the web and marketing consultants, and the actual cost ended up closer to $60,000. However, given the finished product, both Pat and I had no trouble accepting this amount. Our marketing initiatives would clearly become crucial, and we intended to lead the marketplace in terms of bringing on new franchisees and bringing in new tax return clients for those franchisees.

In mid-July, in conjunction with my marketing consultants, we'd placed advisements in both the employment and "businesses for sale" sections of twelve newspapers. We'd developed the slogan: "Arguably America's Leading Accounting Franchise—That's Our Claim, Anyway."

Beneath that, we then highlighted the profit opportunities, along with the comprehensive franchise package provided to franchisees of The Tax Refund Shop.

The plan was to hold six informational evenings for potential franchisees in six different locations over a two-week period in early August. I'd developed a two-hour presentation to showcase The Tax Refund Shop franchise offering, which included complete disclosure of the figures associated with my initial Santa Monica office.

I'd done a lot more analysis of the franchise offering of America's largest accounting franchise – and our biggest potential competitor, A & C Tax Refund. I'd even applied for a franchise with them using a false name and address. I'd purchased a different cell phone and set up a new email address specifically for that purpose. For my interview with the head of their franchise sales, I wore a disguise that went so far as to incorporate makeup and a wig. I even changed the tone of my voice. When I examined their franchise offering, I realized what The Tax Refund Shop had was literally streets ahead of their offering.

Pat and I were becoming more and more excited about the potential of our accounting franchise. When I examined the complete package we'd produced, I knew that I'd have purchased one of these franchises if they'd been available back when I'd completed college.

For the last few months, Pat and I had been living off our respective savings. I'd been funding all the start-up costs of the franchise, along with the cost of the office and associated overheads. There'd been no money coming in, only money going out. By this point, I'd already spent almost all of the money I'd made during the January to April tax season, so it was crucial we sold some franchises during the coming information sessions, otherwise we were going to run out of money.

I didn't want to alarm Pat about our cash flow issues, or the fact I was having sleepless nights about all the extra money we'd been spending at such a rapid pace. All I knew how to do when money was tight was to simply work harder.

In the end, though, my worries about cash flow and the resultant sleepless nights would be all for nothing.

CHAPTER 11

PAT AND I arrived at the Fairmont Hotel in Santa Monica at four o'clock to set up the room for the first of the six franchise information sessions. We had another two information sessions booked at different locations in Los Angeles the same week, followed by a further three in San Francisco the following week.

These events weren't cheap to run. The cost of the venue, with additional light refreshments, and across six different locations, came close to $20,000. I didn't share this news with Pat, but after paying all the venues, I was down to my last $5,000. It had now become crucial for the survival of the business to sign up some franchisees quickly.

We were hoping to get anywhere between five to ten people at each venue, and from this, aimed to sell fifteen franchises across the six sessions. The smallest room available at each venue was for forty people, with a minimum cost of catering based on twenty people attending. The arrival time was advertised as 5:30pm figuring a six o'clock start time, and we intended for the presentations to finish at around 8pm. Pat and I had done upwards of ten full rehearsals of the presentation. We planned for me to do the bulk of the presenting, with Pat providing a twenty-minute segment toward the end in which he discussed the franchise agreements.

Pat had a complete understanding of the franchise code. His last three years at McIntosh & McIntosh had been spent as a senior member of their thirty-team franchise division. Pat had designed every piece of information we were legally required to provide to interested parties, along with all the required disclosures and disclaimers, from scratch. His expertise in franchising was an invaluable asset to our business model. For interested parties, we had an 'Expression of Interest' form to be completed on the night.

All attendees who'd completed an 'Expression of Interest' form would be sent a Franchisee Questionnaire within forty-eight hours by email or post. It was a detailed questionnaire, which required various supporting documentation to be returned by the potential franchisee. Pat had also prepared the complete kit of information we required from each potential franchisee. We had many detailed background checks developed to hopefully ensure that the people we recruited as franchisees were fit and proper individuals to own and operate a franchise under our brand.

As part of our strategy session in May, we'd also identified the top twenty risks potentially facing our franchise. The reason we did this was to mitigate those risks. The number one liability we'd identified was having unsuitable franchisees who'd potentially give our business a bad name, effectively destroying the image and associated goodwill of the brand. A saying I'd come to use throughout my business career was: "You're only as strong as your weakest link." Hence, Pat and I had developed a detailed set of criteria that potential franchisees had to meet to become part of our business.

By 4:30pm on the day of our first presentation, Pat and I had tested all the equipment we'd brought with us - from the audio, lighting, projector, and clicker, to the actual presentation itself. Pat and I were now ready for our first Tax Refund Shop Franchise Information Session – and we waited with both excitement and trepidation for the arrival of the first attendees at 5:30pm. We were like two nervous schoolkids about to attend their first day.

"Nervous?" I asked Pat.

"A few butterflies in the tummy," Pat nodded, with a worried look on his face. "What if no one turns up, Billy?" He placed his hands on top of his head.

"Well, it doesn't matter, we still have another five sessions over the next two weeks." I tried to display a positive attitude, but deep down I was similarly concerned that no one would turn up tonight – or any other night, for that matter. I'd started to worry we'd bitten off more than we could chew.

With self-doubt swirling around in my mind, I thought that perhaps I should have given the Santa Monica office a couple more years of operation before I embarked on this franchise model – or even that I should have stayed at LDN.

No, that was a stupid thought.

What was also troubling me, though, was that Pat had given up his promising career at McIntosh & McIntosh based on the initial success of my Santa Monica office, even though that had been after only four months of operation.

Since Pat had joined me in business, he'd shared with me the news that Steve Menzies, the partner he previously reported to at McIntosh & McIntosh, had contacted him after he'd resigned to try and persuade Pat to return to the legal firm. Steve had told Pat that, before he'd resigned, his name had been going to be put forward to the other partners of McIntosh & McIntosh – to discuss the potential of him becoming a partner. The starting partner salary was $300,000, plus bonuses, and the salary package would only increase in future years.

Pat had recently confessed to me, after a few too many drinks, that he was getting low on his savings, too. He'd been supporting his mother as well as his two sisters, whose husbands had both disappeared and left his sisters with young families to support. He'd raised the possibility of perhaps me lending him some money if we didn't start to get some profit share from the business soon – but of course I'd said yes, not letting him know the truth about my own finances. I was running out of money and the success of these six franchise information sessions was absolutely crucial to the survival of our business. If we didn't sell any franchises, we'd be out of business.

At 5:25pm, I nodded to Pat as eight, middle-aged guys in suits walked up the stairs busily, chatting loudly. I said to Pat, with a big grin on my face: "Here we go – the first of the attendees."

After a quick shaking of hands and introductions, they apologized for being late. I replied: "You're not late. We don't start until six."

The oldest of the group then said to his colleagues: "I thought it was a five o'clock start? With dinner at seven?"

"Yep, it is," his colleague replied. I then realized they were at the wrong function.

"You guys dentists by any chance?"

"Yep," they said in unison.

I sighed. "I think your meeting may be on Level 3. This is an information session for accountants that starts at 6:00pm." I pointed to the lift.

"Bean counters," one of the guys replied, as they made a quick exit for the elevator.

I was nervously looking at my watch now. It was 5:45pm and no one had turned up. Pat was busily pacing the front of the room, hands on his head, muttering to himself. Even during our school days, whenever Pat was stressed or worried, he'd always pace back and forth. Before every high school exam, you'd find him pacing out in the front for fifteen minutes before the doors to the exam room opened. I could never understand why he got so nervous. He always finished top of the class in any exam we'd taken.

At 5:55pm, a single, middle-aged, well-dressed woman – wearing spectacles and carrying a green handbag – approached the registration desk where I was standing. Pat was still down at the front of the room, nervously pacing.

"Is this The Tax Refund Shop information evening?" she asked.

"Yes, it is," I replied, full of excitement. "You're the first to arrive. We're expecting thirty people this evening, but I believe there's been a major accident on the freeway, which is causing chaos." Of course, I was lying – trying to explain why no one else had arrived yet. "Come in and take a seat at the front of the room." I escorted the lady in.

Then, I heard a group of muttered voices coming up the stairs and turned around to see another fifteen or so people coming toward our registration desk – a mixture of men and women of all races and ages. Some were dressed in suits, while others wore smart, casual attire.

"Come on in and join us," I grinned, handing each attendee our glossy information kit, along with a pen and the Expression of Interest form.

Seeing the influx of people, Pat came to join me at the registration desk – a big smile on his face.

"I told you they'd turn up, Pat," I reassured him. "Let's wait another ten minutes or so until we start, just in case we get a few more people."

"More coming up the stairs, Billy," Pat whispered. I turned around to see another twelve people walking up the stairs.

At 6:15pm, I announced to a room packed with over fifty people: "Ladies and gentlemen, welcome to the first of six planned information sessions about this tremendous opportunity with what is arguably America's leading accounting and tax franchise – The Tax Refund Shop. My name is Billy Houston and to my right is Pat Gabriel, one of the leading franchise experts in America." I saw Pat frown, a look of concern on his face as I said that. It was something I'd just made up on the spur of the moment, full of adrenaline.

I continued: "I apologize for the late start this evening, but with the traffic chaos outside I felt it best to delay this important information session to give everyone the chance to hear in full. Tonight, you'll learn about what is arguably the most exciting opportunity for people with passion, motivation, and a desire to build large, profitable businesses in the tax and accounting market. For those of you standing at the back of the room, we've organized for hotel staff to bring in some extra chairs to ensure you're comfortable for the presentation."

As the attendees looked up at me, I announced:

"Tonight, you're going to see the most comprehensive, automated tax preparation system for Form 1040 tax returns ever developed in America. With the training program we've developed, along with our state-of-the-art automation process, we can have anyone prepared to complete a fully compliant and correct Form 1040 return after only three weeks. We can also help you find staff and have them trained within the same three weeks to prepare a Form 1040 return themselves, in less than twenty minutes. You don't need to be a qualified accountant to prepare a Form 1040 return using our system, and your staff don't need to be qualified accountants to prepare a tax return with our system, either." I had a big smile across my face, my heart pounding with excitement.

"How about this? If I can show you this evening how you could make a net profit, before tax, of $140,000 – only working four months out of the year, for a minimal investment, would you be interested?"

I surveyed the room.

"Raise your hand if you *are* interested."

I could tell I had the audience on the edge of their seat. Every hand in the room went up in the air. The attention of everybody in the room was focused on me and what I was saying.

Pat would later tell me: "It was like you were one of the world's leading motivational speakers, Billy. You had them in the palm of your hand for the entire presentation."

Back in the moment, I was bursting with excitement as I told the room:

"I'm also going to share with you the actual figures from the pilot office of The Tax Refund Shop, which we achieved during January and April of this year—a business I started from scratch, with zero clients and three housewives as my staff. My staff were people who'd never worked in the accounting profession before – just three housewives who'd been busy raising families and had been out of the workforce for over eight years at that point. Using our franchise marketing kit, here on Main Street in Santa Monica, the pilot Tax Refund Shop completed 3,200 tax returns and generated a profit of $180,000 during four months of work."

For the next hour and forty-five minutes, I had the audience mesmerized with the potential of becoming a franchisee with The Tax Refund Shop. I was in my element, discussing The Tax Refund Franchise opportunities with passion and excitement.

Of the fifty attendees from that first night, forty-eight said they were interested. We had similar results during the next five franchise information sessions, with just over three-hundred attendees and 265 Expression of Interest forms completed.

The biggest problem Pat and I then had was how to follow up with all the Expressions of Interest. In keeping with my methodology, though, we'd automated the process so within forty-eight hours of attending an information session, each person who'd completed an Expression of Interest form would receive our detailed Franchisee Questionnaire to complete.

I'd explained this process at the end of each of the franchise information sessions. I'd then revised the number of franchisees from fifteen to forty on the first night, much to Pat's dismay. I concluded the first information session with these words:

"The response to tonight's information session has been overwhelming. We have a further five sessions to be held over the next two weeks and will be expecting more than three hundred attendees."

I was buoyant with enthusiasm at that point. Life is funny sometimes, since at 5:30pm that same evening, I'd been despondent with the concern that no one would turn up.

I told the attendees: "We're limited to just forty franchises opportunities, so it'll be a matter of first come, first served. So, the sooner you complete the detailed Franchisee Questionnaire, the sooner we can offer you a franchise in your territory, assuming you meet all of our requirements. We've already detailed them tonight, and they're also are included in your information kits. Unfortunately, we expect many people to miss out on a franchise with The Tax Refund Shop."

Over the next month, Pat and I signed up the first forty new franchisees for The Tax Refund Shop, generating instant cash in the bank of over $2 million dollars, after paying out all outstanding expenses. Over a couple of beers one night, I shared with Pat how I'd also been running out of money – and had spent many sleepless nights worrying about our future. I shared with him the guilt I'd felt in having him join me in this business – giving up what could have been a very lucrative legal career – given how our newly fledged business had been so rapidly running out of money. Fortunately, the business was now loaded with cash – and the world appeared to be our oyster.

The success of our business also brought many new challenges. We now had forty franchisees to train, as well as all their staff, during only the months of September, October and November. We also needed to assist all these new franchisees find suitable storefronts ready to commence operations in January.

After we'd signed up our first ten franchisees by late August, I told Pat we needed to find larger premises to operate our business from – as well as bringing on several new staff members to assist us.

By the end of September, we'd moved to a large, swanky office a few doors down from the old storefront on Main Street. It was already outfitted with a boardroom, offices, and a training room big enough to comfortably seat forty people. We now had a full-time receptionist, three office staff, and a trainer who'd worked extensively in corporate training for over six years. Her name was Emma Baggott, and she proved to be a blessing in disguise. Emma had been a qualified accountant who'd worked in her father's local accounting firm for four years before moving to a corporate training role in the IT industry, so she understood the industry. Her role would be to assist me in training all the new franchisees and their staff.

Pat and I had also completed a strategic review of the business, including a review of what each of us were especially good at, what we were less good at – and which skills the business needed to acquire to successfully start the first forty franchises.

This review helped us decide that Pat would become the operations manager and head the onboarding of all new franchisees. I was to oversee the sales and recruitment of new franchisees, along with the training of all the franchise owners and their staff. Within six months, I'd completely delegate the training part of my role to Emma Baggott and Jesse Samuel, our most recent employee – who'd had seven years of experience working as an accountant at my old firm, LDN.

One of the greatest business skills I've mastered over the years is the power of delegation. As long as I'd built the systems and processes for team members to follow, to ensure the consistency and quality of their work, it freed me up to do what I did best – which was recruit new franchisees.

Pat said to me at one of our daily catch ups: "Our biggest problem is going to be getting all of these franchisees set up in their premises ready for the January tax season."

I replied, with a big smile on my face: "Already on top of that, Pat. I caught up with Brian Norris last week for breakfast— the partner at LDN. He likes to catch up with me every few months to chew the fat and hear how our business is going. Truth be told, I reckon he's sorry LDN didn't back me with my franchise model. Anyway, I shared with him the fact we'd signed up forty new franchisees and were busily trying to assist them in setting up storefronts."

"Do you think that was wise? Sharing the biggest problem we face, Billy?"

I grinned: "I did it on purpose. One of Brian's clients is a guy called Griffith Peters. Griff is the national leasing manager of Westport. Do you know what Westport is?"

"Of course, I do," Pat nodded. "They're the biggest shopping center owner on the west coast." I could tell he already knew what I was thinking.

"Exactly. I'm meeting with Griff for coffee tomorrow morning to pitch a plan to set up The Tax Refund Shop in some of their shopping malls."

"How many malls do they have in California?" asked Pat, knowing full well I'd have already researched everything there was to know about Westport in preparation for my meeting the following morning.

"Sixty-one, plus another twenty or so in other states. They also have a mall in every single franchise territory we've just sold businesses in – but I imagine they'll want to start small and trial the process first. The benefit for them is that with a Tax Refund Shop storefront in each of their malls, they'll automatically drive upwards of two thousand people into their shopping centers to have their tax return completed – and those people will probably shop in one of the stores in the shopping mall while they're there. Of course, they can also charge the tenant a percentage of their turnover, so they potentially pick up extra rent revenue that way, too. They'll also receive extra rent revenue from The Tax Refund Shop itself."

"What about the cost of setting up the storefront for four months? Who's going to pay for that, Billy?"

"Already got that under control." I turned my laptop around to Pat to show the mock booth for a Tax Refund Shop set up in one of the Westport Shopping Malls.

"Looks sensational, Billy."

"All done for $2,000. I suggest we pay for each booth."

"Agreed."

• • •

THE MEETING WITH Griff Peters went exceptionally well. I briefly showed him our franchise kit, marketing material, and franchise agreements – along with details of where each of our current franchisees was located. In addition, I showed him a map of where his shopping malls were and where our franchisees would be. I told him: "Griff, all forty of our franchisees are located where Westport malls are."

After forty minutes of pitching to Griff, he finally said: "Billy, I'm very impressed. I can see the benefits to Westport. It's something we'd already been considering for a while now, given that some of our competitors on the East Coast have already started this process. I can make the decision here and now. We'll start with twenty of The Tax Refund Shops during January to April. In May, we'll review how things have gone, and if both parties are happy, we'll expand that to all seventy-nine of the shopping centers we own and manage. Assuming, of course, you'll have seventy-nine franchisees by then. I'll have my team put together a list of the twenty chosen sites from the forty areas you've shown me. You'll be required to pay for the booths, of course – which look great, by the way."

Griff glanced at his watch.

"Okay, I've got an eleven o'clock meeting to get to. I look forward to doing business with you, Billy." With that, Griff shook my hand and departed.

CHAPTER 12

"YOU KNOW, BILLY, I'm somewhat astonished just how well this business has gone. We've onboarded forty franchisees, trained over a hundred tax preparers, completed close to 80,000 tax returns, and really, we've had no major problems," Pat said.

"If I might add, Pat – we've also moved to a brand-new office, hired seven new staff, negotiated the successful set up of twenty Tax Refund Shops in Westport malls, plus we have over $1 million in the bank," I added.

It was the second week of May, and Pat and I were undertaking a strategic review of what we'd achieved since Pat had joined my business twelve months earlier. After nearly collapsing due to lack of cash flow prior to our first franchise information session in August of last year, the business was now rolling in cash. I wasn't going to make that first million by the age of thirty, but I wasn't going to fall too short of that initial goal.

A week earlier, Pat and I had our meeting with Griffith Peters and his team from Westport Shopping Malls to review how the twenty franchisees in their shopping malls had performed.

Griff and his team were ecstatic. The shopping mall tenants thought it was great having The Tax Refund Shop located in each complex. The storefronts had brought more customers into their malls, which meant both the tenants and Westport were happy.

The great news was that Griff wanted our franchise in every one of their shopping malls by January of the following year. Not only their malls in California, but also in Oregon, Nevada and Arizona – a total of seventy-nine locations.

As part of our strategic planning, Pat and I aimed to recruit a further forty franchises between now and December. Our seven-year plan was to have two hundred and eighty of The Tax Refund Shop franchises across America. It wouldn't make us the biggest tax preparation business in the United States, but it would put us within the top five. It was also going to make Pat and I a truck load of money – or so we hoped.

I ended up making that first million just short of my thirty-first birthday—one month short, to be exact.

• • •

JUST OVER SEVEN years after I first started The Tax Refund Shop, my net worth had grown to more than $8 million, excluding the value of the tax refund business itself.

I'd bought some properties that had all increased in value, and I'd invested wisely in stocks and shares.

Over those seven years, I'd also got married again. I'd met my new wife, Annabelle, at one of our franchise information sessions. She'd been working in banking and was looking to become self-employed. She'd attended one of my sessions and I'd been immediately taken by her glamorous looks – and the next day, I'd made a point of calling her to follow up on the Expression of Interest form she'd completed.

At our first meeting, I'd asked her out for dinner. Pat was furious with me – as he believed, quite rightly, that you should never mix business with pleasure. Three weeks later, though, Annabelle and I had become an item. We were married six months later.

Looking back, perhaps our marriage was a bit rushed – and, in the end, Annabelle never even bought a franchise. As we'd started to date, I took Pat's advice and told her it wouldn't be appropriate for the girlfriend of the boss to own one of his own franchises.

In quick succession, Annabelle and I had three children – two boys and a girl. You'd think I'd be happy. I had a very successful business that made a lot of money, as well as three beautiful kids and a super-attractive and intelligent wife.

The problem was: I was a workaholic.

I loved growing my business. I loved the thrill of the chase. I loved making deals, and I loved bringing on new franchisees. This all meant a lot of traveling and time away from home. The Tax Refund Shop was now a national business, and I was traveling all across the country with my team, hosting franchise information sessions from coast to coast. I worked long hours, but to me, it wasn't like a job – it was fun. Pat repeatedly told me I was a business builder, and a bloody good one at that.

The truth be told, though, my marriage was falling apart. Annabelle wasn't happy. We tried counseling, and it didn't work. It probably didn't work because of my personality, if I'm honest about it. I mean, I hated people telling me what to do and why I was wrong – and especially how I needed to change my ways.

The counselor would say: "Billy, if only you slowed down and spent more time with Annabelle."

The truth was, I was in my element right then – chasing new franchisees. It meant I had to travel across the country constantly, because not only was The Tax Refund Shop in Westport Shopping Malls, but we were now also in a trial phase with Viscount Shopping Centers, which were predominantly based on the East Coast in New York, Connecticut, New Jersey, and Vermont.

In the end, just after my thirty-sixth birthday, Annabelle told me she wanted a divorce. She'd received legal advice from Whip & Skinner, a blue-chip firm of lawyers in New York, and she wanted custody of the kids—who were all under seven at that point. She was entitled to ninety percent of all our assets – which, in her eyes, included ninety percent of my two-thirds share of The Tax Refund Shop.

I'd later learn that one of the partners of Whip & Skinner was a regular golfing partner of her father – a retired, but prominent trader on Wall Street. Her father was meddling in her affairs and offering advice to both

Annabelle and the partner at Whip & Skinner about what he thought was a fair settlement. He'd developed a dislike for me and blamed me completely for the breakup of my marriage to his daughter.

Believe me, I didn't take too kindly to her initial demands – and I'll admit I broke one of my first rules of business: I lost my cool in front of her and let her know, in no uncertain terms, what I thought of her settlement demands.

I mean, I was the one who'd built The Tax Refund Shop from scratch – and it had started long before we'd met. I was the one who had the sleepless nights worrying about cash flow before we'd met, and with all due respect to Pat – who was a great operations manager – I was the one who brought in all the new franchisees, who were the lifeblood of our business. Without franchisees, we *had* no business – which meant I had to work all those long hours and travel repeatedly across the country.

Pat wasn't too happy when I asked him how he'd feel about Annabelle owning ninety percent of my shares in The Tax Refund Shop if I agreed to her divorce settlement request.

"Well, you tell her if she takes ninety percent of your shares – which means, in effect, that she'll own sixty percent of the business – then I'm going to walk away completely; and I suggest you do the same. She knows fuck all about how to run this business, so tell her she'll have ninety percent of fuck all. She'd also better relay the same message to her old man." Pat laughed sarcastically.

Pat had never liked Annabelle. He'd thought she was going to be trouble from day one, and that she'd only wanted to be with me because of the lifestyle I could provide her with through the success of our business.

In the end, common sense prevailed, and I gave Annabelle ownership of all our property, cash, and shares – excluding any ownership of The Tax Refund Shop. So, Annabelle walked away with assets of just over $8 million, and we agreed I'd pay her $20,000 per year, per child, indexed by inflation until each our of our kids turned twenty-one. I had access to the kids every second weekend.

That was the hardest part for me, because while I might have worked long hours and traveled a lot, I always made a point of being home on weekends and being hands-on with the kids. I'd play games with them, joke around with them, take them out – all the things a doting dad does with the children he loves. Hell, they were my best friends. So innocent, so eager to learn, and not yet spoiled by any of the problems of the world. It was important that I was a role model for them.

Truth be told, for the twelve months following the breakup of my marriage, I lost quite a bit of my zest for growing the business. We'd lost a couple of franchisees by then, which wasn't uncommon. People left for several reasons—they got sick, had other personal pressures, or simply wanted a change. However, I'd only picked up eight new franchisees over the previous twelve months, so our franchisee numbers were still at the same level as they'd been twelve months earlier.

This came after me signing up an average of more than forty new franchisees every year for the last seven years – and, believe me, it had been much harder getting franchisees in the early years, because nobody knew about us in the early days. These days, we were so well-known and respected in both the accounting and franchise industry that it was a lot quicker and easier to convert leads into new franchisees.

Late one Thursday night, Pat called me and suggested we get together for lunch the next day. Over the previous twelve months, I'd been taking Fridays off. I liked to take the kids to school and pick them up in the afternoon on Fridays. We'd go down to the park and have an ice cream before I dropped them back with Annabelle – or, of course, if it was my weekend to have the kids, it meant I'd have three days with them instead of just two.

• • •

"HEY, BILLY," PAT had a big, welcoming smile on his face as he sat down next to me at Barry's Steak House – a favorite haunt of ours. The oysters there were the best I'd ever tasted.

"Hey, mate," I replied, glancing across the waters of Landmark Beach. "Such a beautiful day here on the pier. You know – you, me, Chook, and the Dodger… We were all so lucky growing up here and having this as part of our backyard. We spent so much time down here as kids, hanging out and chasing girls."

Pat snorted, remembering those days.

"Remember that concert they had for all of us kids on the beach, in the summer of 1983? We were all of fifteen, going on sixteen, and you hadn't even been at Santa Monica High that long." Pat was in between fits of laughter. I knew what was coming next.

"Ah, yes, I remember it well," I grinned. "We'd all been drinking at Chook's house, as his parents were away – and Steve, his older, moose-head brother, was having a party with his mates – something his parents had told him he wasn't allowed to do. He'd agreed to let the four of us join the party only because Chook had told him if he didn't, he'd do him in to their parents."

Pat nodded along, a big smile on his face – reflecting on that eventful night.

"Then, of course, the four of us – you, me, Chook, and Roger the Dodger – all decided at about eight, and after drinking far too many beers, that it might be a good idea to come down here to the concert and chase girls." I said pointing out across to the park.

"…and at fifteen, it didn't take us many beers to feel intoxicated," laughed Pat.

"Well, lots of other kids in this neck of the woods must have had the same idea," I reminisced, "since they had five times as many kids here than they'd expected. Only one set of toilets, too, despite hundreds and hundreds of people."

"Keep telling the story, Billy. You know it cracks me up every time."

"Well," I continued, in my best speaking voice, "I – the one and only Billy Houston – had just met the love of my life. I'd spent all of twenty minutes with her, kissing and cuddling and professing my love to her, in a totally intoxicated frame of mind."

"Tell the rest of the story, Billy," Pat was now roaring with laughter – and other people in the restaurant were now looking over to see what all the laugher was about.

"I'm dying for a pee," I continue, "so I tell the lady of my dreams to wait and that I'll be back in five minutes. I head toward the one and only set of toilets, and what do I see? A line a hundred yards long of guys waiting to pee. So, I decided to go and have a pee in the bushes instead. I mean, I'm really bursting for a pee at this point and I just can't wait. So, I stumble over to the bushes, undo my pants, drop them to my knees, and just start peeing. I remember thinking to myself: 'Gee, this feels good," as I relieved the pressure on my bladder. The problem was, though, that I couldn't stand due to my intoxicated state. I was still peeing while stumbling out of the bushes onto the pathway – and that's when something a million-to-one happens."

"Keep going, Billy," Pat had tears of laughter streaming down his face.

"There were three uniformed police officers walking down the pathway. My timing was perfect. As the officers walked past the bush I was peeing in – or, rather, the bush I was peeing *on* – I miraculously appeared out of the bush on the pathway right when they were walking down it."

I sighed.

"Picture this Pat: I'm still peeing, and I ended up peeing on one of the officer's feet."

At this moment, Pat was bouncing about in fits of laughter, about to fall off his chair. All the guests in the restaurant were staring at us, wondering what was so funny.

"Keep the noise down, Pat – people are looking at us!"

He settled down a little, so I continued.

"The next minute, I've been hiked up under the armpits by an angry officer, and he and his mate dragged me to the police van, where I spent the next three hours locked up before I was taken to the Santa Monica Police Station and held until sunrise. Of course, I never saw the love of my life again."

"Ah yes – I'm pretty sure she thought you must have been a major criminal, given you'd just been dragged off by three cops. She had no idea what you'd done." Pat was still in fits of laughter.

"I remember being locked in the van and hearing Chook Burns argue to the cops that a person was innocent until proven guilty – demanding they let his mate out. He pointed at you, Pat, and said you were studying law and would be a judge real soon, and the police would be in a lot of trouble if they didn't let me out." We both started to roar with laughter once again.

"Oh yes," Pat nodded, "except we were all under-age and just as drunk as you, Billy. I remember the officer saying he'd lock all of us up if we couldn't walk ten paces in a straight line – and Chook, Roger the Dodger, and I all bolted from the scene."

"Leaving me all alone in the police van!"

"A very funny night. Not funny at the time though."

I laughed. "No. Luckily for me, when they let me out the next morning, the guy who'd filled out the paperwork at the police station literally pissed himself with laughter at my charge. I mean, pissing on a policeman's foot? He let me go scot-free. My mum, of course, wouldn't talk to me for two weeks when she found out what had happened and why I hadn't come home that night."

"Ah yes, Billy – so many fun times we all had hanging around here. In those days, we had no work pressure, no marriage pressure – life was just one big party."

"We've both done well since those days," I nodded, "but we've both suffered tragedy, of course – with the loss of Tommy in that car accident. I guess I went off the rails for a couple of years after the armed robbery, too – while you graduated top of the class. You had a promising career with McIntosh & McIntosh. You'd have been a partner if you'd stayed."

Pat nodded. "It's been eight great years together, Billy. I don't regret one bit of it."

I paused.

"That sounds like a farewell speech, Pat."

"In a way, it is, Billy. I think it's time we both moved on from The Tax Refund Shop. You're the driver of this business. You're the heartbeat of this business. You're the one with the passion and the sales skills. But I can see it in your eyes, and I can see it from your mood. You've lost your passion for this business, Billy. You've becoming bored with the day-to-day grind – the day-to-day travel. You and I have taken this business as far as we can. We've worked hard – so, so hard – but let's both get out while we're still on top."

I paused, mulling this suggestion over. It didn't take me long to nod, and say:

"You're right, Pat. We're a bit like the coach of the Dodgers. We can get the team to the semis, but we can't win them the championship. This team needs a new leader – a new direction."

"You mean you really agree with me, Billy?" Pat had a look of bewilderment on his face.

"Yep, I agree with you. It's actually something I've been thinking about too."

"I know what it means when you say it's something you've been thinking about? It means you've done more than thinking, Billy. It usually means you've already got a strategy in place," Pat laughed.

"I do have a strategy in place," I nodded, and a big grin stretched across my face.

"Well, I'll be," Pat gave me a high five. "Share your strategy with me, Billy – I'm intrigued."

"Yep, mate, I've had enough, too. I had an inkling this may have been why you wanted to catch up. Another failed marriage for me, and I've been having a tough time for the last twelve months. You're quite right – I've lost the drive. I've lost the motivation. Once I lose the thrill of the chase – the thrill of doing deals – I know it's time to exit and move on."

"I hear you."

"Well, remember how I said I'd met Gabriel Darcy, the CEO of A & C Tax Refund for dinner at the CPA National Convention in Chicago twelve months ago?"

"Yes, of course – and that he wanted to buy our business that night, and was ready to give you a check then and there for $10 million – but that was after he'd consumed about twelve scotches," Pat added jokingly.

"Well, not actually twelve scotches. Maybe five," I laughed. "But I think, deep down, he was serious about wanting to buy our business – and he'd deliberately come in with a low-ball figure to see how I'd react. You see, Pat, we've got two things going for us that they don't have. We've got a far superior automated system than they do, despite them being in the game for three times longer than we have. We've also got distribution on the west coast, with over two hundred of our two hundred and eighty franchisees located west of Texas. If they bought us, they'd have complete penetration across all of America – with over nine hundred franchisees."

"So, what's our business worth, Billy?"

"The last valuation completed by an investment bank, twelve months ago, gave us a valuation of $20 million, based on the last three years of earnings, and a rate of return of sixteen percent after tax. Now, though, I reckon A & C would pay a premium for our software and west coast footprint. I reckon we could ask for $35 million." I took a deep breath. "It's like a game of chess. They'll come back at $25 million. We negotiate and get to $30 million." I had a serious look on my face.

Pat nodded. "Of course, they'll want a non-compete clause for a minimum of five years to stop us setting up a similar business."

"That's no concern to me, Pat. With $30 million, I'll walk away with about $12 million after tax, and you'll have $6 million. I'm happy with that if you are."

"Agreed"

With that, Pat and I shook hands on the deal. That's how Pat and I always agreed on things – a simple shaking of hands. We spent the next hour over lunch thrashing out how we'd approach Gabriel Darcy, the CEO of A & C.

Finally, I told him: "We're done, Pat. I'll call Gabriel on Monday and set up the meeting with him at his New York office."

"Now, back to the old days," Pat grinned, as we both looked out across Landmark Beach. "Let's get together next weekend with the old crew from school."

"Sounds good to me. I caught up with Chook Burns a couple of weeks ago for a few beers. He's doing well for himself. He's now got a team of about twenty lawn mowing contractors working for him. Still off the drugs. He's given Roger the Dodger ten percent of all the profits and made him his right-hand man. Roger's been doing it a bit rough – drinking a lot. Chook and I think he's still torn up about Tommy's death – but Chook said Roger still turns up every day and puts in a big day at work."

"Yeah," Pat nodded. "I caught up with Roger for dinner one night a few months ago. He confided in me that he'd forever regret that night. He said he replays it every night in his mind, trying to get to sleep."

CHAPTER 13

PAT AND I flew into New York late on Sunday afternoon for our Monday morning meeting with Gabriel Darcy and his team at A & C.

I'd phoned Gabriel the Monday morning after Pat and I had our meeting. It was a very positive phone call – and, in a way, I sort of felt like he'd been expecting it.

"Hi, Gabriel. Billy Houston, here, mate. How are you doing?"

"Ah Billy," he said, in that sharp New York accent. "My favorite Australian. G'day, mate. How's it going?" Gabriel loved trying to impersonate an Australian accent whenever he spoke to me.

I just laughed. "Gabriel, don't take this the wrong way – but that's the worst Australian accent I've ever heard. Plus, I've been in America since I was thirteen. I sound just as American as you do."

"Still sound like the man from Down Under to me," Gabriel retorted, "and I love your country. I love that game you call Australian Rules. Can't believe those players wear no padding." He paused. "So, what can I do for you, Billy?"

"Do you remember our conversation from twelve months ago?"

"Certainly do, Billy."

Good. I'd been hoping Gabriel had only been five scotches deep that night, not the twelve Pat had claimed. I wanted him to remember what we'd discussed.

"Let me guess, Billy. You've decided to explore my offer of $10 million?"

"Actually, Gabriel, Pat and I would like to come to see you in New York and take that conversation farther."

"We at A & C would love to talk to both you and Pat. When can you get to New York?" Gabriel's voice was now very serious and businesslike.

I didn't want to sound too eager and say tomorrow, so I replied: "We've got a fair bit on this week. We've been approached by a couple of other groups to buy our business." I was lying, but if I'd put the word out, I'm sure there'd be interest. "I felt, out of courtesy, that I should phone you first – given that you made the initial enquiry twelve months ago. How would next week be? Say Monday?"

"How about 10am on Monday, at our office on Chambers Street?"

"Lock it in, Gabriel. Pat and I look forward to catching up with you."

"I'll have Steve Taylor, our legal counsel, and Paul Cunningham, our CFO, attend as well," Gabriel added. Then, he said: " Billy – one more thing."

"What's that, Gabriel?"

"Please don't sign a deal with anyone else until you've met with us."

• • •

A & C HAD A very impressive mahogany boardroom on the forty-fourth floor of the T & C Building in Manhattan, with a board table that could comfortably seat twenty people. Pat and I arrived five minutes early and were ushered straight into the boardroom – where we were left waiting by ourselves for fifteen minutes.

This was often part of the power game corporate America played to try and exert superiority. It was all about trying to get the upper hand.

What they perhaps didn't realize, however, was that over the previous twenty years or so, I'd become something of a master negotiator myself – going right back to my days of running that raffle business at Santa Monica High.

I'd also – without any formal training whatsoever – become a master salesman. I'd never read a sales book, I'd never attended a sales course, and I'd never formally studied any literature on human behavior – but I'd just been born with this innate ability to pick up body language early on in a conversation, and based on that body language instantly develop rapport with the person or people I was talking to.

When I was selling franchises, I could meet with ten different individuals looking to buy the exact same franchise from The Tax Refund Shop. Emma and Jesse, who'd often sit with me during these initial sales meetings, would tell me that it was amazing to watch – because even though I was selling the same product to each person, the sales process I used was quite different depending on which individual I was talking to.

I'd say this stemmed from understanding the needs of each customer I was selling to. Each person had a different need and a different personality. Some of these people want a lot of details, while some just wanted the bigger picture and would leave the details to their spouse, partner, or business advisor to look at later.

If you didn't go through the details with the person who wanted them, you'd lose the sale – and vice versa if you sold the minute details to the big picture customer.

I was a big believer that the most important part of any meeting was the initial twenty minutes. You could gauge your understanding of the type of personality you were dealing with during that time.

Over the years, I'd taught both Emma and Jesse some of my tricks – which allowed them to use this strategy quite effectively. They weren't as good as me at making sales, but they were certainly better than they'd used to be.

After the initial meet and greet, exchanging formalities – along with some small talk about each other's businesses – it was time to get into the details of why we were there.

I knew from my previous meetings over the last four years or so that Gabriel Darcy, the CEO of A & C, was a big picture person. He wasn't too concerned with the minute details. That's why he'd brought Steve Taylor and Paul Cunningham with him, so they could look at the details later.

I also knew from the research I'd undertaken that Gabriel had a very heavy-ended bonus package based on achieving certain KPI. One of the KPI was establishing new franchises. The more the business grew, the more Gabriel got paid. I also knew that Gabriel had a wife who thrived on being part of the New York social scene. She liked the expensive apartment, expensive clothing, and to be seen at all the right restaurants.

Through my contact at one of New York's major investment banks, I'd also learned that Gabriel was heavily in debt. His wife was spending money like it was going out of fashion.

That's how I knew Gabriel wanted to buy The Tax Refund Shop before we even started our meeting. It meant more bonuses for him, purely because the transaction would add a further two hundred and eighty franchisees to A & C, almost overnight.

A & C was owned by three wealthy New York families. The business was started over twenty-four years ago and had a long-established record of steady growth for its first ten years. With a change of CEO after that first decade, Ern Grist had been appointed. Under the stewardship of Ern Grist, growth had slowed dramatically – until, after six years at the helm, he'd been replaced by Gabriel Darcy. Gabriel was appointed with a clear mandate: To grow and rapidly expand the business by adding new A & C franchisees.

Steve Taylor, the legal counsel for A & C, was in his fifties – gray-haired and well-spoken. Pat had done some research on him and didn't expect too many issues. Pat felt he could deal with any questions he might ask.

Paul Cunningham, the CFO for A & C, was a typical accountant. I'd seen lots of his type at LDN and the various accounting conferences I'd attended over the previous eight years. Paul would want to see a lot of details. I'd prepared a comprehensive seventy-page analysis of our business for him, including a complete set of financials for the last eight years, and month-by-month projections for the next five years. This was all summarized in the PowerPoint presentation I was about to deliver to the three of them.

So, I had two hours of presentation time to deliver to three different personality types – all to try and get a deal completed.

Gabriel would want to see the headline figures in relation to the number of new franchisees, and the addition to bottom-line profit. He'd then immediately number crunch his expected bonuses in his mind and compare them to the debt he'd accumulated maintaining his lavish lifestyle.

Conversely, the more detail I provided to Paul Cunningham, the easier it would be to get him across the finish line. I'd leave it to Pat to work his magic on Steve Taylor, with lawyer talking to lawyer.

Despite this challenge, I was in my element as I presented the first slide of my PowerPoint presentation. I was just about to complete the biggest deal in my short business career – and I thrived on making deals happen. Pat would later comment that watching me deliver that two-hour presentation had been like watching a conductor with a symphony orchestra. The subtle use of hand gestures as I'd engaged the three of them, the use of pauses as I spoke, the eye contact I'd made, and the passion I'd displayed as I shared the accomplishments of The Tax Refund Shop all worked their magic together.

The killer blow had been the final thirty minutes – during which I'd shared the value that The Tax Refund Shop would add to A & C, and why A & C *needed* to buy our business.

Of course, Pat and I had practiced this presentation numerous times before we'd even entered the boardroom. There was no substitute for being prepared when doing business.

Gabriel, Paul Cunningham, and Steve Taylor would never have known that Pat and I had rehearsed this presentation countless times before presenting it to the three of them, though. To them, it all looked natural, yet professional.

By the end of the presentation, Gabriel was practically jumping out of his seat. If he hadn't had Steve Taylor and Paul Cunningham at the meeting to restrain him, I believe he'd have signed a contract right then and there for whatever price we wanted. He was like a kid in a candy store, mesmerized by the possibilities flashing in front of his eyes.

Of course, both Pat and I both knew he was mesmerized by the potential bonuses he'd achieve by cementing the acquisition of The Tax Refund Shop.

Paul, the CFO, reined in Gabriel's enthusiasm.

"Gentleman," he told us, "that was a very impressive presentation. Congratulations on what you've achieved over the last eight years. I'll need time to number crunch your figures and projections before I report back to Gabriel and the A & C board."

By this time, Gabriel Darcy had regained his composure. "Very impressive, Billy and Pat. Always been hearing great things about your operation. I like your automation process, the marketing, and the training process. $35 million is a lot of money, though – so let us have some time to pore over the details."

"Not a problem," I replied. "Just to let you know, we have two other offers on the table and have ten working days from today to either accept or reject those offers." That was a lie, but deals like these were like a game of chess. You never showed all your moves at once. You bluffed wherever possible.

• • •

FIVE DAYS LATER, Gabriel Darcey phoned me to offer $25 million dollars to purchase The Tax Refund Shop. I lied and said: "That's a lower offer than the other two we've received, Gabriel. We'll have to decline your offer." Pat and I had already agreed that $30 million was our number.

The next morning, at 9am Los Angeles time, I received another call from Gabriel.

"Billy, our final offer is $30 million. I can't go any higher. You have until 5pm Los Angeles time to accept or not. Terms as per our original offer, settlement in ninety days, all in cash – with five-year non-compete clauses for you and Pat to sign. Steve Taylor is sending an email for your signatures, if you accept the offer."

"Okay. Thanks, Gabriel. Let me talk to Pat, and I'll come back to you with our decision by 5pm today."

I immediately rushed into Pat's office with a big smile on my face. "We've got it. $30 million in cash, five-year non-compete clause."

Pat gave me a high five and uttered words I'd never heard him say before:

"You little bloody ripper."

It was an Aussie expression I used a lot to describe when something great or fantastic happened.

We agreed we'd wait until later in the day to phone Gabriel and accept his offer. We didn't want to sound too eager.

At 4:30pm, I called Gabriel.

"Hi, Gabriel. Pat and I have agreed to formally accept your offer of $30 million. Agreements have been signed and emailed back. The originals have been couriered by Fed Ex to your office."

"Great news, Billy! Delighted you and Pat have accepted our offer. Once again, congratulations on what you guys have achieved in building The Tax Refund Shop. Imagine – one store, eight years ago, to the two hundred and eighty franchisees across the country you have now. We now look forward to welcoming The Tax Refund Shop to the A & C Family."

• • •

PAT AND I organized for some of the old crew from high school – namely Chook Burns and Roger the Dodger –

to come to Las Vegas with us the following weekend to celebrate our success with a fun weekend of partying, drinking far too much, and reminiscing about some of the fun we'd had when we were all much younger.

Of course, Pat – like always – insisted I tell the story about pissing on the policeman's foot. The great thing about friendships dating back all those years was that your close friends didn't become jealous of your success. They shared in it with you.

Once we were back in LA, though, it was time to ponder what to do next.

"Your plans, Billy?" asked Pat.

"No plans. Not really sure what I'm going to do. I'm nearly thirty-eight. Just need to chill for a while." I turned to my friend. "What about you?"

"Well, Sue is expecting our third child in three months. She's been onto me about buying a nice house in the Hollywood Hills for our growing family. I've already been searching local properties, and I've organized a couple of inspections."

Pat had been happily married for over twelve years. He and Sue had both gone to high school together, but had never been never an item back then. She'd had a different group of friends, and their paths at school had never crossed, other than the occasional hello. It was years later, after Pat had graduated, that he attended a friend's party and they'd hooked up.

I was somewhat jealous of Pat. He'd managed to settle down. He was as wild as me in our younger days, but now had a beautiful wife, two lovely kids, and was the complete family man – while being a very successful businessman at the same time.

Me? Well, I'd had two failed marriages and always appeared to be chasing the next opportunity. I was the sort of guy who jumped out of bed everyday full of excitement, not knowing what adventures lie ahead for the day – who I might meet, or what might transpire.

"I can't imagine you doing nothing, Billy," said Pat.

"Yep, you're right, mate. Eventually I will do something else, just not sure what it is yet. I am buying that pad in Malibu, though. Signed the contract yesterday and I'll settle in ninety days."

I'd seen a beautiful house on the ocean at Malibu. It was only a twenty-minute drive away from the ex-wife's home, so it was nice and easy to pick up the kids every second weekend.

I'd decided I was going to have twelve months off, doing not much of anything at all. I was going to enjoy a life of surfing, catching up with Chook Burns and Roger the Dodger for the occasional drink, and just chilling out. Pat and I had agreed to continue to catch up every month for a long lunch to chew the fat.

Pat knew me well, and said: "Billy, I know after having a break, your mind will be looking for new business opportunities. You won't stay idle for too long. Just promise me when that when the next opportunity comes along, please run it past me. I want us to remain in business together, no matter what that business might be."

"Of course, mate. You're my business partner. We work well together." With that, we shook hands and agreed to catch up at the same time, same place, the following month.

In twelve months, Pat and I would indeed be in business together again – a business as far removed from tax and accounting as one could ever imagine.

CHAPTER 14

"IT'S A FASCINATING story, Pat," I continued. "The town my mum used to holiday in as a kid is a small surf town in Australia. It's where three global surf clothing brands all started in the late 60s and early 70s."

We were walking along the pathway toward Venice Beach.

"I've been researching these companies and their history," I continued. "Mum used to spend every summer holidaying at her aunt's house there. Don't you reckon it's fascinating that three of the most popular surf clothing labels in the entire world all started in the same little beach town in Australia?"

"Not sure if I get the significance of where this conversation is going, Billy – but knowing you, I'm sure you have an angle somewhere," chuckled Pat.

"Look around you, Pat. What do you see?" I gestured toward Venice Beach. "Not just young kids, but their parents and grandparents – all wearing surf label clothing. It's a fashion statement. It's a clothing revolution. There are now some very large global surf clothing companies. Not just those that originated in Australia, but also from Europe and America."

I pointed.

"Look over there! Those young kids are all wearing well-known surf brands. There's an opportunity in this whole surf fashion industry. The market is enormous, with so many big players – and guess what, Pat? These big players have a track record of buying the smaller players at incredible prices."

"Billy, you still draw stick men – you have no artistic talent whatsoever," Pat laughed. "Not that I should brag, as I have zero talent myself."

"I don't mean you or me designing clothes, Pat," I laughed back. "I mean we employ designers – people with lots of experience. I've been doing the research, Pat. There's an opportunity for us to make some serious money. In fact, I've been doing more than research over the last six months. I'll fill you in over breakfast tomorrow and share what I've been up to."

"What you've been up to, Billy?" Pat's eyes widened. "The mind boggles – and knowing you, it'll be something I never expected. Yep, let's do breakfast tomorrow."

• • •

THE NEXT MORNING, Pat and I met for breakfast at Santa Monica Pier – and I shared the vision for my next business venture: A global clothing company based in Huntington Beach, California.

"I've set up a company called Huntington Beach Surf Company Ltd. I've put trademarks in place for a clothing label called Shortfuse. I've got trademarks lodged in America, Europe, UK, Australia, and New Zealand."

"Shortfuse," said Pat. "I like it. It's catchy."

"I've also got a designer called Stevie Williams working for me. This is the label." I pulled out the images I'd received from the designer I'd hired six months earlier.

"Looks really good, Billy. So, tell me the story about Stevie Williams."

"I met Stevie through an old LDN client of mine, Georgia. She owns one of the largest medical practices in LA. I was sharing with her my idea of Shortfuse and the work I was doing in looking to build a global surf clothing company. By coincidence, her younger brother, Stevie Williams, was working with Acrabada – one of the largest clothing companies on the East Coast."

Pat listened as I continued:

"He's college-educated and lead on one of the design teams at Acrabada. He's a young guy in his late twenties, and very ambitious. She said he wasn't entirely happy where he was – so, I phoned him out of the blue on his private cell phone and had a good chat with him about what I was looking to do, who I was, and my story. I said if he was interested in hearing more about my vision, I'd fly to New York and meet with him. By chance, he was actually coming over to Los Angeles for a family wedding. So, seven months ago, we met. He's since quit his job with Acrabada and has been working for my clothing company for the last six months, designing a range of clothes."

"So, you've been operating now for six months, Billy – and you've kept this completely to yourself. Never once over lunch for the last six months have you mentioned anything to me about it. You're fucking unbelievable, Billy."

Pat sat with a look of astonishment on his face. I rarely saw Pat angry, but I was seeing it now.

"Yep, correct." I laughed, trying to ease the tension developing between us.

"Billy, you're unbelievable," he repeated, shaking his head.

"Listen, I didn't want to get you involved until I got things up and running – to see if my idea had potential, much like I did with The Tax Refund Shop. You have a young family, Pat. I didn't want you to lose any money if my idea failed."

Pat didn't seem entirely satisfied, but he said: "So, tell me the whole story, Billy."

"Well it's a long story, but it's also a fun one – and so different from our corporate life running The Tax Refund Shop. It started when I met with Stevie Williams and offered him a job. Base salary of only $50,000, which is much less than the salary he was receiving while working for Acrabada, but I've given him ten percent of the company on the basis that he stays with Shortfuse for a minimum of five years."

I pulled a sample of various board shorts and tee shirts out of my duffle bag.

Pat took the samples and examined them, whistling softly.

"Holy cow – this stuff looks great. Love the board shorts." He paused. "What this?" Pat was now holding a package seven inches long by three inches wide, wrapped in plastic in the shape of a surfboard.

"You like the design?" I said pulling out another three similarly shaped packages, all with different motifs on them.

"They look really cool, Billy. What are they?"

"Well, young Pat, believe it or not, if you take the contents out of the plastic wrapping and put it in the washing machine, it turns into this." I pulled out a full-length, fluffy beach towel.

"You're kidding me! Incredible. So soft. So large. You mean this package turns into this?" Pat was now holding up a beach towel as tall as he was.

"Yep – twenty minutes on a cold machine wash and you have that."

"Unbelievable – and this one guy, Stevie, has done all this?" asked Pat.

"Well, no. Now, I have six other people involved in the business, too."

"Six other people, Billy, and you haven't mentioned one thing about this to me until now?"

I could still see the look of anger on Pat's face. Pat rarely lost his cool – but was obviously upset that I'd kept this new business opportunity from him for over six months.

"Yep. You see, after a month of working for me and designing these incredible clothes, Stevie was getting a bit overwhelmed. He came to see me and said he loved my vision and where I was going with Shortfuse, but that he'd been working six, sometimes seven days a week designing them – and for only $50,000 a year. True, he had a ten percent share of the company, but his payday might be years away. He mentioned there were two guys he'd worked with at Acrabada. They were brothers—Billy and Bobby Jones. Billy was referred to as Billy J."

Pat nodded, listening as I continued.

"Stevie told me they're absolute legends in the clothing design game and – like he was – not entirely happy at Acrabada. He said he'd showed them the stuff we'd been doing at Shortfuse and shared my vision with them. They wanted to meet with me to talk about the possibility of joining the company as well."

I shrugged my shoulders.

"So, just like that, four months ago, I hopped on a plane and met with Billy and Bobby Jones in New York. Stevie came with me. Long story short, they joined Huntington Beach Surf Company as designers nearly four months ago. They're working from their apartment in New York."

"How much do you pay Billy and Bobby?"

"Well, I only pay them $50,000 each – and I've given them each five percent of the company."

"So, let me get this straight, Billy. You've got three experienced designers – Stevie, Bobby, and Billy J. – working for you right now, with salaries of $50,000 each, and you've already given away a total of twenty percent of the company?"

"Correct, Pat. I've reduced their salaries from what they got paid at Acrabada, but I've given them shares in the business."

"Carry on with the story, Billy. I'm fascinated."

Pat said that, but he was still shaking his head – not looking happy with me.

"Oh, it gets better, Pat, believe me," I promised with a chuckle, trying to lighten the atmosphere between the two of us. "So, the guys are busy designing the clothes, and the range is getting bigger and bigger. It's looking impressive – but Stevie, Bobby, and Billy J. are designers, not businesspeople. I mean, they know all about designing – but bugger all about production. They came from working for a large clothing brand with hundreds of employees. Acrabada had a whole, separate division looking after production in China and Indonesia. It wasn't something they ever had to worry about."

"That's what I was about to ask, Billy. Where and how do you produce this clothing?"

"That was my dilemma. I knew bugger all about production until I met Sammy."

"And who might Sammy be?" Pat had a look of intrigue on his face.

"Well, I'm a big believer that things happen for a reason, Pat. A couple of months ago, I was running on the beach at Malibu, and this guy walking the other way stopped me and asked me if I was Billy Houston."

Pat raised an eyebrow. I continued:

"He introduced himself as Sammy. He told me he was the guy who'd imported all those gifts for you and me a few years ago." I nudged my mate in the ribs.

"Remember when we organized the Christmas gifts for all the franchisees and their staff? About seven hundred gifts in total?"

"I remember it well," Pat nodded. "That company in South Pasadena organized it all. Made in China and imported across here. The franchisees loved the gifts."

"Well, Sammy is the owner of that company, so I asked him if he knew a lot about importing from China, and he said it was what he did for a living. Then, I asked him if he knew anything about having clothing manufactured in China – and he said he had three main factories in China on contract with him. Through them, he supplies clothing to some of the biggest retailers in Canada and parts of the United States. He said he's in China every month, checking on quality and conditions at the factories. I told him I wanted to discuss this with him, so the next day, I met him for coffee and shared my vision for Shortfuse."

I was smiling so hard that my cheeks hurt, excited about the story.

"I showed him some of the designs that Stevie and the team were working on, and I told him I needed someone who could source production facilities and organize production. I asked him if he was interested – and told him I'd give him seven percent of the company."

"Let me guess, Billy. Sammy accepted." Pat snorted. "I mean, I know how persuasive you can be and how you can paint a picture. I know what you're capable of, Billy – but this is like something out of a Hollywood movie."

He was frowning, now – and that didn't change when I replied:

"Yep, Sammy accepted. I mean, it compliments what he's already doing in China. He helps grow Shortfuse and, in exchange, gets seven percent of the company. He gets paid nothing for his time though."

"But if Shortfuse works out as planned, he'll get the upside of seven percent of the sale price – and, of course, I assume you plan to sell Shortfuse one day, right?"

"Exactly – and I'll come back to the endgame for Shortfuse in a moment. First, I need to tell you about Gonzales—a Mexican guy I hired, who lives here and has worked with Sammy before. He reports to Sammy and does all the grunt work on the production side."

"So, that's four – plus Stevie, which brings it up to a total of five people, Billy." Pat narrowed his eyes. "You mentioned six, though – plus Stevie. Who are the other two?"

"Yep, seven people, including Stevie – and, of course, a design shop on Huntington Beach Road overlooking the ocean." I said, laughing. "The other two are my two sales representatives on the road—Gus McLeod and Stewie Saunders."

"Never a dull moment with you, Billy."

True enough. I shrugged.

"I've been bored, Pat. It's now been twelve months since we sold The Tax Refund Shop, and I've been looking for something new, and challenging, and fun. Something different from tax and accounting. Something different from running a franchise business. These design guys think differently than you and I do.

We're controlled – calculated in what we do, always measuring risk, return, and payback periods. These designs guys are free-spirited, laid-back creatures."

"So, how much clothing have you sold so far, Billy?"

"Well, please understand that clothing manufacturing is a different beast to selling accounting franchises. It works like this: We show the sample range to surf stores—I mean Gus and Stewie do this. If the store likes the sample range, they place an order with us – ten percent paid up front. Even though it's five months until summer, we're already selling the summer range right now. We've got another two months with Gus and Stewie selling on the road. Sammy already has a factory sourced in China, ready to go into production with fabric. We've booked the factory for a couple of weeks to manufacture our order book. Once it's manufactured in China, we'll then ship it all back to the States, to Huntington Beach, and from there send the merchandise to the surf stores by freight."

Pat's eyes widened as I continued.

"So, I'm budgeting our first summer sales to be around $700,000. We've nearly already reached that level, so we'll be closing the order book real soon. Once that's done, Stevie, Bobby, and Billy J. will start on developing the following winter range with new, fresh designs."

"So, if you have more people like Gus and Stewie on the road, generating more sales, the order book gets bigger and bigger," Pat said.

"You hit the nail on the head – but the key is the designers. If they can design something different and cool, the surf shops will want to buy it, which makes it so much easier for Gus and Stewie to sell the clothing range. The margins we make are enormous, once we get the volume up. It's a bit like the chicken and the egg, Pat. We must slowly get a reputation for being a cool brand, which costs us a lot of money until we get the volume up. Then, we ramp up production and move into profit territory fairly quickly."

"So, what's the endgame here, Billy? I mean, you always start with the end in mind – I know how your mind works."

"Good question. The endgame is quite simple: We go hard for seven years, building distribution not just here in the States, but in Canada, Australia, New Zealand, and Europe. In seven years, we'll sell to one of the global players for around $30 to $50 million. In the last three years, six of the biggest players in the surf industry spent a combined $500 million buying twenty, smaller clothing labels. The big players buy out the smaller players – they've worked out that it's cheaper and simpler for them to let people like us put in the hard work, make mistakes, and build the label. Then, when it gets to a certain volume, they'll pay a premium to buy that label."

"I don't understand how they make money doing that."

"Because, young Pat," I laughed, "the big players produce in such immense volume in the overseas factories that their cost of production is ridiculously low – even compared to ours. They can produce at a lower per unit cost than I'd ever be able to. In many cases, they'll also own the retailer, as they have their own shops. Its what's called vertical integration, and their margins are enormous. They have no middleman."

I gestured around us.

"Pat, look around you. Vertical integration is a new phenomenon across numerous industries in this country. It's a sign of the times and it will only get bigger."

"What's the total cash burn over the next seven years, before someone buys the business?"

"By the end of year one? I'll have put in close to $1 million. By year three, it peaks at $5 million, then it becomes profitable. If my projections prove right, by year five, the sale value of the business may be $15 million, and if we hold out until year seven, it could be anywhere between $30 and $50 million." I opened my laptop and shared my seven-year, detailed cash flow with Pat.

A sudden sense of déjà vu hit me.

"Pat – remember? It was at this same café, nine years ago, that I did the same thing we're doing now – only I was sharing the cash flows for The Tax Refund Shop, not Shortfuse."

"A bit eerie, Billy. That decision nine years ago turned out to be the best decision I've ever made. So, count me in if you want me on board as a business partner."

"I've already given away twenty-seven percent of the company to Stevie, Billy J., Bobby, and Sammy – so I'll offer you one-third of my remaining seventy-three percent of the company. That gives you roughly twenty-four percent of the shares. I've spent $500,000 over the last six months, so for $160,000, you can have one-third of my shares, Pat."

"Deal."

We shook hands.

"Oh, by the way," I told him, "you'll also be required to put in a third of the $5 million over the next three years to fund the growth."

With that, Pat and I started our next business venture – which would have far different financial results than those of The Tax Refund Shop.

CHAPTER 15

"MAN, WE NEED to go real slow. We're a cool label. If we start mass producing clothing now, we'll destroy the brand."

So said Stevie, our designer.

"Totally agree. We're soul-based," added Billy J. "A pure, free-flowing clothing label not caught up in the idea of making money. Not beholden to any corporate animal, driven by ideals of sacrificing design and trying to be cool just for the sake of money."

I looked at Pat. He knew I was about to lose it – but I held myself together and remembered one of my ever-important business principles: Never show your anger in a business meeting. If you do, it simply gives the other party the upper hand.

"Stevie? Billy J.? I appreciate your thought process and understand that perhaps you come from a different angle than Pat and I do – but, please understand that while you guys and your design team sit in that lovely studio overlooking Huntington Beach, working out the colors, pictures, and designs for the next label without a worry in the world, it's me and Pat who have to constantly worry about how we pay the bills."

I put my hands on my hips as I continued.

"Despite me repeatedly reminding you that cash in the bank is king, you guys still don't seem to get it. If we keep on burning through cash like we have been, we won't have a clothing company – full stop."

"Man, we told you this has to be a slow, slow process," Stevie rolled his eyes. "We appeal to a niche market. This market then becomes the tipping point – when the general mass market starts to buy our goods."

"I get that, Stevie. It's what we decided from day one," I nodded. "That's why I hired your mate Tommy from Acrabada to head our marketing strategy – as you know, he doesn't come cheap. What I'm saying is that the strategy we agreed on is years behind schedule because you guys continue to try and build the perfect board shorts. I mean, your design team spent six weeks continually redoing the bloody eyelets on the whole board short range! We nearly missed the summer production run last year as a result, and we had to pay the factory in China a large fee to reschedule it."

"Man, but those eyelets are a work of art," said Billy J. "Plus, if you're so concerned with the marketing strategy, why don't you have Tommy T. in this meeting as well?"

"Because this is a shareholder's monthly meeting, not an operations meeting," I replied coldly.

For the last eight months, I'd been running these monthly shareholder meetings with Stevie, Bobby, Billy J., Sammy, Pat, and myself. Pat and I believed we needed to make Bobby, Billy J., and Stevie have some understanding of the financial side of the business. We'd hoped it would help them achieve a balance between the creativity of their designs, while also understanding the importance of sales and cash in the bank.

It didn't seem to be working.

Sammy, who ran his own successful business, fully understood. He supported what Pat and I were trying to do.

Stevie complained: "We have over a hundred and fifty stores in America and Canada stocking our clothes already, plus nearly another forty in Australia and New Zealand – and we're just about to push into Europe."

"Correct. But go back to the original budget we put together over two years ago – which, twelve months ago, you said was still achievable, even though we were miles behind schedule. We're so far behind schedule it's a joke."

I shook my head.

"Guys, I'm going to share with you the current state of The Huntington Beach Surf Company Ltd., or what we all affectionately know as Shortfuse."

"I'm sick of looking at figures," Billy J. rolled his eyes again. "Man, I just want to design clothing. You guys can worry about the figures."

"I'll cut to the chase, Billy J. You guys *need* to look and understand what I'm about to show you – because if Pat and I decide to cut funding to this business, then the three of you, along with your design teams, are out of a job. You get that?"

"...*and* your shares become worthless," added Pat.

A look of concern suddenly appeared on the faces of Stevie, Bobby, and Billy J. I knew they were happy to work for minimal salary in the belief that Pat and I would achieve with Shortfuse what we'd achieved with The Tax Refund Shop. They were looking forward to their big payday when we sold the business in five to seven years. It was the payday we were all hoping for.

I opened the PowerPoint presentation and saw the look of approval on Pat's face. He knew I was in my element when I took to the floor to demonstrate my point.

As it happened, the point I was making was quite simple. If we didn't turn this business around in the next twelve months, Pat and I were going to close it completely and walk away – with our tails between our legs. If that happened, Stevie, Bobby and Billy J. would be out of jobs – and their shares would be worthless.

After my forty-five-minute presentation, I said to the shareholders: "So, in a nutshell, that's it. Pat and I have invested $6 million over the last three years in this business, and we've achieved less than fifty percent of our sales targets. We've spent a million dollars more than we'd originally budgeted. Yep, we've become known as a cool brand – but our following is a minority, not the majority. We keep talking about the tipping point, but I'm concerned we'll never reach that magical tipping point."

There was an ominous hush throughout the room.

"Based on the forecasts Pat and I have completed," I continued, "we'll be required to inject another million dollars over the next twelve months just to keep the doors open – hopefully breaking even and making a small profit by year five. We know we have over two hundred stores stocking our goods, but they only place small orders. We need to be more than doubling our sales targets, guys – and we need to do it *now*."

A glum look appeared on the faces of both Stevie and Billy J., while Bobby gazed into space as though he wasn't even interested in being part of this meeting. These guys had little understanding of business. They were great designers, but they much preferred to spend day after day hunched over a drawing board, sketching the next clothing range. To them, this was our problem, not theirs. I think they thought Pat and I had a magic wand that would appear out of nowhere and fix everything.

After a minute or two of silence, Billy J. piped up: "So, you and Pat would close shop just like that?"

"Why would you do that? Then you'd lose six million dollars."

"Yes, Pat and I would close up shop, just like that – if we didn't believe the business could achieve its targets. You're quite right, Stevie – it means we'd lose six million dollars – but I'd rather lose six million than keep going and end up losing ten million."

I shook my head.

"Listen, guys. One of the secrets Pat and I have learned in business is that for every ten ideas, only six ideas will work out, on average. We just don't know which of those ideas will work until we try them. The secret, gentlemen, is to know when to call it quits with the ideas that don't work."

Pat then spoke:

"Guys, we started this business with an end game in mind – to ultimately sell this business in five to seven years, going from inception to selling to one of the big players. We shared our vision with you. Billy gave you guys shares in the business, so you'd share in the upside right along with us. The vision hasn't changed – but the financials have. Billy is simply saying that unless we massively increase our sales in the next twelve months, we'll have to call it quits."

Sammy, who was normally quiet and reserved – a man of few words – spoke up:

"There are at least sixty surf stores that you guys, along with Tommy T. and the sales team, have refused to stock our clothes in. In your words: 'They're not the right fit. They're not cool enough to sell Shortfuse.' Guys, after hearing what Billy and Pat are saying, I think it's time to change direction – and I mean *now*."

"I'm not sure that's the type of business I want to work in," Billy J. scoffed. "I'm a designer, guys. I don't prostitute my work. I don't prostitute my soul. I'm not driven by the almighty dollar."

"Well, Billy J., I guess you'll need to do some soul searching – because as of today, Pat and I have decided we'll only continue to fund this business if we change the sales strategy. We now sell to the masses. We've given you guys three years to reach this so-called tipping point, and it hasn't worked out yet. Tomorrow, I will be having this same conversation with Tommy T. and the rest of the design team. If you won't embrace our new strategy, then I suggest you resign. Of course, as per your employment contract, if you cease being an employee within five years, you lose your rights to shares in the business. Correct?" I looked directly at Pat.

"Correct, Billy," he nodded. "You all have non-voting shares, which are only vested after five years of service. The same applies to you, Sammy."

"I'm fully aware of that," Sammy nodded. "It was explained in full when we joined the business."

"Guys, before we finish here today, I just want to add one more piece of wisdom. In life, there are three types of people. First, we have people who *make* things happen. Second, we have people who *watch* things happen. Third, we have people who wonder *what the fuck happened*."

This earned some thin smiles.

I continued: "Pat and I are in the first category – we give things a shot. We're big believers that success is based on five percent of the right strategy and ninety-five percent the implementation of that strategy. Pat and I believe that reaching a tipping point isn't going to work – it's the wrong strategy. We have a great design team. We have great clothing, but it's now time to open up the range to the masses and move away from being a niche player."

• • •

BY THE END of the week, Stevie, Bobby, Billy J. and Tommy T. – along with three other designers – resigned from Shortfuse, never to return. They had their knickers in a knot, so to speak – or, to put it more bluntly, they were pissed off with the direction Pat and I had chosen to take Shortfuse.

Over breakfast on Saturday morning, at our favorite haunt on Santa Monica Pier, Pat said: "Well, Billy – this week hasn't quite gone according to plan."

"No. Shit happens, I guess. I'm a big believer that life's a learning experience and that everything happens for a reason."

"Well, what do you suggest we learn from this, Billy?" asked Pat.

"It's a big lesson for us. One big thing I learned is that we never, *ever* get involved in an industry we don't understand. I mean what the fuck do we know about clothing?"

"Fuck all," admitted Pat.

"Correct. Yet, here we were – or, more correctly perhaps, here we are : Thinking it would be easy to reap the same rewards the other surf brands were, by building a clothing label from scratch. We've had some great designers, and I know hindsight is a wonderful thing, but we should have been tougher on the whole design and marketing team from day one. We should have said: "Fuck this tipping point notion." We couldn't afford the cash burn for however long it took to reach that tipping point – and I believe we still realistically have another two to three years of burning more cash, which could take our losses to close to $10 million. That's nearly $7 million for me and $3 million for you."

"It means we've both just blown a large chunk of the money we made from The Tax Refund Shop," Pat gave a sarcastic laugh.

"Exactly."

"So, what do we do, Billy?"

"Good question. I believe we have two options right now. Option one is quite simple – we close shop now and walk away – and vow never to get back into the clothing business."

"So, we've blown $6 million, then," Pat said.

"Perhaps, a better way to look at it," I laughed bitterly, "is to say we've saved $4 million by only losing $6 million and not $10 million."

"What's option two?"

"We continue the business with the reduced design team. I mean, they're young and inexperienced, but all of them are talented. We still have our production team and sales team in place. We'll just change the distribution focus – to move away from being a niche, cool label to a label that appeals to the masses."

"Perhaps we 'prostitute ourselves by selling our soul' to one of the low-end, mass selling department stores," replied Pat, using Billy J.'s pretentious words.

"Exactly. Slash our margins, reduce our profit, but dramatically increase our volume. You and I could approach some of the largest discount department stores in the country. We could do a whole sales pitch with their buying heads about how Shortfuse could become their in-house surf clothing label."

"It has some appeal – but it'll probably be a lot of hard work for us."

"Yep, that it would. Traveling the country, meeting the buyers, coming back with our designers and showing them the range – all hoping that one of the big department stores take us on."

"But no guarantee that they will," added Pat.

"Yep, no guarantee that they will take us on," I said, echoing the same thoughts Pat had. "Let's sleep on it for the rest of the weekend. We'll talk again on Monday when we've both had time to digest this tumultuous week."

"Just one more question for you, Billy. You recently purchased the freehold of the Huntington Beach Studio. If we were to close shop, what would happen to that?"

"No drama there. I'd simply lease the building. I mean it's a great location that overlooks the ocean. It would make a great office for someone."

• • •

AT 9AM THE following Monday morning, Pat and I met to compare our thoughts about the next steps for The Huntington Beach Surf Company Ltd.

"You go first, Pat. Is it option one or option two? Or is there a third option we haven't thought of yet?"

"Option one, Billy. I suggest we walk away and close the business."

"I agree with you. Option one it is then."

With that, Pat and I shook hands and planned the closure of The Huntington Beach Surf Company Ltd.

A staff meeting was called that afternoon, and the staff were informed that the business would be closed within fourteen days. All staff and suppliers were to be paid in full. Fortunately, the factory in China hadn't commenced the next production run for the upcoming summer range, so it was quite an easy process to halt.

Pat and I would never, *ever* again get involved in an industry we had no knowledge of. We'd learned a valuable, if expensive lesson: Stick to the businesses you know. Pat and I knew the tax and accounting industry, but we'd known bugger all about clothing.

My total cash losses, after paying all the bills, were $4,253,456.

Pat's was one-half of mine.

There was, of course, an upside for both Pat and me. We still had a warehouse full of board shorts and t-shirts, which meant our family and friends would be receiving Shortfuse merchandise as birthday and Christmas presents for the rest of their lives.

Even today, some nine years later, I still see the odd person wearing Shortfuse clothing and feel a touch of nostalgia. I'm tempted to ask them what they think of the clothing – but then I think of four million, two-hundred-and fifty-three thousand, four-hundred-and-fifty-six reasons why I should move on and forget about it.

CHAPTER 16

"BILLY, I HEAR you've been doing a lot of walking along Malibu Beach the last few months. I know you do your best thinking when you're walking along the beach. So, what are you up to?"

Pat asked me that question over the phone.

"You're quite right, mate," I told him. "I've been restless and I've been looking, researching, and thinking about what to do next. Let's catch up at the usual place for breakfast next Wednesday. I'll share my ideas with you. I reckon I'm onto something."

"Well, as long as it doesn't involve clothing, I'm happy to hear your ideas," laughed Pat.

It had been six months since we'd closed Shortfuse. While both Pat and I had lost a lot of money in that ill-fated business venture, I still had the burning desire and get-up-and-go attitude to launch a new business. I was approaching forty-two years old and I couldn't afford to retire yet, not given the money I'd lost in the clothing business. Plus, I was still required to pay my ex-wife Annabelle sixty thousand a year for the maintenance of our three children.

I did my best thinking while walking alone along the beach. I think it has something to do with the soothing sound of the waves and the feeling of soft, wet sand beneath the soles of my bare feet. Over the last six months, I'd been walking every day along Malibu Beach, pondering my next business venture.

I could walk for hours along that beach, engrossed in deep thought and thinking of new ideas, somewhat oblivious to the people walking both past and toward me. It was the time when my creative juices flowed best – when I felt like I could solve just about any problem I'd encountered in my life in a clear and concise manner. In fact, it had been a joke for many years between Pat, Chook Burns, and Roger the Dodger that when I was seen walking along the beach alone, it meant I was pondering a new marketing strategy or a new, weird and wonderful business idea.

Over the past three months, I'd started to date a woman who lived in the local Malibu neighborhood. I'd met her on one of my many walks along Malibu Beach. Her name was Isabella, and she was thirty-eight years old and recently divorced, with two children aged ten and twelve. We'd later get married. Unfortunately, the marriage wouldn't last beyond eight years – once again because my workaholic nature consumed me. Isabella would be my third and final marriage. After three failed marriages, I vowed never to get married again.

• • •

"MATE, WHERE WE lost it with Shortfuse was by getting involved in a business we knew fuck all about."

I was explaining my new idea to Pat Gabriel.

"I mean, what did we know about the intricacies of building a clothing label? We had to deal with overseas factories, designers, buyers, retailers – so many different moving parts, and we had such tight deadlines to meet. Then, of course, we also had to deal with the different seasons and organize a spring range, a summer range, and a fall range. Added to that, in Australia and New Zealand, we had a summer and winter range in complete opposite to the American seasons."

"You forgot the European seasons, and the forex exchange issues, Billy," said Pat.

"Ah yeah." I sighed. "We had to quickly learn about hedging currency across China, Europe, and Australia – all an absolute nightmare." I shook my head. "And, of course, I got us involved in a business where I didn't put in place the three most important ingredients – the three things that led to the success of The Tax Refund Shop".

"Leverage, process, and distribution," said Pat.

"Exactly," I replied. I looked at him earnestly. "Let's go back and look at the great business we built and sold for $30 million. It was a business built on those three principles, Pat. We streamlined and automated the whole accounting and tax process, so all anyone had to do to have a successful franchise was simply follow our process. We built the marketing kit for them, the operations kit, we trained the franchisees and their staff. Remember our saying? For any task done more than once, there must be a documented system and process – because why the fuck would you do the same thing ten times, in ten different ways?"

Pat nodded sagely as I continued.

"The beauty was that we put in place the franchise model. They paid us a fee to join our franchise, and we took a clip of the ticket based on every dollar of revenue they produced."

"And, of course, if they didn't follow the process, we had the right to terminate their services and take back their franchise. We had control over what and how they did things."

I nodded. "After eight years, we understand the franchise model in tax. I mean, we were recognized as one of the leaders in the tax franchise business in America. We built the business around innovation and automation. There are currently about 300 million people living in America. There are so many Americans between thirty and fifty-five years of age, Pat. That's where my idea comes from."

I leaned in closer.

"Here's my thought: They need investment advice, so they can plan for their retirement. They need life insurance, in case they pass away prematurely. They need accident insurance, in case they get sick and can't work for a long period."

"I get that, Billy," Pat nodded. "Most Americans spend more time planning their next holiday than planning for retirement."

"Imagine if we had an army of financial advisors providing advice to the average Americans about investing and planning for life after work. A whole army of advisors ensuring the average American had adequate insurance in place."

"So," Pat asked, "are you suggesting we employ advisors to look after the financial needs of the American masses?"

"I'm suggesting that we do to the financial advice industry in America what we did to the simple tax return: We set up a franchise business model for financial advisors. Imagine that you're an advisor looking to start your own business. You pay us an upfront franchise fee to become part of our group. Let's not call them financial advisors or financial planners – let's call them Wealth Advisors. You join us as a Wealth Advisor, and we provide a complete automated advice kit. We provide your marketing kit. We have twelve different web sites and you – the Wealth Advisor – simply pick the web site you want from our menu, along with all letterhead and stationary designs. We provide the Wealth Advisor with the complete kit – including training, business coaching, accounting, compliance, and legal assistance."

Pat nodded as he listened along.

"I understand the concept, Billy – just like we provided to the Tax Refund Shop franchisee. But the biggest issue will be how the Wealth Advisor gets to see Mr. and Mrs. Average American. How do we design the marketing kit? I mean, there are some big players in this industry across America."

"Pat, whether you're an accountant, doctor, dentist, motor mechanic, plumber – whether you belong to any occupation in the world, for that matter – the biggest issue you'll face is being getting qualified leads, and meeting with enough of them to make a buck. The problem is finding people who want to use your services."

"And your plan to address that?" Pat snorted. "I mean, I know you already have a plan because I know how much strategy and planning you put into these weird and wonderful business ideas."

I grinned.

"A & C Tax Refund now has over 1,200 tax franchisees across the country. Let's assume each franchise is seeing roughly 1,500 people a year. That's nearly two million average Americans they're talking to during January to April each year. Imagine if the A & C franchisee was rewarded financially by referring some of those people to one of our Wealth Advisors. Also, imagine if we duplicated the search engine optimization techniques we developed for The Tax Refund Shop, only for retirement planning and insurance, instead. So, if you're a suitably qualified advisor looking to start your own business, we could provide you with qualified leads to meet with throughout the year. We'd automate the advice process and systemize the whole model for you."

"Slow down, Billy," Pat laughed. "I can see your passion about this. So, what you're suggesting is to take The Tax Refund Shop model and convert it for the wealth advice industry?"

"Exactly."

"I'm with you so far, Billy, and I follow your logic – but why would A & C Tax Refund allow us access to their franchisees?"

"You know what I've always preached: When you start a business, start with the end in mind. You have an exit strategy before you've even entered it."

"Okay."

"So, let's imagine that our plan is to list our business in eight years on the New York Stock Exchange – on Wall Street."

"An IPO?" Pat asked.

"Yep, an IPO – an initial public offering underwritten by one of Wall Street's investment banks. I won't show you the cash flow and modeling that I've completed yet, but let's assume the business is making a net profit, after tax, of $30 million in eight years. On a multiple of fifteen times earnings, we could list that business on the stock exchange for $450 million."

Pat whistled appreciatively. I continued:

"So, my pitch to the owners of A & C would be to offer them thirty percent of the shares in the business for the right to let us use their franchisees to refer clients to one of our Wealth Advisors. The upside for the franchisee is that they'd also receive a clip of the ticket for every successful referral."

"So, by referring them to us, it empowers the franchisee financially." Pat rubbed his chin, pondering this thought. "I assume you and I would run the business and set it up, and the owners of A & C would get to own thirty percent of the company right out of the gate?"

I nodded.

Pat continued: "And, based on an IPO value of $450 million, they'd make $135 million?"

"You got it, Pat. I'm suggesting that I own thirty percent, you have twenty percent, and A &C has thirty percent – with the other twenty percent held aside for some of our future key staff. Initial start-up capital required will be $2 million."

"Holy shit," whistled Pat.

"We need twelve months to build the advice model, Pat. We need the marketing kits, the franchise model, and everything else that goes along with it – all built and developed from scratch. We'll need to hire a couple of programmers and a couple of high-quality advisors, too – along with some support staff to assist us. I suggest you and I each get paid $200,000 over the next twelve months to run the build."

Pat sat there silently, considering this. I leaned toward him.

"I want you to think about this over the next few days, Pat. Are you able to come and see me at my office in Huntington Beach on Monday? We'll spend the day running through the business plan I've built, along with projections and cash flows, which I've taken out to eight years. If you like what you see, we'll then work out the next steps to approaching the owners of A & C about the idea."

The following Monday, Pat and I did exactly what I'd suggested – spending the best part of ten hours going over the business plan and detailed modeling. Pat wanted to spend the rest of the week understanding and researching the franchise code in relation to financial planning in America. We believed that what we were about to launch would be the first type of franchising model for financial services in America.

• • •

"BILLY, WHAT YOU'RE proposing can be done. It's all legal and all above board."

Pat had a big smile on his face when he told me the results of his research. He continued:

"I suggest you phone Gabriel Darcy to see if he'd like to meet with us in his New York office to discuss this potential business opportunity. I suggest we only share this with him. Let's not get their lawyers or other key decision makers involved just yet. Let's see what *he* thinks about the idea."

Pat continued: "Billy, you're a fucking genius, you know that? All that walking along the Malibu Beach certainly does something to your mind." He gave me one of his customary high fives.

CHAPTER 17

"So, THAT'S THE model, and how the business works," I said, shutting down my laptop after nearly two hours of presenting a detailed overview on the big screen to Gabriel Darcy, the CEO of A & C Tax Refund.

"Think of it like this, Gabriel," added Pat. "You are, in effect, putting a fence around the clients of the A & C franchise – because if your guy, the A & C franchisee, doesn't have someone he can refer the tax client to for their retirement and insurance planning, there's a good chance that the client of A & C will see a financial advisor that your franchisee has no connection with. That financial advisor may provide good advice or bad advice – but, more importantly, there's a good chance that the financial advisor already has a connection to a different tax accountant. He or she might chip away at your client base – to try and get the clients of your franchisees to leave A & C Tax Refund and go to their guy, instead."

"It's a win for your franchisees, too," I added. "They make money from their referrals, and just like Pat said – it puts a fence around their client base to keep them coming back to their A & C Tax Refund shop."

Gabriel Darcy peered at us from across the board-room table.

"No disrespect to you both," he eventually said, "but what the fuck do you guys know about running a financial planning business? I mean, you're an accountant, Billy – and Pat? You're a lawyer."

"A good question, Gabriel," I'd been expecting this objection. "You're right – we don't know a great deal about retirement planning or insurance advice. We plan to hire the right talent to run that side of the business."

I passed him the resume of Mike Arnold.

"Mike has been a leading financial advisor for over twenty years. He's a very successful man, and he's won many awards for the financial advice business he built. He retired twelve months ago and is currently lecturing part time about financial planning – but he's bored. After a year of being retired, he wants something challenging to sink his teeth into again. He's one of the people we're currently talking to about joining us and helping build this model from scratch. He, and others like him, provide the financial skillset we're missing; which will enable us to build the system and process."

"And that," Pat spoke up, "is one thing we do know about, Gabriel. We know the ins and outs of franchising. We built the franchising model for

The Tax Refund Shop from scratch – and you bought it off us for $30 million. Before that, as you know, I was a senior manager for five years at McIntosh & McIntosh, on their franchising team."

Gabriel nodded. There was no questioning our accomplishments, or Pat's qualifications.

He continued: "Over the last couple of weeks, I've reviewed the franchising requirements for financial planning in a fair amount of detail. It's not really that much different to the tax and accounting model."

I chimed in: "This business model is built on processes, leverage, and distribution. Over twelve months – with the help of the computer programmers and in-house financial planners we'll hire – we can build the process from start to finish. We'll automate the advice system exactly like we did at The Tax Refund Shop, and we'll provide the best automated advice process in the country."

Gabriel was now nodding in agreement.

I continued: "We'll build the process for marketing, for referrals, and for operations – the complete franchise kit. It'll be a kit so powerful that we'll have financial planners lining up to buy a franchise and become a Wealth Advisor with Future Wealth. The kit will give us the leverage to duplicate the process with countless Wealth Advisors. Our distribution model will be in the form of advisors all across America – and while we'll have a great franchise model, in terms of our systems and processes, the key will become the referral system. That, of course, is where A & C Tax Refund comes in."

"Gabriel, how many tax returns did A & C complete last year?" asked Pat.

"Across our 1,200 odd franchisees? About two million."

"So, there are potentially two million average American mums and dads who may want to meet with a Wealth Advisor from Future Wealth," I added.

Gabriel held up his hands.

"Guys, I get it. I see the potential. It's more the matter of me running this past the heads of the three families who own A & C. As you already know, they're three families with extensive business and property interests in New York. I've scribbled down a couple of figures from your presentation, Billy. Let me check if I've got this right: Thirty percent ownership of Future Wealth to A & C; initial working capital of $2 million, so $600,000 required by us; IPO listing in eight years with targeted value of $450 million, which makes our share worth about $135 million."

"Your numbers are spot on," I grinned. "I'll send you my presentation from today, along with all my projections via email."

"And, of course, we'll require confidentiality agreements to be signed before we send that information," Pat added.

"Understandable, guys. Each family that owns A & C has two family members sitting on the A & C board. Steve Taylor, our legal counsel, also sits on that board, along with me. The figures you've presented, and the endgame result, are self-explanatory. We'll need to number crunch the figures and see if they're achievable. The key to the decision to come on board with Future

Wealth will be whether the three families believe that the two of you can build Future Wealth to its endgame over the next eight years. The families have all seen firsthand the great business you both built with The Tax Refund Shop – and that's been a great acquisition for A & C. The technology you guys built to automate the tax return process was far superior to our own technology. It's enabled us to substantially reduce the staffing costs to each franchise, which of course has made them far more profitable, much to the franchisees' delight."

"So, $30 million for The Tax Refund Shop was too cheap, then? We should have asked for more?" Pat was only half-joking.

"No, no," Gabriel quickly responded, "$30 million was around the mark – but these families are very wealthy. They're extremely smart with their money. They do their research, and if they're going to go into business with you as partners, they'll have your backgrounds checked thoroughly to ensure there are no hidden skeletons."

"We fully understand and respect that, Gabriel," I replied.

"One more thing," Gabriel's face was stern. "Guys, I'll be up front. They'll want to know what happened with Shortfuse – and why it failed."

Pat and I looked at each other, somewhat bewildered. How the fuck did he know about Shortfuse?

I turned back and nodded.

"Gabriel, let me tell you about Shortfuse, and why we closed it. Ever hear about the tipping point?"

For the next hour, Pat and I shared the full account of our failed business venture, including the full extent of our losses and the concept of the tipping point marketing strategy; which had ultimately failed.

"Guys, I get it," Gabriel nodded when we'd finished. "Thanks for being so frank, open, and honest about that. I believe once I report back to the board, the three families will want to meet with you both and discuss your proposition in relation to Future Wealth. They'll be fully aware of Shortfuse from the research they do on you both before that meeting. I suggest you jump in first and share with them what you've just told me – the reasons why that business failed and what you've learned from it."

Then, Gabriel leaned forward and reassured us:

"Trust me, there have been businesses that the three families have invested in before that have also failed. They got involved in a big investment involving credit swaps in the Global Financial Crisis (GFC) that have all gone pear-shaped. The actual losses are still unknown today – and may be unknown for a few more years. I'm sharing that information with you on a confidential basis – not to be discussed outside these four walls – but at least you'll know you won't disgrace yourselves when you tell them the story of Shortfuse. The families will appreciate your honesty." He paused. "Assuming A & C decides to invest, when would you be looking to start the build?"

"I think we can complete the build in about nine months – but to be conservative, I've allowed a timeframe of twelve months. I have the computer programmers already set up to commence the IT build once I give them the go-ahead. Mike Arnold has three other financial advisors ready to join him and assist in building the advice model. Pat and I have flowcharted the process week-by-week over the next twelve months. Six months in, we'll start to hire the staff to run the advice model, which includes legal, compliance, and finance. We have a shortlist of six people we've already had preliminary discussions with about becoming the CEO of the advice business. All are experienced in the ins and outs of running large, financial advice businesses."

For a moment, Gabriel processed all that information. Then, he asked:

"What would the board of Future Wealth look like?"

"I'd be Managing Director, and fellow board members would be Pat, a representative from A & C, the CEO, and an independent chairman."

"We actually have a chairman in mind," Pat added. "He has a lot of experience on Wall Street, and he'd assist us in helping the business achieve its goal of an IPO within eight years."

I opened the laptop and turned on the overhead projector to show Gabriel the proposed organizational structure – from the initial build, along with further staff recruitment six months and twelve months out.

"This shows initial expenditure over the first twelve months of $1.2 million, and we've allowed an additional ten percent expenditure for any one-off expenses in that total. So, you can see we've been quite conservative. We've budgeted initially for two offices – one in Huntington Beach, where ten staff will be initially located, and another office in New York, with twenty staff. The CEO is to be based in New York, with Pat and myself based in Huntington Beach, commuting between both offices."

"And the day-to-day roles for the both of you?" asked Gabriel.

"Billy will oversee all initial recruitment," Pat explained. "The guy's the best salesman I've ever seen. Billy single-handedly recruited all the franchisees for The Tax Refund Shop. Meanwhile, I'll be looking after all franchising requirements of the business, using my previous experience from The Tax Refund Shop. The CEO will run the advice side of the business, to ensure the business and its wealth advisors are always compliant. Billy will manage the sales and marketing teams, and I'll work on operations, including finance and HR."

"Okay, guys – this is a very comprehensive and appealing proposal," Gabriel smiled, "and it just so happens that A & C has its monthly board meeting late next week. If I can sign a non-disclosure document today or tomorrow – and if you can provide both hard and soft copies of what you've shown me today – I make sure it's tabled at next week's meeting. As you know, A & C does move quickly when it comes to acquisitions. If the board has an appetite for this investment, I'd expect they'd want you guys back in New York as soon as possible for a full and frank presentation of the proposal." He paused, before admitting: "Gentleman, I think A & C will be interested in at least further exploring this potential opportunity."

With that, we all rose from the table and shook hands.

CHAPTER 18

TWELVE MONTHS LATER, with all thirty staff on board at Future Wealth, we held our first ever combined team meeting in preparation for the launch of our business.

Over the past year, Pat and I had led the build of the franchise model for Future Wealth. We were fortunate to have some incredibly talented IT people on the team, who – along with an equally talented team of experienced financial advisors – had developed a revolutionary and seamless, totally systemized advice process.

Pat and I had supervised the development of the model, with weekly Monday meetings taking place throughout each of the past twelve months. Building the franchise model had taken a tremendous amount of hard work and had meant long hours for the whole team – and we were all so proud of what they'd developed.

Two of the IT team members were now staying on to run the Future Wealth IT division. We had also decided to keep Mike Arnold on as a full-time consultant to enhance, tweak, and further develop the financial advice intellectual property. Mike was already well-respected in the financial planning world from the business he'd previously built.

I'd used the old marketing contacts who'd assisted with the development of The Tax Refund Shop marketing kits. It was over four years since we'd sold The Tax Refund Shop, and the new marketing opportunities that had been developed in the digital space over that time were remarkable. We had a marketing kit that rivaled anything else in the financial services world – a kit specifically designed to bring new clients to franchisees of Future Wealth.

It all stemmed from that meeting with Gabriel Darcy, twelve months earlier. After many detailed and long discussions, the founders of A & C Tax Refund had agreed to invest in Future Wealth.

Looking back, Pat and I had little doubt that we'd presented a compelling investment for them. The numbers stacked up, and over the last twelve months, we'd developed and built a great team to help achieve our goal of an IPO within eight years.

Our initial CEO was Bill Treloar. Bill was an experienced and seasoned individual in the financial services world, having worked in a similar role for the last nine years at one of the largest wealth businesses in the country. His position there had become redundant when the business he was running had been taken over by a large institution.

Bill was fifty-eight, and both Pat and I – along with the board of Future Wealth – had viewed Bill as a safe pair of hands for the initial launch of the company. Given his age, and given that we had a vision of listing on the NYSE within eight years, we viewed Bill as only a temporary CEO for the next five years. Closer to listing the business on Wall Street, we felt we'd require a younger CEO. Bill was aware of this and realized his tenure was unlikely to be for more than five years, which fit in with his own retirement plans.

We now had a team of thirty staff in place, consisting of an accounting team under our CFO, Alex Gordon. The compliance team was large – comprising seven experienced staff to ensure all financial advice was correct and met our rigorous legal obligations. This team was headed by Simon Russell.

I oversaw a sales team of six assistants who'd be working closely with me on recruiting new Wealth Advisors and looking after the needs of the A & C accounting firms.

Pat Stevens headed our Wealth Advisor coaching. He was an experienced individual who'd worked in investment banking on Wall Street for the past eight years, advising mums and dads on where to invest. Prior to that, he'd been a lecturer at one of the top colleges in America. At only thirty-eight, he was viewed as part of the long-term growth of Future Wealth.

The last two months had consisted of intensive training for all the staff on our tools and processes, as well as sharing individual KPI. The team was ready and raring to go.

Our first team meeting was held in our New York office, with the Huntington Beach team in California joining us via Skype. Bill Treloar, our recently appointed CEO, addressed the meeting by saying:

"Well, ladies and gentlemen, as employees of Future Wealth, I'd like to introduce the founder of the company, Billy Houston, to share with us his vision for the company and the big-ticket items we need to focus on over the next twelve months."

I rose from my chair and stood in front of the staff at our new office, on 36 West Street in Manhattan.

"As you all know," I told the team, "Pat Gabriel and I built one of the largest tax franchise systems in the country. What started as a single storefront for The Tax Refund Shop in Santa Monica quickly grew to over two hundred and eighty franchised Tax Refund Shops over an eight-year period."

There was a hush. The team knew all this, but it was still an impressive achievement.

I continued:

"We've seen an opportunity to repeat this model in the financial advice world across America. Importantly, we've partnered with A & C Tax Refund – one of the largest franchised preparers of tax returns in the country, and they've taken equity in our business in exchange for allowing us to use their franchised tax and accounting shops as referrers to our franchised Wealth Advisors. This provides a great lead generation opportunity for people looking to start their own financial planning business."

I was in my element as I addressed the team.

"Over the past twelve months, Pat and I have led a team of IT experts, along with some experienced financial advisors, to build what I can only describe as a revolutionary financial planning system."

As I spoke, I looked around the room, making eye contact with everyone in the New York office.

"Like we'd done with The Tax Refund Shop, we've systemized the advice process to make it quick and easy for Wealth Advisors to provide financial planning advice to the mums and dads of America. Backed with our training program, our digital marketing tools, as well as our compliance framework, we've built something that no one else in the marketplace has ever built for the financial services world."

I gave the room a glowing smile.

"Over the last month, we've signed one hundred and eighty of the A & C Tax Refund franchisees as referral partners on the east coast. In the next four weeks, we'll host ten Future Wealth Franchise Information Sessions that are designed to recruit experienced Wealth Advisors for our business."

"The information sessions will be two hours long and will showcase the Future Wealth franchise model in full. Our focus for the next month is the east coast, and then we'll move onto the west coast and repeat the process." I laughed. "So, lots of traveling for me and Pat."

There was a polite ripple of laughter.

I continued: "Alex and Simon – while we're on the road, we'll undertake weekly Skype meetings. It's important, Alex, that you and your team are closely monitoring our financials – and, more importantly, our cash flow. While we've got over $600,000 in the bank, our cash burn with two offices and thirty staff is high."

I saw the concern flicker across people's faces, and reassured them:

"But trust me – Pat and I have done this before with The Tax Refund Shop. We know how to do it, don't we, Pat?"

Pat nodded in agreement.

"It'll be Pat and I speaking at the Franchise Information Sessions – which, as mentioned, run for two hours. Pat will run a twenty-minute segment explaining the Future Wealth Franchise Agreement and the follow-up process."

I paused to make eye contact with everyone seated in the New York office.

"Currently, we're top heavy in staff. We have thirty staff and no advisors." I added a grin to my face. "Don't be alarmed, though – you're not about to lose your job. It was always planned this way – to first put our infrastructure in place with the accounting function, compliance, sales, onboarding, legal, and operational areas. These are our growth projections over the next five years."

I turned on the overhead projector to show our budgets in detail.

"You'll find that Pat and I have always been very transparent in sharing the key metrics of our vision and plans with our staff from our previous businesses, and we plan to do the same with the staff of Future Wealth. Headline numbers over the next five years are 480 wealth advice franchises signed up, working with eight hundred plus A & C Tax Refund Shops. The total number of staff spread across the two offices will be about a hundred. We are, we believe, the first in America to set up a franchise model for financial advice. The franchise kit, which you've all been trained on over the past month or so, is revolutionary – the best in the business. You should all be proud of being part of this new business venture. We're about to do something unique – something truly special."

I took a sip from the glass of water in front of me.

"Our endgame is to list Future Wealth on Wall Street within eight years. By then, we should have about 800 franchised Wealth Advisors. We've previously discussed our bonus system with each of you. To reiterate, twenty percent of the shares in Future Wealth have been set aside for staff to receive as a bonus. You don't get a bonus just for turning up to work – that's what you get paid for. You get bonuses for doing extraordinary things. With our combined hard work, the shares allocated through the bonus system should become *very* valuable once we list the company on the New York Stock Exchange.

There were plenty of grins from the people surrounding me.

"We have a lot of hard work ahead of us," I warned. "There'll be times when you'll love working for Future Wealth, and there'll be times when you will want to chuck it all in. There'll be times of laughter, there'll be times of stress. There'll be times when we disagree, and there'll also be a lot of fun. I ask you to enjoy the experience and the journey, because you'll find the next eight years will fly by quickly."

I watched the nods from the New York team.

"A very important part of what Future Wealth is about is the word 'culture.' The culture of this business comes from me, Pat, and Bill – the Future Wealth board. It comes from you, our team here in New York and in Huntington Beach. It also comes from the advisors who'll join our great company. We're all on a journey together to make this a great work environment and a great business. To do that, we must have the right culture among us all: A culture of respect, fun, innovation, and sharing. A place you look forward to coming to work. If we get the culture wrong, we won't be successful. Bill, Pat, and I have an open-door policy. If you have any issues or problems, please come and talk to one of us."

I made eye-contact with the team to ensure they understood that point, and then continued:

"You've all been hired for your unique skillset, for the role you'll undertake in our business. We're only as strong as our weakest link."

I saw the smile on Pat's face. I could sense then that Pat knew I had the team motivated and ready to jump through burning doors to follow us into the launch of Future Wealth.

"Next Tuesday, at the Ivory Bar, we'll have the first of ten planned Future Wealth franchise information sessions. I'd like all staff on the east coast to at least attend one of these sessions. It's an important way to experience first-hand who we are and what we do."

For the next hour, Pat, Bill, and I shared the vision and goals of Future Wealth with the Future Wealth team. You could see the look of excitement on the face of every team member. They were pumped and ready for business – raring to go.

CHAPTER 19

BOTH PAT AND I had a sense of déjà vu at our first Future Wealth Franchise Information Session. It started out the same as it had gone for The Tax Refund Shop.

As 6pm quickly approached, no one had turned up. I could see the worried look on Bill Treloar's face. I was relaxed, as was Pat – which was such a contrast from how he'd been at our first franchise meeting for The Tax Refund Shop. Back then, he'd been busily pacing up and down the front of the room, hands placed firmly on his head, looking extremely stressed.

"Don't worry," I said to Bill, "people will turn up shortly." And they did.

By 6:15pm, we had over seventy-five people in the room. I welcomed our guests.

"Ladies and gentlemen, welcome to the very first Future Wealth Advisor Franchise Information Session to be held in the United States. Over the next two hours, what you're going to see is described by many as 'revolutionary'. I ask you all to please turn off your cell phones and ensure no pictures are taken of the intellectual property you're about to see."

"Imagine a world in which you have qualified people to talk to about their retirement and insurance needs every day. Imagine a world in which the provision of quality and compliant financial advice become turnkey – with the use of the special algorithms we've developed. Imagine a world in which you're provided with the latest, state-of-the-art digital marketing campaigns. Imagine a world in which, if you work hard and simply follow the system we've built for you, you could earn yearly incomes of $200,000, $300,000, or $400,000 and above."

That clearly impressed some of the attendees.

"Imagine a world in which you receive the latest training and coaching – where if you simply follow our model, your success is assured. Welcome to the world of Future Wealth."

Once I saw the smile on both Bill and Pat's faces, I knew I had this audience in the palm of my hand.

"He's good," I heard Bill whisper to Pat.

"The best in the business, Bill," Pat whispered back. "He's never had any formal sales training. Never read a sales book in his life. He's actually dyslexic."

"Fucking amazing," said Bill, shaking his head in disbelief. "Fucking amazing."

I turned to the two men.

"Please let me share my credentials and those of my business partner, Pat Gabriel— one of the most distinguished franchise lawyers in this country."

I then shared how Pat and I built The Tax Refund Shop. For two hours, I had the audience mesmerized as I showcased our franchise model and our state-of-the-art intellectual property.

After that first session ended, we repeated these workshops across the country. We had no trouble signing up new Wealth Advisors under our model.

• • •

OVER THE NEXT five years, we surpassed our target of 480 licensed, franchised Wealth Advisors operating under the business name of Future Wealth. In the same period, we got over ninety percent of franchised A & C Tax Refund shops to refer clients to us during the tax season, from January to April. Thanks to the continuously evolving digital marketing kits and client referral programs we'd developed, the Future Wealth advisors had a continued stream of new clients to provide advice to.

Like with anything, at times things went wrong. Some of the franchisees weren't suitable individuals to be part of our business – whether due to a lack of technical skill, a lack of ethical integrity, or a general lack of suitability to run a business. It was a lot different being a business owner than an employee. Anyone who was found deficient in any way was soon asked to leave – and given a partial refund of their franchise fees.

Some of the A & C Tax Refund shops were better referrers than others. Some were hopeless, while others fantastic. One thing I've learned in life is that you can give the exact same business model to ten different individuals – and still get ten different results. With the development and refinement of our franchise model, however, we managed to reduce those odds – but we could never guarantee the success of any individual franchise; which was a fact we shared with any potential new Wealth Advisor.

At the five-year mark, it became time to review the tenure of Bill Treloar. Bill and I had developed a great relationship, and Bill had been outstanding in leading and motivating the Future Wealth team, which now numbered close to a hundred people.

He never micromanaged. Instead, he empowered each team member to reach new heights. He was honest, ethical, and called a spade a spade – the sort of guy you'd be happy to serve in the trenches with. He was an integral part of developing and maintaining the culture of Future Wealth – a true leader, and respected and liked by all his peers, including me and Pat.

When the time came, both Pat and I agreed that Bill should remain as the CEO of our business. We agreed he had the skill, drive, knowledge, and strategic vision to lead our business to its IPO, which was only three years away. Under Bills stewardship, we'd surpassed budget for each of our five years. We were right on track to achieve what we'd set out to do over the proposed eight-year journey towards listing on the NYSE.

Bill agreed, subject to board approval, to stay on and take us through and beyond our listing on the New York Stock Exchange. He enjoyed working with Pat and me – and loved the challenges and opportunities that arose day in and day out. He'd decided he wasn't ready for retirement yet, and had been thoroughly enjoying himself as CEO of our company.

Unfortunately, the other members of the Future Wealth board had different ideas. Our initial chairman, Charlie Cameron – an experienced Wall Street investment banker – had been forced to suddenly resign from the board four months earlier after being diagnosed with prostate cancer.

Charlie had been a great chairman and was a strategic thinker who'd been on the boards of many companies over the past thirty years – companies that had a similar vision to ours; of listing on Wall Street. His experience over the last five years with Future Wealth had been invaluable in terms of putting in place strategies to reach our ultimate goal.

His replacement, Tom Carroll, was a somewhat controversial choice. Charlie Cameron was completely against Tom Carroll being appointed as chairman. He wouldn't elaborate why, other than to say Tom Carroll was a man who couldn't be trusted.

While Charlie was trying to win his battle against cancer, we were reluctant to burden him with discussions about why he was opposed to Tom Carroll's appointment as chairman. Unfortunately, we never had a chance to discuss this matter any further – because three months after resigning from the board of Future Wealth, Charlie lost his battle with cancer and passed away.

The board also consisted of Brian Petty, who was the new legal advisor to the founding families of A & C. He'd replaced Steve Taylor on the board. Now, neither Steve Taylor or Gabriel Darcy were no longer part of A & C, both having retired – or so we'd been told. It was quite weird how one minute, Steve and Gabriel had both been working at A & C and then, in the blink of an eye, they were both gone.

Pat and I used to joke about how we'd made Gabriel rich with all the bonuses he'd received – firstly from buying The Tax Refund Shop, and then from A & C's investment in Future Wealth. His replacement at A & C was Doug Heck – a ruthless and arrogant individual who continued to remind both Pat and I, long after he'd been added to the Future Wealth board, that he was appointed to protect the interests of the shareholders who owned A & C Tax Refund.

About the same time Charlie was first diagnosed with cancer, the A & C owners wanted – or should I say *demanded* – a complete restructure of the Future Wealth board. They argued that since the company had grown so substantially, it was now appropriate to have a six-person board rather than five, and given the fact that they owned thirty percent of the business, they should have two of their people on the board.

Over the last five years, Pat and I had always found the owners of A & C to be good people to work with. They were fair and reasonable and seemed quite switched on. Pat and I had no reason to doubt or question their logic at the time, so after a bit of hemming and hawing, we agreed to their request. Hence the appointment of Doug Heck to join Brian Petty as A & C representatives. In addition, they wanted to nominate Tom Carroll as chairman, citing the great work he was undertaking for their own private investment companies. They backed this up with Tom Carroll's twenty plus years as an investment banker with large Wall Street firms.

So, in the span of a couple of months, the makeup of the Future Wealth board had dramatically changed. It was now a six-person board, with Charlie Cameron and Steve Taylor gone.

One wonders how things would have panned out if Charlie Cameron had never been diagnosed with cancer and hadn't been forced to resign from his position as chairman of Future Wealth. Unfortunately, we'll never know the answer to that.

• • •

"GUYS, AS FAR as I'm concerned, the answer is no. It's time for Bill Treloar to retire. It was always part of the plan that he'd only serve five years. He's done a great job, but we need someone younger – someone more qualified. Someone with more strategic skills to come on board, run this company, and take us to the goal of listing on the New York Stock Exchange."

So spoke Tom Carroll – and both Doug Heck and Brian Petty followed with:

"Agreed."

"I suppose you already have someone in mind?" I said sarcastically to Tom Carroll.

"Well, yes I do. It's my job as chairman to always safeguard the business and think two steps ahead. I've been working with a guy in Chicago named Steve Roberts—an experienced banker."

"Let me guess," I hissed. "You've already met him, and have already discussed the opportunity of him becoming CEO of Future Wealth?"

"Well, I have actually," confessed Tom, "on an informal basis only."

"So, are Brian and Doug aware of this informal discussion?" I looked across the table at both of them.

"Yes," Tom nodded. I'd mentioned that I was going to meet with Steve Roberts to sound him out."

"A major breach of trust, Tom," Pat complained, "and perhaps a breach of your duties as chairman of Future Wealth."

"So, you're telling me that the three of you withheld information from Pat and I about a possible new CEO?" I stared intently at Tom Carroll.

"Listen, you guys work in the business," he replied. "Brian, Doug, and I don't. The three of us feel your opinions about Bill Treloar's abilities are somewhat clouded and less objective because you work alongside him."

"Tom, you only sit in that seat because of the illness and unfortunate death of Charlie Cameron – and the fact that, for some reason, the owners of A & C pushed hard for you to replace Charlie. Just don't forget that I'm the one who founded this company. I'm the one who's been traveling around the country, signing new Wealth Advisors and bringing on new A & C Tax Refund shops as referral partners. It's just about killed me over the last five years. From Monday to Friday, I live in some hotel room in some part of America, and by the time I get home at the weekend, I'm exhausted. Then, I get up early the following Monday and have to do the same fucking thing all over again."

I uttered those words without once raising my voice – never let them see you angry.

"For the three of you to undertake a search for a new CEO without *once* mentioning this to me or Pat is an absolute disgrace." I shook my head.

"Well, as per board rules, we'll have a vote as to whether we reappoint Bill Treloar or look for a new CEO," Tom brushed aside the comments I'd made.

"Well, that's a fair outcome," said Pat. "We'll have the three of you voting not to reappoint Bill Treloar as CEO, while me and Billy wish him to remain. So, its two versus three – and my simple math tells me that you guys win. Or, should we let Bill Treloar have a vote about whether he stays or goes, given that he's a board member? Then, it'll be three votes to three – but, of course, the chairman has the right to a casting vote, so guess what? You win."

"And let me guess, Tom," I added, "you'll then put forward a motion that Steve Roberts – a man both Pat and I have never met or even heard of until today – is appointed as CEO?"

"No," Tom shook his head. "We can have a vote today whether we reappoint Bill Treloar. Subject to that vote, we can – as a board – decide on the next steps."

He looked around the room.

"Those in favor of reappointing Bill Treloar as CEO beyond his five-year tenure – which expires in one month – raise your hand."

Both Pat and I raised our hands.

"Those against reappointing Bill Treloar as CEO beyond his five-year tenure, raise your hands."

Doug, Brian, and Tom all raised their hands.

"Then the decision, by majority, to not reappoint Bill Treloar as CEO beyond his five-year tenure has been decided – three votes to two. Which of you will inform Bill of the decision of the board?"

Tom was looking at Pat and me.

"I suggest you do it, Mr. Chairman, given you made the decision before this meeting even started." I was glaring at Tom, Brian, and Doug. "Might I just add that the functioning of this board has become extremely biased over the last four months."

I pointed directly across the table towards the three of them – Tom, Brian and Doug.

"It coincides with a couple of things. First, the appointment of you, Tom, as chairman. Second, the appointment of Brian to the board in place of Steve Taylor. Steve was a person who looked at things objectively and fairly. He made his decisions based on what was best for the company, because he always believed that what was right for the company would ultimately be right for the shareholders – *all* shareholders, I might add. Third, the expansion of the board from five people to six – with the addition of you, Doug."

"I completely agree with you, Billy," Pat nodded. "I must remind all directors that we're to act in the best interests of all shareholders, not just those we work for."

"Thank you, Pat and Billy," Tom said slyly, "the board takes note of your concerns. As chairman, however, I thoroughly reject the assertion that myself, Doug and Brian don't always make decisions that are in the best interests of all shareholders. Also, please note that I was providing investment and strategic advice to the owners of A & C before I was appointed chairman of this business. It was *they* who convinced me to come on as chairman – and a decision you both agreed to."

"Now, onto the next piece of business. Given the decision by the majority not to reappoint Bill Treloar as CEO, may I suggest we interview Steve Roberts for the role. If, by majority – after the interview process – we agree that Steve is a suitable candidate for the position, we hire him."

"Agree," said both Doug and Brian.

"Pat, Billy?" asked Tom.

"Disagree," both Pat and I replied.

"I'm afraid the majority rules," said Tom, barely concealing a smile. "I'll organize for Steve Rogers to attend a board meeting of Future Wealth for the purpose of deciding whether or not he should be the new CEO of our company."

"May I suggest that we at least advertise the position to ensure we employ the best available candidate?" I asked.

"We don't have enough time," replied Doug.

"The only reason we don't have enough time is because the three of you have delayed any discussions about Bill's reappointment. It was on the agenda for the last two board meetings." I paused: "I wonder if that was on purpose, given you'd secretly been in discussions with Steve Roberts."

"Not at all," Tom shot back. "I'll reschedule a board meeting for next week, subject to confirming the availability of Steve Roberts. I now declare the meeting closed."

• • •

WITH THAT, PAT and I left the boardroom to grab a cab to the airport for our late-night flight back to LA.

"We've been screwed here, Billy," Pat growled. "I don't understand what their agenda is. Why can't they see that Bill Treloar's performance as CEO has exceeded our expectations?"

"I'm not sure what their agenda is, Pat. I mean, all the shareholders are in it to achieve the same goal, which is the IPO and the associated profits from that. I think it's just a case of Carroll being a control freak, and thinks he knows best."

I pondered what had transpired in the boardroom that afternoon.

"You know the mistake we made, Pat?"

"What's that?"

"When Carroll started acting as the investment advisor for the owners of A & C, he created a conflict of interest. We should have refused to accept his nomination to the board on those grounds. He's now too close to Doug Heck, the CEO of A & C, and Brian Petty, the lawyer for A & C. I was tempted to go and see Charlie Cameron to find out why he was so vehemently opposed to Tom Carroll joining as chairman."

"Unfortunately, Billy, we couldn't do that while Charlie was focused on trying to beat his cancer."

"It was strange how both Steve Taylor and Gabriel Darcy tendered their resignations at the same time, and both so abruptly. I mean, one minute they're here, and the next they're both gone."

"Perhaps they didn't resign, Billy," Pat mused. "Maybe they were terminated for reasons we may never know. I've tried to call them both several times, and I've left messages, but no response ever comes back. All quite weird."

"Yes," I nodded. "It is rather strange."

"I agree the whole dynamics of the board have changed over the last few months – ever since Tom Carroll, Doug Heck, and Brian Petty all joined."

"And all three joined at the same time, I might add." I turned to my friend. "Pat, can we request that Carroll resign as Chairman of the Board? On the basis he's faced with a conflict of interests by acting for the owners of A & C?"

"Not sure if we would have any grounds there, Billy. He'll argue there's no conflict. He'll also argue why we waited until now to raise the conflict. He'll ask why we didn't raise it when his name was first put forward to become chairman – as we'd known he was acting for the owners of A & C back then. He'll argue it's just because we lost the vote to reappoint Bill Treloar."

We'd learn only a few years later exactly why Tom Carroll wanted Steve Roberts appointed as CEO of Future Wealth.

• • •

A WEEK LATER, the meeting to interview Steve Roberts for the position of CEO of the company – a role that entailed taking Future Wealth to an IPO in three years – took place with the board of Future Wealth.

Both Pat and I had decided to take an objective view about the suitability of Steve Roberts for the role. We arrived at 9:55am for the ten o'clock meeting. It was being held at Tom Carroll's investment bank at 32 East Street, as the New York boardroom of Future

Wealth was in the process of being repainted. When we entered, we were somewhat surprised that Steve Roberts was already seated at the boardroom table with Tom Carroll, Brian Petty, and Doug Heck.

"You guys all already know each other?" I asked as we entered the boardroom. All four of them were seated together, talking.

"No," Tom brushed off our concerns. "Steve had the time shown in his schedule as nine, not ten. It was my mix-up when I sent the calendar appointment through. I told him to come in. It just so happened that both Doug and Brian were already here for a meeting to discuss some private matters regarding A & C business."

We'd later realize that this was all planned – an opportunity for Tom to introduce Steve to both Doug and Brian to discuss plans and tactics *before* Pat and I arrived.

Steve was a bald, fit-looking guy in his mid-forties. He was well-educated, with two master's degrees from two of the top colleges in America. He was married, but had no children. He'd spent the last ten years working in banking in Chicago. He had one of the worst-looking set of teeth I'd ever seen – something I'd always notice, each and every time I spoke with him. Pat and I would later chuckle that a dentist would have had a field day with those teeth.

For the next hour, it was mainly Pat and I asking the questions. Steve answered all our questions well, with no obvious hiccups or concerns raised about his ability to perform the role. Our initial concerns were more about how his name had been put forward for the position of CEO in the first place, without having gone through a proper recruitment process.

Tom interrupted our questioning after forty-five minutes to say that if Steve was successfully appointed as CEO, he wished to – subject to board approval – bring three of his trusted lieutenants with him. Their names were Mark Hemmings, Errol Archer, and Arthur Evanglass. Steve told us that Mark had been a very successful financial advisor eight years earlier. He'd built one of the most successful planning practices in Dallas, and was the founding partner of a three-partner planning business. He'd sold it when he and his wife had decided they wished to be closer to family in Chicago and had joined Steve eight years earlier. He'd overseen all training of the bank's hundred-plus network of branches. In Steve's words, he was the guy: 'who was always inventing new processes and ideas." He told us the staff loved him and thought he was a legend.

Arthur Evanglass and Steve had attended college in New York together. Arthur had a background in mergers and acquisitions and had joined Steve at the Chicago bank four years earlier, where he'd become responsible for all potential strategies to increase the value of the bank's shares through carefully selected acquisitions.

Errol Archer was a young, qualified accountant who'd been assistant to the CFO at Steve's bank. He was a person Steve believed could one day be groomed to become a member of senior management – perhaps even CFO of Future Wealth.

"I appreciate your thoughts here, Tom and Steve, but with all due respect, let's first have the board do adequate due diligence as to whether you – Steve – are the right person to be the CEO of Future Wealth. Subject to that decision, we can then determine the suitability of the other three gentleman."

• • •

THE DECISION, MUCH to the disagreement of Pat and I, was made to hire Steve Roberts as CEO of Future Wealth. Likewise, the decision would also be made to employ Mark Hemmings, Errol Archer, and Arthur Evanglass as his trusted lieutenants.

Mark would be employed as head of Intellectual Property Development, a role where he was responsible for developing new systems, processes, and IT to enhance the operations of the Future Wealth advisors.

Arthur's role would be to look for any new strategic alliances and acquisition opportunities for Future Wealth over the next three years, which might further enhance the value of the business prior to our initial IPO. Errol would be assistant CFO and be groomed to succeed our long-serving CFO.

All votes at the board level were decided three to two, with Pat and I voting against the appointments of Steve Roberts, Mark Hemmings, Errol Archer, and Arthur Evanglass. Tom, Doug, and Brian all voted for the appointments.

CHAPTER 20

SIX MONTHS PASSED since the Future Wealth board had appointed Steve Roberts as the CEO and allowed him to employ his three trusted lieutenants – Mark Hemmings, Errol Archer, and Arthur Evanglass.

Steve Roberts was an interesting character. He micromanaged the team and had lost the trust and respect of most of the senior management at Future Wealth since his appointment. Pat and I despised the man. He was a liar – the sort of guy who'd say nice things about you to your face, then five minutes later would tell people what a horrible and incompetent person you were. He was also a control freak and acted like he had to be involved in every decision, which often meant nothing got done because nothing got past his large IN tray of things to do. He lacked leadership skills and tended to divide the team rather than bond them together.

Pat and I repeatedly had team members from Future Wealth complain to us about Steve's rude and demeaning manner. When he wanted to admonish a team member, it was normally done by email, rather than a face-to-face meeting. Pat and I had decided early on that he was a man we couldn't trust.

The inner circle of the management of Future Wealth now consisted of the Chairman of the Board, Tom Carroll, plus Steve Roberts and his two lieutenants, Mark Hemmings and Arthur Evanglass.

Interestingly, ever since the appointment of Steve Roberts, our chairman had taken a much greater hands-on role in the day-to-day operations of the business than our previous chairman, the late Charlie Cameron.

Errol Archer, while an appointment of Steve, wasn't part of this inner circle, for some unknown reason. Pat and I – despite being board members – were also not part of Steve's inner circle. None of this made for a very happy place to work.

The board of Future Wealth had become more and more one-sided. We now also had Steve Roberts on the board, which meant votes were always decided four to two. Steve Roberts, Tom Carroll, Brian Petty, and Doug Heck always voted as one block – and normally opposed any ideas or motions that Pat and I suggested or proposed.

This was a very tough and soul-destroying time for both Pat and me. The baby we'd built – the vision I'd shared with Pat, and the vision we'd then shared with the owners of A & C – was slowly but surely being eroded and taken away from us. The culture that we'd worked so hard to build and maintain was evaporating right in front of us.

Pat and I both had an entrepreneurial spirit. We were business builders. I'd recently even been featured in one of the major New York papers under the heading 'A True Business Builder.' The story basically tracked my life from arriving at Santa Monica High School as a teenager from Australia, to the success of the 280+ Tax Refund Shops and the ultimate plan to take Future Wealth to an IPO. Fortunately for me, there was no mention of Shortfuse – my biggest failure in business thus far.

Tom Carroll, Steve Roberts, and his three lieutenants all came from corporate backgrounds. None of them had the skill, vision, or ability to build a business themselves from the start-up phase. They were what Pat and I called "suits" – guys who never got their hands dirty building businesses from the ground up. They just came in and ran the business once someone else had built it for them. They were arrogant individuals who couldn't be trusted – and aside from Errol Archer, they were always self-promoting and looking out for their own interests.

Pat and I stood up to these 'suits' whenever we could, and we'd always support any Future Wealth staff against the vicious and ruthless shenanigans of Steve Roberts and his lieutenants. Pat and I were concerned about what would happen to the management team that we'd put together if Pat and I ever left Future Wealth.

● ● ●

THE COMBINED SHAREHOLDING of Pat and I was now below fifty percent, which meant we no longer controlled the company through the power of our shareholding.

Within two weeks of Tom Carroll's appointment as Chairman of the Board, he approached me about buying five percent of my shares in the company. He explained that he'd be devoting a large portion of his weekly time to help Future Wealth achieve its dream of listing on Wall Street, and only felt it fair that he should be able to buy shares now, so he could benefit from the upside of the IPO. He explained he'd pay current market value for the shares he wanted to purchase from me – and that this would further empower and motivate him to assist the company in achieving its goal of an IPO.

His logic at the time seemed fair and reasonable to me. I've always been a big believer that it's best to have a smaller piece of a big pie, rather than a big piece of a small pie. I discussed his proposal with Pat. Pat's only concern was that by selling five percent to Tom, we'd effectively relinquish control of the company – with our combined shareholding falling below fifty percent.

At that time, Carroll, Heck, and Petty had only recently been appointed to the board, and there were no warning signs about just how bad things would ultimately turn out with their appointments. We'd only later learn that buying five percent of my shares was a move orchestrated after discussions between Tom and Steve Roberts.

CHAPTER 21

THE WORKINGS OF the Future Wealth board become more biased and dysfunctional than ever over the next three years. By then, we were only four months away from listing on the New York Stock Exchange.

"The guy is an absolute fraud," Pat complained one morning. "Completely full of shit."

He was talking about Mark Hemmings. To the outside world – the franchisees of Future Wealth – the guy was a legend. To the senior management of Future Wealth – other than Steve Roberts and his cohorts, of course – Hemmings was a fraud. He never followed through with what he was meant to do, always leaving it for someone else in the team to finish the tasks he was responsible for. Once other team members had completed the things he'd failed to, he'd then stand in front of everyone and claim ownership for the wonderful new intellectual property they'd been instrumental in developing.

It did nothing at all to inspire confidence and trust in him, yet the CEO of Future Wealth lauded him as a genius in front of everyone.

Steve Roberts didn't help to develop and enhance the culture of the team at Future Wealth either. Coupled with the cover-up of Mark Hemmings's limitations, it all but destroyed the senior managements' respect for the CEO.

Pat came to me one day with news.

"I've done some research on the guy, Billy. Yes, he was a partner in a three-partner planning business in Dallas eight years ago – but were you aware he's married to Steve Roberts's sister? Can you believe we were never told about that?"

My eyes widened.

"Things apparently went pear-shaped for Mark Hemmings in Dallas eight years ago," Pat continued, "and the good old brother-in-law, Steve, came to the rescue."

"So, the guy's a fraud," I growled. "He couldn't lie straight in bed."

I shook my head.

"Hemmings has an ego as big as a bus. In most other organizations, he'd have been sacked a long time ago. He's basically incompetent."

"Well, listen to this, Billy. After much researching and a lot of phone calls, I've spoken to two of his former business partners. They're still both advisors, but don't want anything to do with Hemmings again."

"Why?" I asked.

"Well, turns out the guy's a complete shyster."

For the next hour, Pat gave me the complete rundown.

"Unbelievable, mate," I said to Pat, when he'd finished recounting this story, "and Steve Roberts is aware of all of this?"

"He certainly is. In fact, he bailed Mark Hemmings out of potential jail time. I think he's using Mark as his eyes on the ground at Future Wealth. Mark is indebted to Steve for the rest of his life."

So, we knew where his loyalties lay.

"Steve's a control freak with non-existent people skills," Pat continued. I'd rarely seen him this animated. "He assumes everyone working at Future Wealth is untrustworthy. He uses both Mark and Arthur as his eyes on the ground, and Errol Archer too, to a much lesser extent. No one trusts Mark or Arthur, and none of our management team will share any confidential information with either of them because they know it'll go straight back into Steve Roberts's ear. They're hesitant to share information with Errol for the same reason."

"Mark Hemmings's old partners are now practicing in Santa Barbara?"

"Yep, and I suggest that we take up their offer for lunch and head there tomorrow. We'll hear the full story – it's only a ninety-minute drive."

• • •

CHARLIE FAGAN AND Ted Jones were both in their early forties. Hemmings's earlier business partner, Bob Fleming, had passed away six years earlier. Charlie and

Ted felt that Hemmings had been responsible for his death.

"Pat's given me an overview of your business relationship with Mark Hemmings," I said after we'd made introductions. "Obviously, from our point of view, it's important we know the full and complete truth about the guy. As Pat mentioned, we're only four months out from our IPO. When we list on the New York Stock Exchange, we have to be completely clean and have no skeletons hiding in the cupboard. Unfortunately for Pat and me, we've lost control of Future Wealth since Mark's brother-in-law, Steve Roberts, came on board as our CEO. We also have a chairman who appears to be in cohorts with Steve Roberts, for reasons unknown to Pat and me. They're totally opposed to every suggestion Pat and I have."

"It's as though we've lost our baby, guys," Pat lamented. "The baby Billy and I started with our direction and hard work. Then, these corporate cowboys came in. So – please – share with Billy what you guys told me over the phone."

"Hemmings is a complete fraud," said Charlie Fagan. "We were three equal partners in a merger of two businesses. The late Bob Fleming had been in business with Mark Hemmings, and Mark had purchased Bob's shareholding. Bob stayed on as senior manager, earning a salary, to help run Mark's business. Ted and I had a planning business in Dallas as well. Ten years ago, we merged the two businesses to leverage some economy of scale. It turned out to be a disaster because of Mark Hemmings."

"The guy can sell," Ted clarified. "Put him in front of any type of client and he'll have them convinced he's the best financial planner in America. The problem is, there's no substance to those claims at all. His staff would constantly churn because they got sick of the lies he told clients. To his friends and family, Mark portrays himself as the image of success. He wants people to think he's just so smart – like a guru. The sad thing is, guys, he mistakenly believes he really is a legend."

"Yeah, a legend in his own dreams," said Charlie with smirk on his face.

He continued: "The man is a complete liar. The end for us came when our bank threatened to sue us. Mark had always lived beyond his means. He was always running out of money. No matter how much money the business made, it was never enough to fund his lavish lifestyle."

"He was also very lazy – a person who expected others to do things for him. He never took any accountability," added Ted.

"Anyway, the senior management of our bank came to see us about potential fraud," Charlie shook his head. "Unbeknownst to us, our good friend Mark was falsifying cash flows and budgets for the business to finance his lavish lifestyle."

"Yep, the bank had given him $500,000 in cash, up front, based on the false figures he'd given about our business. Of course, Charlie and I never had anything to do with this. Hell, we weren't even aware he'd used the firm as security for the loan – because he'd also falsified our signatures on the bank documents."

"Can you believe that he lied to his two business partners? While we were being investigated by the bank?" Charlie was clearly emotional as he interrupted Ted.

"What a lowlife." Pat shook his head in disbelief.

"Oh, it gets worse, fellas," Ted warned. "After a couple of weeks of investigation, the bank realized that Charlie and I had nothing to do with this little scheme. We were victims of his fraud as much as the bank was. While this was going on, we were just trying to run our financial planning business, with twenty staff relying on us – doing our damnedest to ensure that aside from a couple of our senior managers, no one else knew anything about this."

"Of course, we were also trying to ensure it didn't get into the press, so clients wouldn't be aware of it either," added Charlie.

"So, what happened?" I asked.

"Well, that's where the one and only Steve Roberts comes in," Charlie sighed.

"Steve is Mark's brother-in-law, as you now know. He was a hot-shot banker in Chicago. He pulled a few strings with some of his banking contacts, and the executives of our bank agreed to drop all the charges against Mark on the provision that the $500,000 was immediately paid back," said Charlie.

"The bank also requested that we didn't press any charges against Mark," added Ted.

"I guess the bank didn't want any bad publicity," Charlie seemed incredulous. "I guess they thought it might lead to a lack of confidence, so they settled and dropped all charges. We believe it was only because of Steve's involvement that the charges were dropped."

"Where did the $500,000 come from to pay back the bank?" I asked.

"From Steve Roberts, of course. Mark Hemmings owes Roberts big time. Roberts organized a job for Mark with him in Chicago, and Mark and his wife moved back to Chicago where they were originally from. Mark Hemmings owes Steve Roberts some enormous favors for the rest of his life. He'll do whatever Steve Roberts asks him to do."

"What happened to the business?" I asked.

"Well, the two of us bought Mark's share. Shortly afterward, Bob Fleming – Mark's original partner – got hit with a lawsuit. Mark was being sued by a client for $3 million for some financial planning advice he'd given to an elderly client that was eventually deemed inappropriate."

"This was before we'd merged the two businesses," added Ted.

Pat asked: "I assume Mark and Bob had the required professional indemnity insurance to cover such claims?"

"Well, no – and that's why the shit hit the fan, so to speak," Ted explained. "You see, Bob Fleming had sold his interest in the business to Mark. Mark had wanted Bob to stay on as a manager because Mark was smart enough to realize his own limitations. He realized he had no skills to run a business. He always needed someone else to run and do things for him, so he persuaded Bob to stay on as manager."

"Anyway, Mark – in his normal sloppy way – had failed to renew the professional indemnity insurance,"

Charlie continued. "So, both he and Bob got sued by the client for advice Mark had given a few years earlier – when both Mark and Bob were partners in the business."

"Excuse me for my ignorance," I asked, "but why did Bob get sued? Given he'd already sold his interest in the business to Mark?"

"Because at the time Mark gave the advice, it was a partnership between both Mark and Bob," Charlie clarified.

"Well that shouldn't have been a problem," said Pat. "When Bob sold his interest to Mark, he'd have had proper indemnities in place to safeguard against such actions."

"Correct," Charlie nodded. "So, picture this: Mark, and by association, Bob, were both sued for more than $3 million. Mark had failed to renew the professional indemnity insurance in his normal sloppy manner. So, no insurance means both Mark and Bob are liable – but Bob had already sold his interest to Mark before they were sued."

"So, wouldn't this have been simple matter of Bob using the indemnity clause in the contract he'd signed when he'd sold his interest in the business to Mark? Thus, all damages becoming Mark's liability?"

"Correct," Charlie nodded, "and that's how it should have been – but remember, Mark's a fraud and has no scruples. For a couple of years, Mark had expected to be sued for this advice. He'd known the advice he'd given was inappropriate, but he'd never shared this with Bob. So, Mark had previously and fraudulently transferred all the assets from his own private company to another one of his companies. That meant, when the shit hit the fan and Bob Fleming sought to be indemnified from Mark's company – as per the contract they'd both duly signed – Mark simply liquidated his company. His company was worthless, so the buck stopped with Bob Fleming."

"The buck didn't just stop for Bob's half-share," Ted continued. "Bob was now being sued for the full $3 million – and Mark Hemmings, the slime, was happy to walk away and leave poor old Bob with all that debt, which included legal fees that nudged the amount to over $4 million."

"Surely, Bob could prove that Mark fraudulently transferred his assets? That scheme's clearly designed simply to protect him. I mean, it's a case of blatant fraud," said Pat.

"For the last twelve months of his life, Bob Fleming spent all his time trying to prove to the court that what Mark Hemmings had done was fraudulent," Ted explained. "Bob had spent all his remaining money trying to prove Mark Hemmings was a crook, but in the end, he got diagnosed with terminal cancer before he could – and he was dead within three months of his diagnosis. Both Charlie and I believe the stress of it all led to his cancer. It was a tragedy – and Mark Hemmings is nothing but a crook."

"Wow." I looked over at Pat. "This is the sort of guy we've got involved in Future Wealth? Steve Roberts – and by association Ted Carroll – are obviously fully aware of what a crook he is."

• • •

ON THE DRIVE back from Santa Barbara to LA, Pat and I pondered our options.

"I think we need to call a meeting with both Steve Roberts and Tom Carroll and let them know what we now know," suggested Pat.

"I agree. We also need to mention the behavior of Arthur Evanglass. Last week, Sue Harris came to see me complaining about the guy. He was making sexual advances to her, along with suggestive comments. I mean, I thought the guy was happily married with a couple of young kids?"

"Several people have also complained to me about him. Some of the guys say when he's had a few drinks, he can't keep his cock in his pants around the younger girls. He's the sort of guy who'd fuck his best friend's girlfriend or wife. Not the sort of guy we want on our team."

"What a sleaze." I added: "How did we ever get involved with these people?"

"Because you and I believe that most people are good people. When they tell us something, we assume it's the truth. Unfortunately, some of the people we've surrounded ourselves with are blatant liars."

"If only we'd realized all this earlier, Pat." I sighed, pondering our next steps.

"Billy, let's have the meeting with Steve and Tom as soon as possible. I'll be asking for Mark Hemmings to be terminated. Just so you understand, if they don't do that, I'll be resigning from Future Wealth immediately. I don't want to be involved with people like that."

I was somewhat shaken by Pat's comment. We were only four months out from listing Future Wealth on the New York Stock Exchange. Since the appointment of Steve Roberts as our CEO, nothing had felt right, though. It was as though the culture of this great business we'd worked so hard to build was evaporating right before our eyes.

"I also want us to hire a private investigator," Pat continued. "There's something not right about the whole dynamic of our board ever since Tom Carroll and his two stooges so hastily appointed Steve Roberts as CEO. There's also something not quite right about how Tom Carroll, Brian Petty, and Doug Heck all got appointed to the board of Future Wealth at the same time three years ago. There's a guy we used at McIntosh & McIntosh for high-level private investigative work. His name is Steve Pollard. He's not cheap, but he's one of the best. I think you and I need to hire him to try and uncover what's really been going on."

"Yep, let's do it," I nodded in agreement.

CHAPTER 22

"GENTLEMAN, NO DOUBT you're aware that most of the senior staff of Future Wealth don't believe that Mark Hemmings possesses the required attributes to continue as an executive member. Too many people who work with him say the man's a fraud," said Pat.

I could see the red blush appear on Steve Roberts's face as he leaned forward, over the boardroom table. He was about to let fly with a barrage of words directed at Pat.

"Let him finish what he is about to say, Steve," I warned, as Tom Carroll pulled at Steve's left sleeve to restrain him. I guessed Steve would be a very poor poker player – always letting his emotions show when somebody said something he disagreed with.

"The staff know Mark Hemmings is a fraud," Pat continued, "yet you, Steve, put him out there to join us, saying he was a genius. Do you have any understanding of how this makes the Future Wealth senior staff feel? Do you have any idea what it does for the culture of our organization?"

Pat was staring intently at Steve Roberts.

I then interrupted him, and said: "A few days ago, Pat and I traveled to Santa Barbara and met two experienced financial advisors by the names of Charlie Fagan and Ted Jones. Unfortunately, their good friend, Bob Fleming, had passed away a few years earlier."

I could see the names register immediately on Steve's face. It was hard to gage Tom Carroll's reaction. Perhaps Tom was a far better poker player than I thought he'd be.

"Charlie Fagan and Ted Jones were former business partners of your brother-in-law, Steve," I continued. "They think your brother-in-law is a crook. They told us if it wasn't for you pulling in a few favors with your banking colleagues and stumping up $500,000 to bail him out, there's every chance Mark Hemmings would be in jail even as we speak."

I could now tell by Tom's reaction that he knew the full details of the story that Pat and I were about to share. Both Tom and Steve got up, and Steve started to yell a jumble of expletives across the boardroom table, his fist clenched and the veins on his face standing out. His face was the color of a beet.

Pat – in his best deep, legal voice – warned: "Gentleman, if you don't sit down and behave like proper board members, I'll have no hesitation whatsoever in filming and recording your behavior."

Pat pulled out a camera with a built-in microphone. Tom immediately regained his composure and pulled Steve back, urging him to sit down.

"We never even knew until a few days ago that Mark Hemmings was your brother-in-law," I hissed. "I'm somewhat intrigued as to why you failed to disclose that piece of information to Pat and I at any point over the past three years."

In a soft, nervous voice, Tom explained: "It's irrelevant whether or not you knew that Mark was Steve's brother-in-law." He sighed. "What do you both want? There is no point talking about what happened between Mark Hemmings and his previous business partners. That was eight years ago. Its old news. What do you want *now*?"

"We want both Mark Hemmings and Arthur Evanglass to resign from Future Wealth, effective immediately," said Pat.

"Why do you want Arthur to resign?" Tom demanded.

"You both know Arthur is a sleaze," Pat snapped. "All the staff know he's a sleaze. He's tried to proposition many of the female staff at staff functions. If only his wife knew he couldn't keep his dick in his pants after a few drinks."

"Arthur is crucial to the IPO," Tom retorted. "He's working on several acquisitions that are going to add further value to the business for the IPO."

"Big deal," Pat hissed. "I'd rather work with people who have integrity, rather than fakes and sleazes."

Throughout this exchange, Steve Roberts had grown remarkably quiet. Tom Carroll had one hand on

Steve's sleeve to calm him down the whole time Pat and I were speaking, and his face was red with anger throughout the whole discussion.

"As far as I'm concerned, both Mark Hemmings and Arthur Evanglass must resign immediately," Pat demanded.

"And if they don't?" Steve Roberts finally asked.

"Then I'll resign immediately," said Pat.

"What about you, Billy?" asked Tom.

"I'll also resign," I replied. I couldn't hold back my feelings about Steve Roberts and Tom Carroll any longer. "Steve, in business and in all forms of life, you respect a person who has integrity, honesty, and tries to lead and motivate people. Since you've been here, you've displayed none of these traits. I have no respect for you whatsoever, not as an individual, or a businessman. I think you're a very weak and tormented soul. You bully staff, you micromanage the organization, and you only have Mark Hemmings and Arthur Evanglass working with you because they're your eyes and ears on the ground. You're destroying the culture of Future Wealth – a culture that Pat, Bill Treloar, and I spent years developing."

My eyes narrowed as I turned to Tom.

"You, Tom, have been a very weak chairman. You allowed this man and his cohorts to get away with murder. I think you both have an agenda, although I'm not sure what that agenda is."

"I totally agree with Billy's comments," Pat nodded. "You, Steve, are nothing but a bully. It astounds me that you've gotten as far as you have in the corporate world. I can only suggest it's because of favors owed to you by friends and family."

"So, Mr. Chairman," I added, "I suggest you keep Steve Roberts away from us both. Perhaps not the ideal situation, given we are only four months away from our IPO after nearly eight years of hard work from a lot of people – but having the right morals and ethics, and being able to lie in bed at night knowing right from wrong, are far more important traits than money."

With those comments, Pat and I stood up and left. Pat stopped at the door just as we were about to leave, and turned to say: "Just so we're all clear about the next steps: If Mark Hemmings and Arthur Evanglass aren't terminated immediately, then both Billy and I will resign. If this happens, I guess you can kiss the IPO goodbye, since we're the founders of this company."

Tom sat there, wide-eyed.

"One other thing," Pat added. "We want him gone, too." Pat pointed directly at Steve Roberts.

• • •

OVER THE NEXT two days, several meetings took place between Pat, me, and Tom Carroll. Pat and I had told Tom we didn't want Steve Roberts involved in any of these discussions, for obvious reasons. We'd also told Tom that we wanted both Doug Heck and Brian Petty removed from the board.

Tom advised us that Steve Roberts, Doug Heck, and Brian Petty needed to remain on the board until at least three months after the IPO.

"To remove three board members just four months before the IPO will make investors nervous," he warned. "We need to ensure continuity. For that very reason, it's important that you both remain on the board, too. If you both resign now, it will severely jeopardize the IPO. So, let's take the personalities out of the equation. Forget Steve Roberts, forget Doug Heck and Brian Petty. I will agree to terminate Mark Hemmings now. I also agree to finish up Arthur Evanglass once he completes the next acquisition in two months, and I agree to remove Steve, Doug, and Brian from the board three months after the IPO."

We sat there and listened to this.

"I further agree to review Steve's position as CEO of Future Wealth within six months of the IPO," Tom continued. "Nearly everything you've wanted, I've agreed to."

"We want Roberts sacked now as CEO, or we both resign." Pat spoke in a heated, raised voice.

"That can't happen for the reasons I've just spelled out, Pat – plus, twenty percent of this company is set aside for your team members. Those are people who joined this company because of the vision you both shared with them. For many of those team members, the IPO is the icing on the cake for them. It sets them up for retirement. If you were to leave now, it basically means the IPO won't happen, and those people – the people you've told me are like family to you – will miss out on their payday. Forget the three of us. It's not fair to them."

In all the discussions Pat and I had, our major concern had always been the staff and the shares they would receive in Future Wealth from the IPO. What Tom had just said was correct. The payday for the staff was the IPO. Shares had been set aside for over fifty staff members as a form of bonus for their hard work over the years. In other organizations, they might have been given cash bonuses. At Future Wealth, Pat and I had structured things so that we rewarded staff who performed above and beyond what was normally required with stock in Future Wealth, on the basis that those shares would become incredibly valuable once we listed them on the New York Stock Exchange. Staff were to receive these shares for free in recognition of their hard work.

In the end, though, Pat resigned.

Other than that, we accepted what Tom Carroll had proposed. A very hectic and gut-wrenching few days ensued for Pat and me, with a lot of negotiations going back and forth between us and Tom Carroll, with a bit of give and take on both sides. We'd learned a lot about Mark Hemmings. In a few months, Steve Pollard would provide us with his findings, and we'd learn a lot more about Steve Roberts and Tom Carroll, too.

A large farewell party was held for Pat at my home. We flew in all the senior management team from New York. Of course, we didn't invite Steve Roberts or any of the other board members.

CHAPTER 23

THINGS HADN'T IMPROVED since the meeting Pat and I had with Tom Carroll, three months earlier. We were only one month out from the IPO, which still promised to be a great success. Institutional investors were lining up to invest in Future Wealth, but they had no idea about the inner rumblings within our business.

While Mark Hemmings had been terminated, to the great delight of most of the staff at Future Wealth, Steve Roberts was still acting like a bully and demonstrating to everyone why he wasn't suitable to be running the organization.

Four weeks earlier, the National American Franchising Awards were held in Boston. Future Wealth was a finalist in the Franchisor of the Year awards across all categories. Steve Roberts asked all members of the board to attend – except for me.

Future Wealth won the big award as the National Franchisor of the Year, and with cameras buzzing in his face, Steve Roberts gave his victory speech, thanking the board of Future Wealth for entrusting him to build the business into a truly great venture over the previous three years. There was no mention of me, the founder of Future Wealth, nor any mention of my business partner, Pat Gabriel – who'd shared my vision and helped me build the business model from the ground up. Neither was there any mention of Steve Roberts's predecessor, Bill Treloar – who'd guided and shaped the business as CEO for five years.

Pat and the senior management team knew what a big kick in the guts it was for me to not be invited. They all knew it should have been me up there, accepting the national award and thanking my business partner and the sensational team that Pat and I had assembled over the previous eight years.

"Just hang there until the IPO, Billy – for the sake of the staff and their shares," Pat advised me. "Then, move on. The people who care will always know the truth. They'll know that Steve Roberts was just a fool – out to take all the glory to satisfy his own, warped ego. The man is a psychopath."

• • •

RECENTLY, I'D SPLIT up with Isabella. There was nothing sinister about our breakup. We'd just simply grown apart. I'd spent the last few years traveling all across America to grow the business and help Future Wealth achieve its goal of the IPO, and most weekends

I'd arrived home exhausted. While Isabella was keen to socialize and entertain, I simply wanted to stay at home, have a few quiet beers, perhaps a surf, and then hit the road again early on Monday to travel wherever I was needed next. The time away certainly took a toll on our relationship.

Isabella wanted to seek counseling and try and get our relationship back on track. Me? I just wanted to escape and relieve myself of all the pressure and stress after the IPO. I never shared with Isabella all the issues that Pat and I had encountered since Tom Carroll, Steve Roberts, and their cohorts had joined the company. My logic for that was quite simple: It meant Isabella would never suffer the stress and sleepless nights I'd been experiencing over the previous three years.

Much to Isabella's dismay, I was content for our relationship to end. I vowed after three marriages, I'd never get married again. Fortunately, Isabella and I had no children together, so our breakup was quite simple and straightforward from a financial viewpoint.

Isabella was heartbroken by my decision. She suspected, incorrectly, that I'd been having an affair during my travels across America – something she'd believe for many months.

The last three years at Future Wealth had been very stressful for both Pat and me. We had a board stacked against us, we had a CEO who we couldn't trust, and we'd had his two dodgy lieutenants watching our every move. Even more difficult, I'd been needed to grin and bear it until after the IPO, so the fifty staff would receive their ultimate payday for all their hard work.

Without wanting to admit it to anyone, I was suffering a mental breakdown. I was completely and utterly burned out.

I hadn't told anyone, but once the IPO was complete, I planned to quit Future Wealth for good. I wasn't going to stay on the board. The memories of Choeng Mon on Koh Samui Island in Thailand, where I'd visited all those years ago, were once again fresh in my mind. I'd decided I was going back there to recuperate once this IPO was complete.

Once I get an idea in my head, I become very focused on it – and it was difficult to change my mind once an idea is cemented into it.

• • •

PAT AND I continued our weekly catch ups since his departure from Future Wealth. It gave me a chance to talk with someone openly about the corporate suits who'd taken over our baby.

"Billy, you won't believe what I'm about to tell you," Pat told me the next time I saw him. "Let me just correct that statement: You *will* believe what I'm about to tell you about Arthur Evanglass, but you won't believe who he's done it with."

I was somewhat perplexed by Pat's statement.

"Pat, I've no idea about anything you've just said."

"Arthur Evanglass has been screwing Errol Archer's wife," said Pat.

I nearly choked on my coffee.

"Are we talking about the same Errol Archer? Errol who was brought on board with Future Wealth three years ago by Steve Roberts?" I asked.

"Yes – the same Errol," replied Pat. "Errol and I have become good friends since he joined the company. We catch up every few weeks for a beer when I'm in New York. I took Errol under my wing when he first joined Future Wealth. I guess I was quite intrigued by him. He was so different than the others, yet he came across and joined our business as one of Steve's trusted lieutenants."

"What happened?"

"Errol and his wife, Mandy, split up five weeks ago. Mandy is a very attractive woman," Pat added.

"Yeah, I've met her at various staff functions. I'd always thought they were the perfect couple."

"Like many couples, their relationship had been struggling," Pat shrugged. "I mean, Errol had been working incredibly long hours over the last twelve months, what with the upcoming IPO. Steve Roberts was driving him into the ground."

"I've found Errol to be one of the nicest guys I've ever met."

"Me too – but after ten years together, Errol decided he wanted to call it quits with his marriage to Mandy. For the last few years, they'd been trying to have kids, but without luck. I think Errol shares one of your traits, Billy – in that he's a workaholic."

"Well, being a workaholic hasn't worked for me, Pat, given I've now had three divorces."

"I don't know if you've ever noticed, Billy, but it's always been obvious to me – and some of the others, I might add – that Arthur Evanglass has always fancied Mandy. Whenever we had a social function, he'd always make a beeline for her – and always made certain that he sat next to her. Even Blind Freddy could tell that he had the hots for Mandy."

"Yeah, I guess I had noticed that. I just assumed it was Arthur being his normal, sleazy self. Isabella told me she'd thought he fancied her. He'd told her his marriage was a marriage by name only – that he shared the same bed with his wife, but they never had sex." I rolled my eyes. "I mean, why the fuck would he be telling Isabella, my wife, personal stuff like that?"

"We all know the man is a sleaze and can't keep his dick in his pants."

"So, what happened with Mandy?"

"Mandy had been quite demoralized by the breakup of her marriage. She'd taken it worse than Errol expected. She thought he'd been unfaithful to her, and that he must've had a mistress hidden away somewhere."

"Does he?" I asked.

"No, he gets home late at night and is absolutely exhausted with all the work on the IPO."

"Okay – but how did Errol discover that Arthur was having an affair with his wife?"

"He was aware that Arthur had been paying a bit more attention to Mandy than normal. He noticed over the last few weeks that Arthur's body language toward him at work was totally different, too. He said the guy had become very weird."

"So, he suspected something?"

Pat nodded.

"Errol told me he'd met up with his wife last week for coffee, to discuss how she was doing – knowing she'd been pretty upset by the breakup. She popped out to the restroom and left her phone on the table. While she was gone, Errol opened her phone, hoping she hadn't changed her password – which she hadn't – and then he saw the text messages between her and Arthur. Not all of them, but enough to confirm that something was happening between them."

"What did he say to her?"

"Initially, nothing. He thought he needed to gather his thoughts, so he said nothing at the time. Last week, though, he popped around unannounced to her house. Errol had moved out of the family home, and she was still living there. He asked her to tell him the truth about what was happening between her and Arthur Evanglass. Mandy initially denied everything. He then mentioned the text messages he'd seen. She denied it and gave him her phone to check. She'd obviously deleted the messages since then, but Errol had taken a photo with his own phone of one of the exchanges between the two of them, which he showed her. She then started sobbing uncontrollably and told him everything."

"Of all people, why would she have it off with Arthur Evanglass?" I asked.

"Because the guy took advantage of her emotional state. He somehow knew that Errol had moved out of the family home."

"How would he even know that?" I asked.

"Errol suspects Steve told Arthur. He was the only other person, aside from me, that he confided anything in regarding his marriage problems."

I shook my head as Pat continued:

"Arthur had apparently turned up at the house unannounced, on some false pretense that he had documents for Errol to sign. He told Mandy he'd been trying to call Errol, without any luck. Errol assured me he'd had no missed calls from Arthur – it was all a ruse."

"What a slime," I sighed.

"Anyway, Mandy explained that Errol had moved out and that they'd broken up. It was late afternoon, and Mandy was having a glass of wine all by herself on the balcony. Arthur asked her to tell him what had happened, so she invited him to join her for a glass. She incorrectly assumed that Arthur was a close friend of Errol's. Heck, they'd worked together in Chicago and came across to Future Wealth together as part of Steve Roberts's team. It was a fair assumption."

"Anyway," Pat continued, "so Arthur came in and sat down on the sofa and shared a glass of wine with Mandy. She was an emotional wreck. She couldn't believe that Errol called the marriage off. Arthur told her how much he cared for her, and that he couldn't believe Errol had left her, given how beautiful she was. They started kissing on the sofa, and he told her how he'd fantasized about her."

"You're kidding me! He told her he fantasized about her?" I just about choked on my Coke.

"Yep, he said he'd always fantasized about being with her. He then produced a condom and they had sex – fully clothed, on the sofa."

"You mean, he turned up there knowing full well that she and Errol had broken up, knowing full well that Errol wouldn't be there, and he had a fucking condom in his pocket? What a lowlife! What a down-and-out sleaze."

"It happened again a couple of weeks later. Arthur called her, wanting to know if he could come around. He said he had some chocolates and wine for her. He ended up spending the night with her. Mandy then told him it had to stop. I mean, she knew Arthur's wife from various Future Wealth social functions. He told her – and you won't believe this, Billy – that he was old enough to choose his play buddies."

"What a jerk! You and I, and the others, all know the man is the complete office sleaze." I paused. "How is Errol coping with this?"

"Errol's taken a week off, which I'm told has really pissed off Steve, given the IPO is one month out." Pat narrowed his eyes. "Has Roberts spoken to you about Errol being on leave?"

"I don't speak to Roberts at all. My staff have been told not to put any of his phone calls through."

"Well, unbeknown to Roberts, he'll be receiving Errol's notice of resignation next Monday, which no doubt will really piss him off, given the IPO deadline."

I shook my head.

"I've never understood why Errol has always been so loyal to Steve Roberts."

"It's a simple case of the boss man telling his junior: 'if you stick with me, then one day you'll be the CFO of this company.'"

"What do you plan to do?" I asked Pat.

"Tomorrow, I'm going to march into Tom Carroll's office in New York and tell him the full sordid story."

"Better still, Pat, make sure Steve Roberts is there as well. I'll come with you."

"At a later stage, I plan to tell Arthur's wife what a sleaze she's married to. I feel sorry for Errol. A trusted coworker has been fucking his wife. Admittedly, the marriage had broken up – but it had only broken up a couple of weeks prior, and that sleaze Arthur couldn't wait to drop his pants and hop into hers."

"The marriage probably only broke up because of all the work he was doing for Future Wealth," I suggested.

"Exactly," Pat nodded. "Our company put him under such pressure. It takes two to tango – and Mandy and Errol had split up, which was his decision not hers – but she was still emotionally distraught, and that guy said all the right words to pump her up."

"That bit about having fantasies about her? I mean, that is sick, Pat. The guy has worked with Errol for over eight years. Five years in the bank in Chicago, and then the last three years at Future Wealth."

"He obviously has no respect for Errol whatsoever. He broke up with his wife, and within a couple of weeks, Arthur was around trying to fuck her."

"Not trying to fuck her, Pat," I groaned. "He *did* fuck her."

"The person I feel sorry for is Arthur's wife. Fancy him telling Isabella that he has a marriage 'in name only.' Fancy him telling Mandy that he can 'chose who his play buddies are' and that it's of no concern of his wife."

"One sick dude."

• • •

"THE GUY IS a sleaze," Pat snapped at Tom Carroll the following morning. "He's been fucking Errol Archer's wife. He should have been sacked months ago. You promised Billy and I that he was only going to stay for two months to complete that one last deal, and here we are three months down the line and the guy is still here. Why?"

"So, he's been fucking Errol's wife," Steve Roberts laughed. "Hardly a fireable offense." He had a big smile on his face.

"It's about what's right and wrong, Steve," I snapped at him. "You brought your so-called 'trusted lieutenants' here with you. We discovered through our own investigation that Mark Hemmings – your brother-in-law – was a man of less-than-desirable character. You knew this the whole time, but you'd deliberately hidden it from us. You never even told us he was your brother-in-law!"

"Mark Hemmings was never found guilty of any inappropriate behavior," snarled Steve, "and whether he's my brother-in-law or not is none of your business."

"True, he wasn't convicted of anything – but only because you used your high-level banking contacts to ensure it never went any farther," Pat snapped. "You also paid the $500,000 back to the bank to keep it all hushed up. So, you've had one over Mark Hemmings for the last eight years. He's been your yes-man, happy to do whatever dirty, little grubby things you want him to do."

"You've no proof I've ever asked Mark to do any dirty, grubby things for me," Steve retorted.

"Correct. I can only assume so, but I have no evidence." Pat, ever the lawyer, admitted: "I withdraw that remark, for now. I repeat: For now."

He turned to the man sitting beside the CEO.

"And you, Tom, have been fully aware of what Mark Hemmings had done, and yet – as chairman – you still allowed him to be employed by this company."

"As Steve said," Tom replied coldly, "Mark Hemmings has never been found guilty of any crime. His police record is impeccable – it's completely clean."

"Let's not go around in circles here, guys," I hissed. "We all know right from wrong, and Mark Hemmings should never have been employed by this company in the first place. The fact that it could even happen tells me and Pat that there's something far deeper to all of this than you two let on."

Both Tom and Steve had a glare in their eyes as they stared at me. Once again, Steve – who would've been a shocking poker player – had a red face and his blood vessels were showing. Tom was holding his sleeve, trying to calm him down.

"Countless staff have made complaints about Arthur," I said next. "You both know the man is a sleaze. You even said to me and Pat twelve months ago that the guy had always been a sleaze. So, why do you both surround yourselves with characters like that?"

Thirty seconds went by with no answer.

"I repeat my question to you both," I growled. "Why do you surround yourselves with characters like that?"

Eventually, Tom growled: "Billy, there's nothing more to say. If Arthur fucked Errol's wife – or should I say *ex*-wife – it has nothing to do with this company. It's a matter for Errol and his ex-wife to handle."

"Perhaps this affair was going on while Errol and his wife were still together," laughed Steve. "Perhaps Arthur was fucking her this entire time."

Tom gestured to Steve to hush, and then turned back to me.

"Billy, Arthur will be finishing up in the next couple of weeks. This one last deal he's been working on has just taken a bit longer than expected to finalize. It'll add value to Future Wealth. I've told Arthur that once the deal is completed, his services will no longer be required. He'll leave before the IPO."

I shook my head.

"The fact that you're both prepared to continue to associate with people like Arthur – knowing full well that this is normal behavior for him – says something about your own character. I guess it's all about the dollar, at all costs. Neither of you give a damn about people. I sit here, and I've watched the culture of the business Pat and I built get destroyed. All the staff complain to me about you, Steve – you're a bully and a liar. And you, Mr. Chairman, are a weak soul."

I stared at the two of them, before adding:

"I can only imagine there's something else about the both of you that Pat and I haven't yet discovered. There *is* a bigger picture here. We haven't worked out what it is yet, but believe me, we will eventually. We'll find out about all the untoward things that have been happening at Future Wealth ever since Steve got appointed as CEO. Too many unexplained things have happened since Steve Taylor and Gabriel Darcy resigned, and I believe both of you are behind them."

I could see a worried look on their faces. Steve and Tom now knew that Pat and I were sniffing for information.

"Gentlemen, you know right from wrong," I growled at them. "You know the appropriate course of action to take with Arthur Evanglass. I'll be telling the senior management team what a sleaze the man is. I suggest you inform all potential investors that I'll be resigning from Future Wealth in all capacity once the IPO is complete."

Pat and I left that meeting and we'd never speak to or see Steve Roberts again.

CHAPTER 24

WITH ONLY FOUR days before the IPO of Future Wealth, we finally met with Steve Pollard – the private investigator we'd hired to undertake research into Steve Roberts, Tom Carroll, and their cohorts.

Steve Pollard had spent nearly four months putting together all the pieces of this jigsaw puzzle. It had cost Pat and I close to $100,000 for his services. To say that what he was about to tell us was worrying would be an understatement.

Because of the sensitive nature of what Steve was about to share with us, we'd agreed to meet at my Malibu house, where we wouldn't be disturbed.

"Guys, this has been a very difficult matter to investigate," Pollard explained as soon as we met with him. "There are just so many moving pieces. One thing is certain, though – you're not going to like hearing what I'm about to tell you both. I've been in this private investigation game for a long time, and this has been one of the most complex cases I've ever worked on."

We listened with a growing sense of dread as he continued:

"Because of the complexity and the need for me to double-check everything I've uncovered, it's taken just under four months of nearly full-time research to get to this point. I've had to rely on a few favors from some of my government contacts to chase through the paper trail."

Steve sat on the sofa, facing both Pat and me, and placed folders in front of us.

"I have here a hard copy of my report for each of you. Before you read it, though, I'll share with you both what I've discovered. This may take a while," he warned.

"My investigation has revealed that the founding families of A & C got themselves into a major financial bind just over three years ago – and I do mean a *major* financial bind. They were on the verge of bankruptcy due to some investments they'd undertaken during the Global Financial Crisis, the impact of which reared its ugly head some years later. They'd just about lost everything, and their last remaining assets were their investments in Future Wealth and A & C Tax Refund. They were about to lose those as well, unless they could liquidate the investments in a hurry."

"At about that time, Tom Carroll – who wasn't your chairman at that point – had established his own investment advisory business. Carroll had years of experience in investment banking. To some, he was revered, but to others, he wasn't well liked at all. He was known for having a ruthless streak, and for perhaps doing things close to the line of what was legal and ethical. The impression I've gathered is of a man always motivated by money, and doing what was best for him at the expense of others."

"That must be why Charlie Cameron didn't want him as chairman," I interrupted. Steve nodded.

"The families who owned A & C had approached Carroll's fledging new investment advisory business for help in staving off their impending bankruptcy. They needed to do things quickly – and so they confided in Carroll the full extent of the financial crisis they faced. Carroll is an opportunist, always trying to put together deals that benefited him – deals that aren't always in the best interest of his client. However, these three families had their backs to the wall. They were desperate for help."

Steve paused for a drink of water.

"Carroll and his associates formed a new company, and the owners of A & C agreed to transfer all their shares in Future Wealth to that company. The owners of A & C were in desperate need of cash. Carroll's company paid less than half the market value for A & C's thirty percent share in Future Wealth. Carroll's company also received twenty percent ownership of A & C as part of the deal he'd negotiated. The money the founding families of A & C received from Carroll and his associates enabled them to clear all their debts and stave off bankruptcy."

"I remember signing the paperwork to approve that share transaction," Pat was ashen faced. "The owners of

A & C had told Billy and me it was due to an internal restructure. We didn't think we needed to question that claim. I mean, we'd been in business with them for nearly five years at that point, and we'd never had any reason not to trust them before."

He breathed deeply.

"If we'd known that the company they were transferring shares to was ultimately owned by somebody else, then warning bells would have been ringing – but we didn't even know Tom Carroll existed back then. This all happened before he was chairman."

Steve nodded: "The price the owners of A & C paid was the total loss of their investment in Future Wealth, and they gave up twenty percent of their ownership of A & C – but it saved them from becoming bankrupt."

"All a bit unbelievable," I shook my head, "but now a lot of things that have been happening over the last few years make sense."

"There's more, so please let me carry on," Steve insisted. "The company that bought the shares in Future Wealth was ultimately controlled by Tom Carroll and Steve Roberts. I've found out that Roberts and Carroll were old buddies from years ago. When Carroll was starting to set up his own investment advisory business, he had Roberts invest in that business with him. Roberts got his two lieutenants, Mark Hemmings and Arthur Evanglass, involved as minor shareholders. Consequently, both Hemmings and Evanglass also own shares in both Future Wealth and A &C." Steve flipped open the folder, and added: "Errol Archer, for some reason, was excluded from this transaction."

"Wow," Pat breathed. "Unbelievable."

Steve nodded.

"I believe their initial plan was to simply get hold of thirty percent of Future Wealth at half price, and then sit there silently and let you guys follow through with the IPO. They just had to make sure you guys never found out that A & C weren't the real owners of the shares any longer. Your future IPO is potentially a big payday for Carroll and Roberts."

I nodded my head, adding: "Tom Carroll isn't a dumb man. He'd have learned all about Pat and me, The Tax Refund Shop, and the plans we had for the IPO of Future Wealth. I mean, all that information was provided to A & C when we presented to them eight years ago. Tom Carroll would have had all that information at his fingertips when he was consulting with A & C."

I leaned back in my chair, frowning.

"But Carroll, the opportunistic bastard, would have also been aware of Charlie Cameron's illness. He'd have seen an opportunity to gain control of Future Wealth and demanded – or perhaps even forced – the decision-makers at A & C to put his name forward as future chairman."

"Correct, Billy," Steve nodded. "I believe part of the deal with him rescuing A & C was that they'd put his name forward as chairman of Future Wealth once it became inevitable that Charlie Cameron was going to have to resign. Carroll also forced A & C to make changes to the Future Wealth board by increasing the members from five to six, and he organized the appointment of both Brian Petty and Doug Heck to the senior management of A & C – and, by virtue of that, onto the board."

"Wow. What a tangled web" I added.

Steve continued: "Since Tom Carroll now had control of the Future Wealth board, he could install Steve Roberts as CEO of the company. This is where it gets thorny. I'm pretty sure Carroll and Roberts had an initial plan simply to get thirty percent of Future Wealth at half price, given Carroll would have been aware of the pending IPO a few years down the line. It was a simple opportunity to make some big bucks."

"That's the part of the puzzle I haven't been able to figure out," Steve sighed. "Carroll and Roberts got hold of thirty percent of Future Wealth three years ago, at a bargain price. They could see the potential of the future IPO with the two of you leading the company forward. They could have just sat there, done nothing, and watched you guys do all the hard work – and they'd have still gotten their reward once the IPO took place. Nobody would have been any the wiser."

Pat and I nodded. Steve kept speaking:

"What I don't understand is why they've gone to all this trouble to get Carroll the job as chairman, to get Roberts appointed as the CEO, and to bring Petty and Heck onto the board. All they've done is increase their shareholding from thirty percent to thirty-five percent by buying an extra five percent from you, Billy. Why would you go to all that trouble to get control when it only nets you an additional five percent of the company?" Steve shook his head with confusion.

"That doesn't make any sense," Pat agreed.

"Gentleman, this is of some concern," I narrowed my eyes. "There must be some other agenda here. Why have they gone to so much trouble over the past three years to gain control of the board, and why did Roberts bring his cohorts with him?"

I was thinking out aloud, and continued speaking:

"I suppose it does explain why Carroll wanted to purchase five percent of my shares. Once he saw an opportunity to become chairman, he didn't want Pat and I to own fifty percent of the company and exert control. He purchased my five percent just to take that majority away from us. The story he sold me – about wanting to share in the reward for all the hard work he'd put into taking Future Wealth to the stock exchange – was clearly a lie. I mean, he already owned thirty percent of the shares – Pat and I just didn't know it at the time."

I pursed my lips.

"So, Tom Carroll knew if he controlled the board, and if Pat and I had less than fifty percent of the shares, he'd get control of the company – but why? Why did he want control of the company? Why not just sit on thirty percent, and do nothing? He'd still reap the rewards from the IPO."

"What about Gabriel Darcy and Steve Taylor?" Pat asked. "They were both great guys to work with, and Steve Taylor was a great board member – always making decisions based on what was best for all the shareholders, not just the ones from A & C."

Steve interrupted: "Carroll and Roberts didn't want Taylor on the board precisely because of that – because he supported decisions that were best for *all* shareholders. If they could have him removed from the board and ensure A & C had two places at the table, it gave them control."

I flopped back into the sofa and admitted: "I just haven't been able to determine *why* they wanted to have control."

For a moment, there was silence in the room. Then Steve sat up again and continued.

"In his role as investment advisor to the owners of A & C, Tom had made Gabriel Darcy and Steve Taylor the scapegoats for the bad investment decisions that had nearly wiped out the three families. Since Carroll – and by association, Roberts – now owned twenty percent of A & C, they immediately had Gabriel and Steve terminated. It was part of the deal they negotiated with the three families."

"Both Mark Hemmings and Arthur Evanglass were minority shareholders in Tom and Steve's company – the one that owned thirty percent of Future Wealth. That's why they came across with Steve Roberts to Future Wealth. Mark Hemmings also happened to be married to Steve Roberts's sister."

I interrupted him: "Did you manage to speak to the owners of A & C to find out their side of the story? I mean, they were great people to work with for the first five years – but we've had no contact with them for the three years since. They insisted then that all contact with their company had to be through their two representatives, Brian Petty and Doug Heck. Pat and I found that very strange."

"Well, now we know the reason why they stopped taking our calls – they weren't the shareholders of Future Wealth any longer," Pat said.

Steve nodded in agreement.

"The owners of A & C refused to speak to me," he nodded. "In fact, I received a terse letter from their lawyers advising me to immediately cease and desist in trying to contact them. I suspect – but haven't been able to verify – that Tom Carroll and Steve Roberts were behind that. They didn't want me sniffing around. Likewise, I ceased all contact because I didn't want Carroll and Roberts finding out I was on their case."

"If they did, they'd have immediately known you were working for me and Billy," Pat said.

I snorted bitterly. "I'd love to ask the owners of A & C why they sold at half market price, given we were only three years out from the IPO. I mean, Pat and I could have purchased their shares at full market value, rather than selling to Carroll and Roberts at half what they were worth. That would have resolved all their financial problems."

"They were only weeks away from total financial ruin and would have lost everything, I guess they felt they didn't have time to shop their stock around. Besides, they were being advised by Carroll, and there was no way he was going to let thirty percent of Future Wealth slip through his fingers once he saw the potential payoff after the IPO. I assume he told them that if they didn't accept his offer, they'd go bankrupt. Given things were time-sensitive, it was the lesser of two evils – I mean, either sell for half price, or go broke."

"*And* give up twenty of A & C at the same time," I added.

"Yep, they paid a high price – but still staved off bankruptcy." Steve agreed. "I had this all verified by Gabriel Darcy. I managed to meet with him, at least. Carroll and Roberts paid him off to walk away on the basis he never discussed A & C or Future Wealth with anyone. He's broken that agreement by speaking with me, but he despises both Tom Carroll and Steve Roberts, and he's at the stage at which he doesn't give a damn what those guys do to him if they discover he'd been talking to me."

Pat and I listened as Steve continued.

"Gabriel told me that A & C had been just weeks away from total collapse. They were starved of cash, as the losses in their other investments with the various credit swaps they'd invested in back before the great financial crisis were far greater than anybody had previously thought."

"In Gabriel's words," Steve snorted, "'Tom Carroll is an absolute ruthless prick who'd sell his own mother if it made some money for him. As for Steve Roberts, you wouldn't piss on him if he was on fire.'"

Pat and I laughed bitterly when we listened to that – imagining hearing those words in Gabriel's clipped, New Yok accent.

Steve continued: "Gabriel advised me that he and Steve Taylor were the fall guys who'd been blamed for the impact of the financial catastrophe. The truth was, though, it had nothing to do with them. It was just a way for Tom Carroll and Steve Roberts to gain equity in both Future Wealth and A & C at a price well beneath market value."

"Gabriel also believed that Carroll was forced out of his previous role as director of that Wall Street investment bank for dodgy and shady dealings during the great financial crisis. I just haven't been able to substantiate whether that assertion is true or not."

"May I ask how you've been able to piece all this together?" I asked.

"Let's just say the three families that owned A & C are quite large. There are one or two members of that family who are completely and utterly devoid of all respect for Carroll and Roberts – and what they've done to the families. They believe they've been totally ripped off – in fact, they were more than happy to talk to me about it. It took a few weeks to gain their trust, but once I did, they openly shared their version of events. I was also able to search company records from the government's databases and put together the paper trail that led to my discovery about who owned what. Then, of course, Gabriel Darcy simply confirmed what I'd already pieced together."

Steve looked at Pat and me seriously.

"I'm not sure what you guys want to do now, given everything I've told you about Carroll and Roberts."

"We're only four days out from the IPO," I said coldly. "I suggest we call an immediate meeting with Carroll and Roberts and fly out to New York. I don't think there's been any fraud here, which is going to mean Carroll and Roberts won't serve jail time, but there are serious issues presented by all this."

"Agreed," Pat nodded. "I mean, it'll be very hard to argue fraud – the three families willingly transferred their shares to Carroll and Roberts – but at the very least, Tom Carroll is completely conflicted, acting as their advisor and then purchasing their investments at half price. That demonstrates a complete lack of ethics, morals, and professionalism. It simply demonstrates how ruthless those two are."

"I've been in contact with two members of the families over the past couple of months," Steve said. "They both believe they've got grounds to sue Carroll and his investment advisory business for negligent advice. It appears he gave the families advice that was in his best interest, not that of his client."

"As a lawyer, I absolutely agree," Pat nodded. "This is an example of blatant abuse of power. Tom Carroll and his investment advice business were completely conflicted. He should never have been advising those three families, while actively trying to buy their shares."

He leaned forward on his chair.

"When you speak to them next, please advise those family members to go after Carroll and sue him. He *stole* their shares." Then, Pat turned to me. "In relation to Future Wealth, both Roberts and Carroll have clearly breached their duties as directors. I suggest, Billy, that we contact the US Securities and Exchange Commission."

"We can't pull the IPO with four days to go, Pat," I warned. "Plus, as we've discussed, the IPO is the payday for our own staff at Future Wealth – the ones we rewarded with shares."

I pondered what our next move should be.

"Okay, I agree we can't pull the IPO," Pat nodded, "but we can force both Roberts and Carroll to resign immediately. I'll come back on the board for six months, and you can stay on and assume the role as chairman for six months. The investment banks will love that – you, the founder of the business, assuming the role of chairman. They'll also love it that I'm coming back after four months away from the board."

I took a deep breath.

"Pat, I'm literally burned out, mate. I've been exhausted by all the traveling across America. I'm exhausted by everything that's gone on with the company ever since Carroll, Roberts, and their cohorts gained control. I just need a break."

Pat warned: "Billy, if you walk away now – given that we're going to demand that both Carroll and Roberts resign immediately – it'll kill the company. We list in four days – and when the markets see your resignation, as well as the resignations of those two assholes, we'll get clobbered on Wall Street. Our share price will plunge, and questions will be asked as to why three directors, including the founder, have all resigned on or before the IPO."

Pat was uncharacteristically passionate as he said: "Think of our staff, Billy! This is also their payday. Many of them have been with us from the start. With Carroll and Roberts gone, we can make this company great again. We could get Bill Treloar back as the CEO. The staff love that man. It would become a real, feel-good story."

I took a deep breath, and finally nodded.

"Okay. Call Tom Carroll now and organize a meeting. You and I can fly to New York immediately."

CHAPTER 25

TOM CARROLL CLEARLY had no idea why we were in New York when he welcomed us to the offices of Future Wealth.

"Good morning, Billy and Pat. Pretty exciting time for us all, what with only two days left to the IPO. I just got off the phone with Wall Street. They're expecting we'll be oversubscribed – with a market value of close to $480 million. They're expecting shares to surge ten to fifteen percent once the bell is rung."

Tom had a big smile on his face as he led us to the boardroom.

"Please sit down, Tom," I asked, as soon as the door clicked shut behind us. "Where is Steve?"

"He should be here any moment." Tom saw the tense look on my face. "Is there something wrong?"

Tom was now obviously aware of my body language, and growing concerned by my tone of voice.

"Yes, there is something wrong, Tom," I warned him, "but we'd rather wait for Steve to be here before I share with you what Pat and I have discovered."

"Perhaps get your receptionist to call Steve to see how far away he is," suggested Pat.

"He's probably caught in traffic. He was driving in for this meeting, rather than catching the subway." Tom exited the boardroom to ask his receptionist to make the call.

Fifteen minutes passed before Tom returned to the room. Pat and I assumed Tom might have had an inkling of what we'd discovered. There was no small talk while we waited for Steve Roberts to arrive.

"We've tried Steve's cell and it just goes to voicemail," Tom explained. "I've contacted Gloria, his wife, who said he'd left home ninety minutes ago. It's only a forty-five-minute trip. There must have been an accident or something he's gotten caught up in." Then, Tom's mouth narrowed into a thin line. "Still, I don't understand why he wouldn't answer his phone. It's hands free. I'll just try to call him again."

"Let's not wait any longer," I insisted. "We need to have this discussion now. I'd have preferred Steve to hear this firsthand, but Pat and I will repeat what we're about to say once Steve walks in."

We turned to face the chairman of the board.

"Tom – Pat and I have been concerned for the last three years about corporate governance issues surrounding Future Wealth. This was our baby – I started this business. It was my vision, my idea, and I got Pat involved based on that vision. Together, Pat and I have spent years devoted to growing Future Wealth into what it is today."

I paused to have a drink of water. I could sense Tom's unease.

"Over the last three years," I continued, "things started to change. First, Gabriel Darcy and Steve Taylor abruptly disappeared from A &C. Then, Steve Taylor resigned suddenly from our board. Their replacements were Doug Heck and Brian Petty. As soon as those guys joined A & C, they were appointed to our board – all because the owners of A & C claimed they wanted two representatives on the board, rather than the one representative they'd previously had."

I narrowed my eyes at Tom Carroll.

"It turns out, you've known Doug and Brian for many years – totally unbeknownst to Pat and me at the time."

"At the same time," Pat continued, "the owners of A & C put your name forward as the ideal person to be our new chairman after Charlie got sick and retired. You were subsequently appointed to the Future Wealth board."

"And for those last three years," I followed on from Pat's thought, "you, Doug, and Brian have always voted as one block. The first example of this was the appointment of Steve Roberts as CEO. There was no proper process followed there – the three of you had clearly already made the decision to hire Steve before you even discussed any of this with Pat and me. You also made the decision to allow him to bring his three cohorts along before you discussed it with us."

As Tom sat there silently, I continued:

"We all knew that Bill Treloar was the perfect person to continue as CEO of this business and take us through to the IPO. Thereafter, we witnessed Steve Roberts bully staff, micromanage everything, and basically destroy the culture of this business – a culture that Pat and I worked so hard to develop among the staff and franchisees, knowing full well that if we didn't get the culture right, we wouldn't have a business. Pat and I have repeatedly raised these concerns with the board ever since Steve's appointment, but no action was ever taken."

"With Steve Roberts as the CEO, and therefore having a seat on the board, we've always had you, Steve, Doug, and Brian vote as one block against me and Pat. We've smelled a rat for many years because of this."

Now, it was the time for the kicker.

"Four months ago, at considerable personal expense, Pat and I hired a private investigator to undertake research into both you and Steve Roberts."

Tom's eyes narrowed.

"That's nice," he snorted bitterly. "You don't trust me and Steve, so unbeknown to us, you hired some no-hope private investigator to try and dig up dirt."

"Correct, Tom," I smiled thinly. "For obvious reasons, we don't trust you or Steve Roberts. You forced our hand into this, by the way you ran the business."

I slapped a folder onto the boardroom table.

"Here's a copy of the private investigator's report. Please don't read it yet – I'll let Pat give you an overview of what's contained in this report."

Pat rose form his chair, and in his best lawyer voice, explained: "Tom – we're fully aware of what you and Steve Roberts have been up to. We're fully aware that the true owners of the thirty percent share of Future Wealth are no longer the A & C families, but you and Steve instead – hidden behind an obscure company you both control. We're now fully aware that you acquired these shares at half their market value, along with twenty percent of the shares of A & C, all in one transaction around three years ago. You ensured that the owners of A & C approached Billy and me to increase their board representation from one to two members. You ensured that Doug Heck was made CEO of A & C and Brian Petty made Chief Legal Counsel – as they'd then be appointed to the board of Future Wealth as well. You also ensured that the owners of A & C put your name forward as the possible new chairman of Future Wealth, once you were aware of Charlie Cameron's illness. This was all orchestrated so you could control the board, and hence control the company – since, at the time, Billy and I owned more than fifty percent of the shares."

Tom tried to interrupt, but Pat cut him short with a wave of his hand.

"Let me carry on." He squared off against Tom Carroll. "Within two weeks of being appointed chairman, you approached Billy with some fake story about needing to buy five percent of his shares, so you could share in the upside of the IPO. Billy accepted your story and duly sold you five percent. We now understand that this was a decision you and Steve Roberts made to ensure Billy and I owned less than fifty percent of the shares in Future Wealth. Unbeknown to Billy and me, you and Steve already owned thirty percent of Future Wealth because of the shares you'd ripped off from the A & C families. This meant you and Steve now owned a combined thirty-five percent of the company, which is an important figure in our company's constitution. I'll come back to that in a moment…"

Pat was pacing the boardroom, absorbed in his explanation.

"You organized Gabriel Darcy and Steve Taylor's terminations from A & C and then blamed them for the financial difficulties the company had encountered three years earlier. You knew the financial woes of the owners were due to bad credit swaps they'd got involved with during the great financial crisis, which blew up in their face. You know it had nothing to do with Gabriel and Steve Taylor, but you still used them as a scapegoat because you didn't want Gabriel and Steve at A & C in case they figured out your little scheme."

"Stop right there, Pat!" Tom interrupted angrily. "This is a complete lie! You have nothing on either me or Steve!" He stood up angrily from his chair.

"It's not lies," I barked sharply. "It's all contained in this report, prepared by our private investigator – which runs to over two hundred pages. Included are copies of all the source documents confirming everything Pat has said so far. We're also aware that you threatened to smear the reputations of Gabriel and Steve Taylor if they didn't sign confidentiality agreements about their abrupt exit from A & C and Future Wealth."

"You also paid a lump sum to Gabriel and Steve to buy their silence," Pat added. "They weren't aware of the bigger scheme you were working on." He placed his hands on his hips, and growled: "Tom – you have breached your duties as an advisor to the owners of A & C. I believe some of the family members are even now in discussions about suing you for negligence. Both you and Steve Roberts have also breached your duties as directors of Future Wealth under the US Securities Code. Penalties for those breaches could include jail time."

Tom's face was red. "Load of garbage. We've done nothing wrong. We simply focused on achieving the goal of the IPO."

"You've simply focused on dramatically increasing wealth for yourself and Steve Roberts," I snapped back in a firm tone of voice. "We're also aware of why Mark Hemmings and Arthur Evanglass came on board with Steve. They're both minor shareholders in the company that owns thirty percent of Future Wealth, the shares that *you* forced the A & C families to transfer to you under financial duress."

"None of what you've claimed is an offense under the Securities Act, nor is it an imprisonable offense. There was no fraud involved. The owners of A & C signed the executed share transfer forms properly, and they were approved by the Future Wealth board," Tom laughed angrily.

"Yes, you're quite correct," I nodded. "The share transfer was approved by the Future Wealth board – but only because the owners of A & C *lied* to the board, which comprised of me, Pat, Bill Treloar, the late Charlie Cameron, and their own legal representative, Steve Taylor. They told us the shares were being transferred to another entity that *they* owned as part of an internal restructure. In truth, the shares were being transferred to an entity owned by you and Steve Roberts. *You* put them up to it, Tom. You were the architect of this little scheme."

Tom looked smug as he responded: "If they approved the share transfer put forward by the initial owners of those shares – that being the A & C families – then that's the board's problem, not mine. There's nothing illegal there."

"Because you were acting for A & C at the time," Pat raised a finger, "you became aware of an important company document in relation to Future Wealth. Charlie Cameron, when he first came on as chairman, advised us that we needed to set aside a substantial number of unissued shares in the company for possible future use. With his years of experience in setting up businesses for IPOs on the New York Stock Exchange, this was common practice. It was like a war chest of potential shares the company could issue to other third parties, if required."

Tom stood there and listened.

Pat continued: "The shares could only be issued *before* any future IPO, not after. Charlie advised us that if we achieved our goal of the IPO, there'd be no need to use this parcel of shares – but if we entered a trade sale before the IPO with a major company, or if we required – for some unknown reason – extra working capital, then those unissued shares would need to come into play."

"They were designed as a safety net and nothing more," I continued Pat's thoughts. "Of course, Tom, you'd be fully aware of this process from your years of experience on Wall Street. It's common practice. The exact number of unissued shares set aside were twenty million – or roughly seventy-five percent of the company's issued shares at the time."

I could see Tom sigh and turn away as I continued: "Please let me finish, Tom."

I was reaching the conclusion of what we'd discovered.

"Obviously, any activation of these shares into issued shares would have the effect of diluting the percentage ownership of existing shareholders, if they weren't to receive any of the additional shares that were issued. The issuing of those shares, therefore, required a couple of steps to be undertaken before it could proceed. Charlie Cameron was very particular about this to ensure there'd be no attempted fraud with any unexpected issuing of these shares."

I explained: "He put in place three criteria: First, that shares could only be issued if a minimum of thirty-five percent of shareholders agreed, consisting of three or more shareholders. Second, that a properly convened directors meeting had to take place, with at least four directors present at the meeting and agreeing to the issue. Third, that the company was to have a maximum of six directors, so at least four of the six directors would have to agree to any issuing of shares."

I placed my hands on my hips.

"With those safeguards in place, never in his wildest dreams would Charlie Cameron have believed anyone would be able to manipulate the issue of those shares for their own benefit."

"Of course, Pat and I have been aware of your possible influence of the A & C shareholding because you were providing investment advice to them. We weren't overly concerned at the time, given the issue of shares required the approval of at least three shareholders. We assumed you could never pass that test, given our belief that there were currently only four shareholders of Future Wealth: me, Pat, the A & C families, and yourself. The staff only receive their shares post IPO. However, you falsified our share register and added Steve Roberts's company as a shareholder. We only saw this document for the first time yesterday."

Pat added: "As you're aware, Tom, the transfer of any shares in the company requires the unanimous approval by all directors in a properly convened director's meeting. I have here minutes dated two months ago – purportedly approving the transfer of half the shares you purchased from Billy to a company controlled by Steve Roberts. If these minutes were legal, it would mean that three shareholders – namely you, Steve, and your company that originally purchased the A & C family shares – satisfied both the three shareholder test and the thirty-five per cent test; the first criteria of what Charlie Cameron put in place to allow the release of those unissued shares."

His eyes narrowed: "However, the minutes are a sham – because while they claim that all directors unanimously approved the share transfer, Billy was never actually *at* that meeting."

"Yes, he was," Tom blustered. "It was a normal monthly board meeting, and Billy *was* there. The minutes are signed off by me as chairman."

"I was never at that meeting," I countered. "You knew I'd never have approved the transfer of your shares to Steve Roberts because I don't trust you. You falsified the minutes of the meeting. No properly constituted board meeting ever took place to approve the transfer of those shares from you to Steve. Therefore, you failed the first test, as per the guidelines put forward by the late Charlie Cameron. Specifically, the issue of shares was only approved by *two* shareholders, not the required three." I felt the corner of my lips curl. "You've outsmarted yourself, Tom."

Pat followed by saying: "We now also know why you and Steve Roberts worked so hard behind the scenes to stack the Future Wealth board with Roberts, Heck, and Petty as directors. It was to ensure that you controlled the board – four votes to two. Or, should I say, since my resignation, four votes to Billy's one. It meant you could now ensure four directors would agree with the resolution to activate those twenty million unissued shares."

Tom tried to interrupt, but Pat continued – not giving him a chance to speak.

"I have here a copy of a minute dated one week ago, which purportedly gives effect to an issue of twenty million shares to six people in two days' time – precisely one hour before our IPO. The minute is signed by you, Steve Roberts, Doug Heck, and Brian Petty; four of the five directors of Future Wealth. Billy's name is on the minute, but Billy never signed it because he'd never even seen it until yesterday. While the minute acknowledges that a meeting of directors took place, approving the issue of twenty million shares in Future

Wealth to the six listed individuals, the minute is a sham."

Pat shook his head.

"The meeting never took place – and you specifically engineered the issue of shares to take place just one hour before the IPO, so Billy and I would be powerless to stop this fraudulent action. We'd have only discovered that the share issue took place *after* the IPO – and unless one of you four told the truth about the fraudulent transfer of shares, and the subsequent issue of the unallocated shares, we'd have had no recourse."

Pat gestured towards the report Steve Pollard had given us.

"The document in that folder purportedly allocates eight million shares to you and Steve Roberts, plus one million shares each to Mark Hemmings, Arthur Evanglass, Doug Heck, and Brian Petty. The allocation of twenty million shares has the impact of reducing both mine and Billy's total shareholding from forty-five percent of Future Wealth to just under ten percent. It also reduces the shares reserved for the staff from twenty percent to roughly four percent – *and* increases the shareholding of you, Steve Roberts, and your other cohorts from thirty-five percent to roughly eighty-five percent. With an IPO value of $480 million in two days' time, your shares would have increased in value upon listing to $408 million."

Pat paused.

"I say *would have* because we've managed to stop it."

He looked across the table at Tom, who now had his head buried in his hands.

"You and Roberts tried to steal this company from underneath Pat and me," I hissed. "It wasn't enough to simply have thirty percent of Future Wealth, which would have been worth $140 million. No, you and Roberts saw the opportunity to grab eighty-five percent of the company, which was worth $408 million."

I shook my head.

"It was a simple matter of getting rid of Gabriel Darcy and Steve Taylor and replacing them with two of your yes-men. That gave you complete control of the Future Wealth board. Well, when we notify the authorities, you'll all be facing jail time – not to mention that some of the family members of A & C will be suing you for professional negligence." I narrowed my eyes at Tom. "You're in deep shit."

• • •

AT THAT MOMENT, the door was opened by Audrey, Tom's long-serving personal secretary.

"Mr. Carroll?" Audrey asked.

"Not now, Audrey. Please leave us alone." Tom practically screamed.

Shaken by his tone but standing her ground, Audrey muttered: "It's about Mr. Roberts. There's something important you all need to know."

Before Tom could reply, given he was in quite a state of shock and stress from what Pat and I had just revealed to him, I turned and asked: "What is it, Audrey? What about Mr. Roberts?"

"Mr. Roberts has just been killed in a car accident," she stammered. "His wife just phoned. She couldn't get through to Mr. Carroll's cell phone, so she called me on the main office line to give me the news. She's obviously distraught."

"He's dead?"

A chill descended across the room.

"Audrey, if you can – please get the number of Mrs. Roberts. I'll call her now."

Tom was in no fit state to make any phone calls, his head buried in his hands, visibly shaking.

"We'll have a five-minute break while I go and call Gloria Roberts to find out what's happened," I told Pat. "I'll leave you here with Tom."

I re-entered the boardroom five minutes later. There was stony silence, with Tom still sitting with his head buried in his hands. He hadn't appeared to have moved.

I took a deep breath.

"It appears Steve suffered a massive heart attack while driving his car to our meeting this morning. He veered off the freeway into oncoming traffic and was killed instantly. His wife only found out twenty minutes ago, when the police came to her home to inform her."

"Holy shit," Pat breathed.

"She's very distraught," I continued. "She was trying to contact you, Tom, as you were one of Steve's closest friends. I've asked Audrey to go around and comfort Gloria and see if there's anything we at Future Wealth can do to assist."

Tom raised his head from his hands. I made eye-contact with him.

"While Pat and I have no respect for either you or the late Steve Roberts, death isn't a nice thing, and we'll ensure Gloria is looked after." I turned to my friend. "Pat, will you please outline the next steps from today's meeting?"

"Tom, you're requested to resign as chairman of the board of Future Wealth, effective immediately. At this time, Billy will replace you as the new chairman. I'll also be returning to the board immediately. After this meeting, Billy and I are going to the offices of A & C to meet with Doug Heck and Brian Petty. We'll be sharing with them what we now know, and they'll also be asked to resign from the board with immediate effect. Please don't contact either Doug or Brian when we leave this room to warn them of why we're coming to see them."

Tom said nothing.

"We've also organized a meeting with members of the three families who own A & C, and we'll be informing them of what we now know."

Tom had tears welling in his eyes and both hands planted firmly on the boardroom table. He looked at both Pat and I, trying to maintain his dignity.

Pat continued: "Bill Treloar will be returning to Future Wealth as interim CEO for at least the next two years and will be assuming a board position. Through our Wall Street contacts, we've identified two new people with extensive experience sitting on the boards of public companies to join the Future Wealth board. All these positions will be filled within the next twenty-four hours, so all new board members will be in place before the IPO. A press release will be sent out tomorrow morning, announcing that the founder of Future Wealth, Billy, is assuming the chairmanship role, and that I'm returning as a director. We'll also announce that you're resigning, but no mention will be made of what we've discussed today." Pat took a deep breath. "We'll now also have to add news of the unfortunate death of our CEO, Steve Roberts, to the press release."

Tom blinked. "So... I don't lose my shares in Future Wealth?"

"Currently, you – along with the late Steve Roberts, Mark Hemmings, and Arthur Evanglass – own thirty percent of Future Wealth because of the shares you purchased at half market value from the owners of A & C. You also own five percent in your own company name because of the shares you purchased from Billy three years ago. I think the families of A & C will most likely commence legal action against you and your cohorts to try and recover that thirty percent."

Pat shrugged.

"That will be a matter for your lawyers and their lawyers to argue over, which might ultimately be determined by the courts. Next week, we'll be informing the authorities about the fraudulent transfer and allocation of shares – whereby you and your cohorts attempted to strip away the shareholdings of Billy, me, and the Future Wealth staff. We'll let the authorities take whatever action they deem appropriate against you."

"You can't prove anything," Tom hissed. "Doug Heck and Brian Petty were present at those meetings and will confirm all proper due process was followed.

The transfer of shares was done legally – and was one of many things actioned at that board meeting. You, Billy, simply forget what was discussed and approved. Likewise, four directors approved the allocation of the unissued shares, which was all that was legally required. You've been outsmarted, guys."

Pat and I stared in disbelief. Tom was trying to convince himself that what he and Roberts had done wasn't illegal. Tom, unfortunately, could no longer tell the difference between fact and fiction, as he'd become a man overwhelmed by greed.

"Tom, don't be a fool," I warned him. "Read the report from our private investigator. Every single detail – other than the fraudulent transfer of shares, and the subsequent issue of shares – is covered. As Pat mentioned, the fraudulent transfer and issue of shares is something we only discovered ourselves in the past twenty-four hours. Don't try and fight the issue, Tom. We have proof of what happened. We have a signed Statutory Declaration by someone who has firsthand knowledge of what happened. It was a scheme designed by you and Roberts." I paused. "Do you want to say anything else, Tom?"

"Yes."

Tom shook his head, tears running down his cheeks. "I want to ask one question: How did you find out about the share transfer and the share allocation?"

"Let's just say, Tom, that some people who work with you and Steve don't like either of you. They think you're greedy and you cross the line between what is right and wrong. I can't tell you who the person was – or whether they worked for you in your investment bank, or worked with Steve at Future Wealth – but I can say this: After the report we received from the private investigator, we did some research of our own, trying to understand why you and Steve were hell-bent on gaining control of Future Wealth at the board level."

"Goodbye, Tom." I opened the folder we'd brought with us and pulled out some sheets of paper. "Your letter of resignation is here for signing. Please read it and sign it today, and also email Lenny Bird, our legal advisor." I pulled out another sheet of paper. "Here is a copy of the proposed press release for tomorrow. The only change will be adding the unfortunate death of Steve Roberts."

"And if I don't sign?" asked Tom.

"Then the IPO won't be going ahead, and we'll be informing the press as to the reasons why. Also, Tom – one last thing. Please never try to contact Pat or me. We never want to speak with you, or see you, ever again."

With that, Pat and I stood up and exited the boardroom. There were no handshakes as we left.

CHAPTER 26

TOM CARROLL SIGNED his letter of resignation, as did both Brian Petty and Doug Heck. I guess once Tom read the report from our private investigator and realized we knew the truth, he knew he was in deep trouble – with little room to move or escape.

The listing of Future Wealth on Wall Street was a huge success. As the founder of Future Wealth, I had the privilege of ringing the bell on Wall Street as the market opened, making Future Wealth – eight years after inception – a publicly listed company with a market capitalization of $480 million.

I ensured Pat stood next to me on the podium of the New York Stock Exchange as I rang the bell. If Pat hadn't shared my vision, then perhaps Future Wealth would never have been formed in the first place.

With me as Chairman of the Board, and both Pat and Bill Treloar returning to the company, the morale of the hundred and thirty staff of Future Wealth was pumping. The culture that Pat and I had worked so hard to build had returned. The fact that fifty of our long-serving staff members had made a nice little return on the shares they'd been gifted before the listing of Future Wealth probably contributed to the positive vibe among the staff.

The shares surged upwards of twenty-five percent in the first two weeks after listing, and three months later, they were trading at fifteen percent above issue price.

Pat and I had both made some serious money from the listing of Future Wealth on the New York Stock Exchange – but personally, I was physically and mentally washed out. I'd taken Future Wealth as far as I could. I'd given the company every single ounce of my body that I possibly could.

The first five years of building the business with Pat had been an absolute joy. I'd been in my prime, chasing new franchisees and focusing on achieving our dream of listing the business on the New York Stock Exchange. I thrived on the business-building opportunities.

With the sudden death of Charlie Cameron, our inaugural Chairman of the Board, and the subsequent appointment of Tom Carroll as chairman, the last three years had been an absolute disaster. Looking back, Pat and I couldn't believe how we'd been railroaded so quickly by Tom Carroll, Steve Roberts, and their cohorts. Pat and I had always assumed that what someone told us was the truth. Why would someone tell you something and be blatantly lying?

That was our big weakness; we trusted people to do the right thing.

I'd decided that if Carroll and Roberts were any indication of how the corporate world of big business operated, then I didn't want anything to do with the corporate world ever again.

• • •

"GOOD MORNING, PAT. Looking as fit and healthy as ever." I grinned as Pat joined me at our favorite café on Santa Monica Pier for a Saturday breakfast catch-up.

"I'm feeling good, Billy," Pat smiled. "I'm loving being back at Future Wealth. When I left, seven months ago, I swore I'd never return. I was so bitter with the events that had unfolded. But now, with the new board and the staff all motivated again, looking to further build Future Wealth, I'm just loving being a part of it."

He opened the menu, even though we knew it by heart at this point.

"By the way, Billy – there was a nice article in yesterday's New York press about you." He pulled out the newspaper and handed it to me. "Front page of the business section. 'Billy Houston: Everything he touches turns to gold.'"

I laughed. "Yep – although luckily, they didn't mention Shortfuse."

"Billy Houston is a true builder of businesses," Pat read. He opened his mouth to continue, until I cut him off with a gesture of my hand.

"Enough Pat, I read the article," I laughed. "The press has no idea of what we went through with Carroll and Roberts – or how close we were to pulling the IPO. So, what's the latest on Tom Carroll and the other turkeys?"

"Carroll is in deep shit. The lawyers for the family members of A & C believe they'll be successful in getting back the shares that Carroll and Roberts purchased from them at half market value. There was a blatant abuse of power by Carroll, given that he was meant to be their investment advisor at the time. They hired him to help them get out of their financial mess – and his advice was negligent. If he'd paid full market value for the shares, he might have been in the clear; but he used his power and influence to get those shares at half price, and at the same time, get twenty percent of A & C for nothing. That twenty percent was worth about $15 million. He clearly abused his position."

Pat continued: "The US Securities and Exchange Commission have indicated to me that Carroll, Heck, Petty, Hemmings, and Evanglass can all be prosecuted for breaches of Securities Law. In Carroll's case, there's even the potential for jail time. Everyone will definitely be banned from acting as directors of any companies for a long period of time."

"I guess we have to give Brian Petty some leeway here," I snorted. "If he hadn't rolled over and shared with us what Carroll and Roberts were proposing to do with the issue of those shares, we'd have lost most of our shareholding. We'd never even have known that the meetings that took place between Carroll, Roberts, Petty, and Heck were invalid. We could have protested as much as we liked after the event, but it would have all been for nothing unless one of those four directors rolled over – but by then, they'd have all cashed in their shares and run."

"I agree," Pat nodded. "It's just lucky we got Steve Pollard's report in time, even if it still left unanswered the question of *why* Carroll and Roberts went to all that effort to control the Future Wealth board. It was just fortunate I had a working relationship with Brian Petty, and as one lawyer to another, I made him aware of what we knew – and the potential legal repercussions for him."

Pat sipped his glass of water.

"It was only then that he coughed up the information – the *true* reason why Carroll and Roberts wanted control."

Then, Pat reached down and opened the briefcase he'd brought with him.

"I need your opinion on something, Billy," Pat asked. "Or, to be more precise, I need your approval. I've had two days of roundtable meetings with lawyers representing the families of A & C and the three lawyers from the US Securities Commission who are working on the case. Subject to your agreement, a deal could be worked out on the basis that Carroll and his cohorts transfer all their remaining shares back to the three families of A & C."

"I assume Carroll and his associates have probably sold some of their shares, so they'll have to stump up some cash equal to the value of them."

"You're one step ahead of me as usual, Billy. Yes – they're entitled to thirty percent of the shares at the value of the IPO at listing, plus any subsequent increase in market value. At the current share price, that's a further fifteen percent, or thereabouts. The value is roughly $165 million. They also transfer back to the families the twenty percent share of A & C they'd acquired for nothing."

"Yep, I agree with that."

"Hemmings, Evanglass, Heck, and Petty are banned from being directors of any company in the United States for the next ten years. Carroll is banned as a director for life, and he's also not allowed to practice as an advisor on Wall Street, or in any other jurisdiction in the United States. On the basis that you and I agree to this, they'd not face criminal proceedings, though, and there'd be no further penalties levied by the Feds."

"I assume by doing things this way, it also keeps the whole sordid affair out of the press?"

"Correct."

"On the basis that the owners of A & C get the full entitlement of what they should have had before they ever met with Carroll and Roberts – and that Carroll and his associates all face the bans you mentioned – I'm happy with that."

I paused.

"But what if they've already sold some of their Future Wealth shares and spent the cash?"

"Then the families can chase them personally," Pat answered. "From their private assets, up to the agreed value of $165 million. That'll be a battle between the A & C families and Carroll and his cohorts."

"I agree, then." I reached out to shake Pat's hand, just like we always did when we both agreed on something.

Then, my tone grew more serious.

"There is one more thing to discuss, Pat. I want to resign as chairman of Future Wealth, and I wish to resign from the board completely."

I watched the shock on his face, and explained:

"I'm burned out, mate. Everything that's happened over the last few years has taken its toll on me."

"But, Billy! Things are going so well at the company with you leading the show, and with the new board. The business is humming along perfectly. We're growing, and the staff are thriving with a newfound culture."

"Exactly," I snorted. "The business is humming along, and you don't need me anymore. Initially, I agreed to stay on for six months – but we've already achieved in three months what I'd thought would take six. I suggest *you* take on my role as chairman."

Pat shook his head.

"I know you too well, Billy. You don't just do things on the spur of the moment. You always have a plan. So, what's your plan this time?"

"The kids are getting older," I told him, "and they don't need me in a hands-on father role. I've a long-lost cousin I haven't seen for forty years who lives in this little seaside town in Australia called Noosa. Interestingly, he also owns an accounting firm in Noosa – can you believe that?"

"Must be something in the Houston genes, Billy."

I grinned.

"You want to google Noosa, Queensland, Pat. It looks spectacular. Some great beaches with no high-rise buildings, no traffic lights, and a laid-back lifestyle. I'm just going to pop over there for a couple of weeks. Might even buy a property if I find one I like. I'm still an Australian citizen, so I expect I can do that. Then, I'm going to return to Thailand."

"Let me guess. Choeng Mon on Koh Samui Island?" Pat laughed.

"You got it, mate. Choeng Mon, Koh Samui. I'll see if it's changed from when I was last there, thirty years ago. I'll just spend some time chilling out on the beach, having the occasional massage, along with a nice, cold beer in the afternoon, sitting in a beach bar."

"Billy, you'll get completely bored within three months. You'll be walking along the beach every day thinking of new business ideas. I bet you $10,000 I get a phone call from you within the next three months. The first thing you'll say to me on the phone will be: "Pat, have I got a business idea for us.""

Pat laughed, shaking his head. "I know you too well, Billy. I know how your mind works. I can read you like a book. You're a business builder. Your mind never stops thinking about ideas."

"No, mate," I gestured dismissively. "I'm done with business this time. Future Wealth was my final business – and you're about to become the new chairman of the board."

I reached over and shook his hand again, acknowledging we were both in agreement with this idea – and in sealing our bet of ten thousand dollars.

• • •

I HADN'T TOLD Pat, or anyone else, that for the past three months I'd been having weekly meetings with Dr. Sam Draper – a Clinical Psychologist based in downtown Los Angeles.

I'd been having problems sleeping and was always feeling restless. Something deep within me told me that I needed help. Dr. Draper had previously helped my third wife, Isabella, overcome some of her issues when our marriage had broken up.

I'd had twelve sessions with him so far. He'd told me my problems were quite common in successful business people, because they were always looking for the next opportunity. They were never satisfied with what they'd already achieved.

That had been the story of my life – from the failure of my three marriages and the building of two very successful businesses, to the failure of my clothing venture. While Dr. Draper didn't put a label on my condition, deep down I realized I was experiencing some form of a breakdown. It was as though my brain was fried.

It helped talking to Dr. Draper, and it reinforced the idea that I needed to escape my home in Malibu – escape from America, in fact. i needed to relieve myself of all business-related stress. I needed to pause and enjoy life. I'd told Dr. Draper about my car accident and the armed robbery some thirty years earlier, and how – back then – I'd felt I needed to get away for a few weeks to deal with it all. Then, I'd mentioned my trip to Choeng Mon, Koh Samui, in Thailand.

Dr. Draper asked me how I'd felt while I was lying on the beach, soaking up the sun. I told him I'd felt sensational. It had enabled me to forget about the loss of my mate in the accident. It allowed me to forget about having the sawn-off shotgun pointed at my head and about being tied up. It was such a different place and a different culture than America – so relaxed, so carefree, and such a beautiful environment.

His words to me were: "Get back to Choeng Mon for a few months, Billy. Relax. Enjoy the sunshine, and walk along the beach. You can do all those things over there. Just take time out and reflect on what you've achieved and what you want to achieve with the rest of your life. Take a pause in your hectic life and smell the roses, Billy."

I listened as the doctor continued:

"Given everything you've told me so far about your life, perhaps you should write a book. Writing a book about your life might be part of your healing process." He said it to me jokingly – or perhaps he wasn't joking. Perhaps, in his own way, he was setting me on a future journey.

Dr. Draper was one hell of a smart guy – a man who could lead you down a path without you even knowing he was doing so. In my case, that path was about to become a whole, new career.

CHAPTER 27

LIFE IN CHOENG Mon, Koh Samui was idyllic. I'd managed to rent a bungalow on the beach on a twelve-month lease, which included a daily maid service.

It had been thirty years since I'd last been at Choeng Mon, but the village hadn't changed much. Of course, there were more shops in the village – and more villas on the hillside, overlooking the beach – but it had still maintained its village charm. No high-rise buildings and very little traffic.

I'd left Malibu to travel to Noosa, Australia for a few weeks, then on to Choeng Mon two days after a farewell dinner with Pat, Chook Burns, and their wives. I was still single, and for the moment happy to remain so. For Pat, Chook, and me, that last night had been one spent reminiscing about the old times. I wasn't too sure how Pat and Chook's wives felt about all the scandalous memories!

It was also a time for the three of us to reflect on the recent passing of our fourth mate, Roger the Dodger. We'd been four very close mates from those days back at Santa Monica High, and Roger was the first of us to pass away.

• • •

I'D BEEN AT Choeng Mon for four months. My life consisted of early morning walks along the beach and through the village. My running days had ceased a few years ago due to my aching limbs, but I still loved walking along the beach.

I'd normally then take the stand-up paddleboard out across the bay for thirty minutes or so.

I'd found a little café that had exceptional coffee, so after that, I'd normally venture there mid-morning with the Bangkok Times in my hand. The day's newspaper didn't arrive until after lunch time from the mainland, so most days I was reading yesterday's news – but that didn't worry me because I was living a simple, laid-back lifestyle.

I'd then head back to the beach bungalow to write a few pages of my upcoming book, followed by an early afternoon massage on the beach.

In the late afternoon, I'd pop into the local bar on the main street, which was owned by a Frenchman who'd lived in Koh Samui for over twenty-five years. He was married to a local Thai lady. The bar was a hangout for many expats. People from all over the world – either living or vacationing in Choeng Mon – went there. There were lots of Italians, Germans, French,

Norwegian, and Danish people. I'd become especially good friends with a Norwegian there named Lars.

Lars had retired to Choeng Mon some twelve months earlier. He'd been taking his annual holidays to Choeng Mon for the last ten years, vowing to one day retire there. In his words, he was sick of freezing his balls off in the cold Norwegian winters.

Lars was similar in age to me and had a beautiful, Thai girlfriend eleven years his junior. Her name was Dao, which Lars informed me meant "star."

"Mr. Billy, its Dao's fortieth birthday party next Saturday," Lars greeted me one afternoon. "We're off to a little bar in Chaweng to celebrate. Lots of Dao's girlfriends will be there." He laughed. "An opportunity for you, Mr. Billy, to meet a lovely Thai lady."

"Mate, I'm happy being single and just relaxing here in Choeng Mon," I told him. "Believe it or not, I'm pretty busy writing this book."

"Ah yes, the book. Tell me how it's going, Mr. Billy?" Lars spoke with a thick, Norwegian accent. Depending on Lars's mood, he alternated between calling me Billy or Mr. Billy.

"I find it pretty easy to write," I told him. "I thought I'd have to spend months putting together an outline of what I was going to write about, but it just comes out so easily. I mean, I just sit on the deck of my beachfront bungalow, turn the laptop on, and the words flow from my fingertips." I laughed. "Although I'm not sure if what I write is any good. The reader will be the ultimate judge of that."

"From what you've told me about your life, Billy, you're a creative individual."

"I don't think I'm creative, Lars. I can't sing, I can't dance, I can't play a musical instrument, and I can't draw or paint."

"But you built those businesses in America, which took vision and creative foresight. You *are* creative – in ideas and imagination."

"Yeah, I guess so – but I watched a guy play the keyboard at a bar in Lamai Beach the other week. He was Thai, in his mid-twenties. He sat on his stool, cigarette hanging from his mouth, eyes shut, and he made the most incredible sounds come out of that keyboard."

I leaned back in my seat, and thought:

"It's a bit like that for me when I'm typing the words onto my laptop. It's as though the words just flow from my fingertips. The thoughts and ideas just come to me, then and there. It's as though I'm in a special zone, oblivious to everything else around me. It's weird."

"It's because you're creative, Billy."

I snorted, shaking my head.

"Well, I will come to Dao's fortieth birthday party – but please don't match me with any of her friends."

• • •

HOW I CAME to be writing a book was somewhat unexpected. I'd only been at Choeng Mon for seven weeks when Pat phoned me, all excited.

"Billy, you won't believe this. I've just been having lunch with a lady named Cynthia Fleming. Cynthia is a publisher who works for World Focus Publishing, based in downtown LA. She's been researching Future Wealth. Well, you in particular."

"What do you mean, researching me? I've never heard of her."

"She read the article in the press a few months ago," Pat explained. "She's always looking for stories, fact or fiction, to publish. She'd heard that you'd left the US and were living somewhere in Southeast Asia. She thought you'd be hard to contact – but since I was briefly mentioned in the article, she phoned me out of the blue and shared with me *why* she was doing some research into you."

"Oh?"

"Yeah, and she wanted to meet me for lunch to elaborate further," Pat continued. "I was quite intrigued by her approach, and with what she told me, so I agreed."

"Well, now you have me intrigued, too – so, please, tell me more."

"She knew lots of stuff about you. She knew about the car accident, the armed robbery, the success of The Tax Refund Shop, the failure of the clothing business, and the success of the IPO of Future Wealth. She knew a little bit, too – but not too much – about Tom Carroll and Steve Roberts. She wanted to know more about you."

"Why?"

"Well, you wouldn't believe this, Billy, but she thinks your life story is something that should be published. The story should be told right from arriving in Santa Monica as a teenager, through to retiring in Choeng Mon on idyllic Koh Samui island, a couple of months ago. She wants to meet you, Billy, and hear more about who you are and what you've done in your life – to see if there's merit in publishing your story. She also said it could be quite lucrative."

"Mate," I laughed, "I've never written a book in my life, and I don't need the money."

"Billy, you have a story to share. You don't see it as a story because it's your life. You're entwined in what you do and don't see it as something special. But me? I've known you since you were fourteen. Of all your friends and family, I'm the one guy who's seen your life story unfold first-hand. Without your drive, passion, risk-taking, and vison, The Tax Refund Shop would never have happened."

I shrugged. Pat continued:

"You built one of the most successful franchised accounting groups in America. Your vision and drive led to Future Wealth. You built something very special and empowering for so many people. For sure, there were setbacks, Billy – but most people quit when they have setbacks. That's one of your most admirable traits. You never give up. You never accept failure. Every day, I think about the three key secrets of building a successful business: Leverage, processes, and distribution. You also taught me and others about the importance of culture in a company."

"I'm not sure, Pat," I laughed nervously. "I mean, I flunked English in high school. I always struggled with adverbs, adjectives, and proverbs – and I still don't get how they all work."

"Have a long think about it, Billy. You've got a great lifestyle over there in Thailand. All you need to do is write one page a day, and in twelve months you'll have your life story finished. Please, don't take that the wrong way, Billy. I don't mean yours is a short life story – but in twelve months, writing one page per day gives you a whole book."

"I don't know, Pat. I'm not a writer."

"Cynthia will be in Bangkok in a couple of weeks. Just meet her and have a chat. It's not as though you don't have time. I'll text you her number."

"Let me think about it. Talk soon, Pat." With that I hung up the phone.

The next morning, on my daily walk along Choeng Mon Beach, I thought about what Dr. Draper had said to me, and the words echoed in my head:

"Writing a book about your life might be part of your healing process, Billy."

When I got back to my bungalow, I sent a text message to Cynthia Fleming telling her to call me about a possible meeting when she was next in Bangkok.

I ended up having three meetings in Bangkok with Cynthia. The first was simply a meet and greet – a chance to eyeball each other and have a brief discussion about my life and what she already knew about it, with me filling in a few of the gaps.

Cynthia outlined how the writing and publishing process worked. I said I'd think about it.

After my first meeting with Cynthia, I then had both Chook Burns and Bill Treloar phone me. I assumed Pat must have put them both up to it.

"Billy, you need to tell your life story," Chook insisted on our call. "I ran into Pat, and he mentioned the publishing lady. Without you, I wouldn't be who I am today. I'd have been living on the streets, taking drugs, and still sulking about not becoming a professional surfer. You got me involved in your lawn mowing business. You didn't have to do that, but you did – because you were worried about me and where I was heading. You've made me the person who I am today."

Chook, with a bit of help from both Pat and I over the years, now had a successful lawn mowing franchise operation in Los Angeles.

Bill Treloar, the CEO of Future Wealth, also called and said to me: "Billy, I've never seen two people work so well as a team together as you and Pat. Without your passion and drive and never-give-up attitude, Future Wealth would never have existed. You *need* to tell your story, so others can learn from your successes and failures – and, more importantly, let others know that failing is how you learn. You've always said to the team that without the failures you'd experienced in your life, you would never have been successful."

Bill also added: "You need to share your wisdom about building a successful business – how it's only five percent of the right strategy and ninety-five percent implementation. I clearly remember you standing up in front of the Future Wealth team at our very first meeting and telling them all that. You also told them that there are many people with great ideas in this world, but most of them are never successful because they can't implement their ideas. You used to say they were dreamers – and, unfortunately, there are many dreamers in this world. Well, it's time for you to stop dreaming. Give this a go, Billy, and tell your story. It'll motivate people to become successful and teach them to never give up, no matter what challenges they face."

After the phone calls from Chook and Bill, along with another follow-up phone call from Pat, I agreed to have a second meeting with Cynthia. This turned into a third meeting, as I recounted my life story to her.

She told me she needed to fully understand my story to ensure it was something that readers would actually want to read. She also needed to understand my life story to determine commercial arrangements.

• • •

OUR FOURTH MEETING took place at Choeng Mon, at a little restaurant I frequented.

"Thanks for flying to Koh Samui to meet me, Cynthia," I said, shaking her hand.

"I wanted to see this idyllic seaside village you've retired to, Billy," Cynthia smiled. "Pat told me he was here a month or two ago – and that it's one of the nicest places he's ever seen. I must say, I agree with him. Plus, you've flown to Bangkok to meet me the last three times, so I thought it was only reasonable that I come here."

After a bit of small talk over lunch, Cynthia then said: "Billy, World Focus Publishing would like to publish your story. It's an incredible story of highs and lows. We want you to tell it all, warts and all. We want the story to come from your heart and soul. We're not going to tell you how to write it, other than it needs to start from when you arrived in Santa Monica and ends with how you ended up living here in Choeng Mon, Koh Samui."

"As I've said numerous times, Cynthia," I laughed, "I've never written before. I actually flunked English at school - plus, as I've mentioned, I'm dyslexic."

"Not to worry," Cynthia grinned. "Our editors will correct your grammar and spelling. Leave that stuff to us. We'll tidy up all the loose ends."

She reached into her bag and pulled out a stuffed envelope.

"Enclosed in this package is a contract for you to sign, if you wish to accept our offer. It gives us exclusive worldwide publishing rights to your life story. I've also attached some writing tips. Note – no more than eighty thousand words, which is roughly three hundred pages. We have a ten-month timeframe, so if you accept our offer, we'll want the final manuscript by the July 31, so we can complete final editing in August and September, for publishing in October. If all goes according to plan, it'll be in bookstores by the second week of November, ready for Christmas sales. In this document, you'll also find the detailed schedules for completion of the final manuscript."

"A bit of light reading for me," I chuckled.

"Finally, Billy," Cynthia continued, "if you accept our offer, once we've received the signed contract, we'll pay you $500,000 upfront. The calculation of your ongoing royalties is included in the attached schedule."

"$500,000?" I said, showing no emotion. I've always said business transactions are like a game of chess. Most people get beaten in business because they let their emotions get the better of them. Cynthia had no way of knowing if I thought $500,000 was too high, or too low – and I wasn't about to make any comment or show any emotion to reveal that information.

Because she couldn't read my body language, Cynthia then added: "We've never paid a first-time author anywhere near this amount of money, Billy."

"Thanks, Cynthia. Let me read the contract and go through the information you've provided, and I'll get back to you soon." As we got up, I shook her hand and added: "Once again, thanks for coming all the way down here."

I hailed a taxi to take Cynthia back to Koh Samui's airport.

With that, my new career as an author commenced. If it hadn't been for the words of Dr. Sam Draper, along with the gentle nudging from Pat, Chook Burns, and Bill Treloar, perhaps my career as a writer would never have happened.

CHAPTER 28

"CHIMLIN. THAT'S A nice name."

I introduced myself to the woman I'd just met, who was one of fifty or so people gathered in the bar at Chaweng Beach, celebrating Dao's fortieth birthday.

"Where are you from, Chimlin?" I asked.

"I live and work in Bangkok," the beautiful woman replied, speaking perfect English with the usual Thai accent.

"And your connection to Dao?" I asked.

"We went to school together in Bangkok. While studying at university, we shared a flat together. We go back a long way. Dao is one of my closest friends, so there was no way I was going to miss her fortieth birthday party."

She appeared as intrigued with me as I was taken by her.

"Billy, where are you from? You sort of sound American, but with a strange accent."

"I was born in Australia," I explained, "but I came to America with my mum as a teenager. I've lived in America ever since."

"Australia," she replied wistfully. "I've heard so many nice things about that country."

Chimlin and I spent the next hour or so talking. At midnight, it was time for me to depart and grab a taxi for the twenty-minute ride back to my bungalow at Choeng Mon.

Chimlin gave me her phone number, and we agreed I'd call her to have dinner in the next few days. She was staying at Chaweng for the week, which turned into two weeks after our first encounter.

Sometimes, when you first meet a person of the opposite sex, you just know that things could develop further if you got to know each other. Well, that's what happened between Chimlin and me. That first dinner turned into many more dinners over the next few weeks.

Chimlin was an interesting lady. She was university-qualified, with a degree in commerce. She owned her own small fashion business, with six clothing stores in Bangkok. She'd been married for five years, but had separated six months earlier from her German husband – with whom she had an eighteen-month-old daughter. She was eleven years younger than me.

Like many Thai women, Chimlin had a dark, olive complexion, large brown eyes, and long, dark hair. Ours became a long-distance romance, with me based in Koh Samui and Chimlin in Bangkok. She'd often catch a flight down from Bangkok to Koh Samui on a Thursday night and return to Bangkok late Sunday evening. The flight time between Bangkok and Koh Samui was only an hour, but her ability to get away depended somewhat on the availability of her ex-husband to look after their daughter.

Our time together in Choeng Mon was largely spent strolling along the beach, hand-in-hand, and having cocktails in the evening before dinner at my favorite little beach restaurant. I taught her how to swim – because, at age thirty-nine, she'd never learned how.

Before too long, Chimlin was joining me paddle-boarding in Choeng Mon Bay on her regular visits.

When Chimlin wasn't staying with me at the beach bungalow, I'd spend my spare time thinking of new business ideas, in between writing my book.

• • •

"BILLY, WE'VE BEEN together now for five months. Why don't you come and live with me in Bangkok?"

"I don't want to live in a city," I told her. "I like the relaxed beach lifestyle here, plus our life is good together the way things are."

"But we only get to see each other for a few days each week," Chimlin complained. "Or sometimes a few days each fortnight. As my daughter gets older, it's going to be increasingly harder for me to visit you here. If you want to be with me for the rest of your life, you need to make sacrifices, so we can be together every day. I'm tied to living in Bangkok, because my ex-husband would never let me bring my daughter to live in Choeng Mon. Plus, I have my business in Bangkok, which I need to manage. You have nothing to tie you to Choeng Mon. You could live anywhere in the world and write your book. Please, I want you to consider coming to live in Bangkok with me."

This conversation would be the beginning of the end of our relationship.

Perhaps I'm selfish, but at the age of fifty – about to turn fifty-one – I didn't want to be living and raising a two-year-old daughter. Deep down, I probably realized that the idyllic lifestyle I had with Chimlin wouldn't last forever. At some point, I knew she'd want us to be together. While I thought that perhaps she could sell her business, move to Choeng Mon, and have her ex-husband look after their daughter for a lot of the time, I knew I was kidding myself.

In the end, the ultimatum came from Chimlin. "Move to Bangkok and live with me, or we'll have to stop seeing each other."

After six months together, Chimlin had told me she was not coming to Choeng Mon to see me any longer. Deep down, neither of us wanted to end the relationship – but I think we both knew that I couldn't give Chimlin the relationship she wanted or deserved.

I'd later learn that Chimlin returned to live with her ex-husband. At the time, I thought I'd never see her again. As it happened, that wasn't to be the case – but that's a story for another time.

With the breakup of my relationship with Chimlin, I sort of lost the desire to write the book. I'd completed twenty thousand words by that point, but I still had about another sixty thousand words to write. I thought perhaps I might simply phone Cynthia Fleming and let her know I wasn't cracked up to be a writer. Tell her: "Thanks for the opportunity, Cynthia, but I might call it quits – and, by the way, I've transferred the $500,000 back to your account."

But then, I thought to myself: I'm not a quitter. I never give up.

I still had a few months left to complete the book, so I decided I might just park the book-writing to the side for a month or two and get back into it later.

With Chimlin no longer flying down to see me each weekend, I now had a lot of spare time. I was doing a lot of walking up and down the beach. Over a couple of weeks, I'd started to develop a business idea. I was getting excited about it, and that meant it was time to give my old friend Pat a call.

• • •

"MATE, HAVE I got a business idea for us," I said to Pat.

"Billy, I love talking to you, but its midnight here in Los Angeles."

"Don't worry, Pat, this will be the best midnight phone call you'll ever get." I realized that in my enthusiasm, I'd failed to consider the time difference between Thailand and LA.

Nevertheless, I continued:

"The top two searched book topics in the world are health and fitness, Pat. Do you realize that in Southeast Asia – I'm talking Indonesia, Philippines, Thailand, Malaysia, Singapore, and Vietnam – there are roughly

600 million people? This region currently has the highest uptake of new Internet connections anywhere on the planet, too. This region is about to go through a digital boom."

"Not sure where you're going with this, Billy," Pat yawned. "It's late."

I continued with no loss of enthusiasm.

"I've worked out the secret of building a beautiful, seamless business, Pat. You need a lot of people paying you a small sum of money each week, which is automatically deducted from their bank account and deposited into yours."

"So, you're going to illegally hack into people's bank accounts, Billy?" Pat laughed. "That's fraud, and I have no intention of going to jail."

"No, of course not. Nothing illegal. I'm speaking about the world of health and fitness. Everyone is getting focused on being healthy and fit. People are watching their diet. People everywhere are exercising and wearing fitness clothing. There is a revolution coming, and it's about to hit Southeast Asia hard."

"I still don't follow where you're coming from, Billy."

"Imagine if we had some people design a new fitness program for us. Something people could download for a small weekly fee on their phone, iPad, or laptop. Something we could license to gyms in Southeast Asia for a weekly fee. We build four or five fitness programs that are updated weekly or monthly. We hire some social media and digital experts to get the message out to the masses about this new and exciting fitness program. Say we get a million people signed up, each paying only twenty cents a week. That's roughly $10 million in annual revenue. We get two million people signed up? Revenue becomes $20 million. Costs are minimal, Pat."

"Billy, we know fuck all about gyms," Pat laughed. "Correct me if I'm wrong, but I don't believe you've ever even stepped inside a gym."

"Correct. I never have – but I enjoy being fit and I've always exercised. Pat, we knew bugger all about financial planning, but we hired experts who did. We need to hire some smart, good-looking gym junkies to appear in the exercise videos. We need a sports scientist to build the programs. We hire a video company to produce professional videos. Then, we have our social media gurus work their magic and we get it out to the masses. We sign people up on year-long contracts for twenty cents, American, per week. We build a continued, recurring income stream, Pat."

I paused to catch my breath.

"People won't cancel their subscription," I continued, "even if they stop using the services. It's more hassle to cancel the subscription than to keep paying twenty cents per week. We build a substantial recurring revenue stream with minimal costs – and then we move into diet, yoga, and sports clothing. That's stages two, three and four."

"Where do you plan to launch this service?"

"Given I'm living in Thailand, I'll launch it here. Once we've tested and refined the model in Thailand, we'll take it across other parts of Southeast Asia. The real big market, a few years down the track, will be China, with its ever-increasing hordes of middle-class."

"Ah, Billy, I can hear and feel the excitement in your voice – but why don't you stop?" Pat laughed. "Why start up another business? You've got enough money to live a life of luxury ten times over. Future Wealth burned you out. It's time to stop and smell the roses – slow down, and just enjoy life."

"Pat, I like building businesses. It's what keeps me alive. I've been down here for over ten months now. Choeng Mon feels like home to me. It's where I want to base myself – but I *need* to build a business. Something new and different. Since I broke up with Chimlin, I'm restless."

"Perhaps you and Chimlin should get back together."

"No," I snorted. "I heard from Lars's girlfriend, Dao, that she's back with her husband. She was too young for me, anyway – and I'm too old to raise her daughter."

"Billy, I'm really enjoying my life. I'm happy being the chairman of Future Wealth. Life is good and reasonably stress-free. If you want something to do, why don't you return to America and rejoin the Future Wealth board? I'm happy to relinquish my role as chairman of the board and hand over the reins to you if you return."

"No, Pat. I want to remain in Thailand. We'll talk later."

I hung up, somewhat peeved that Pat apparently didn't share my enthusiasm for this new business idea. Unfortunately, I doubted if Pat and I would ever be in business together again.

• • •

TWO DAYS LATER, I was in my favorite bar in Choeng Mon having a quiet beer with my Norwegian friend Lars, recounting my discussion with Pat and outlining my business idea. I shared my sadness at Pat's lack of enthusiasm.

"Ah, Mr. Billy, you need to meet with Cheyenne Holly," Lars told me. "She's an Australian girl backpacking around Southeast Asia. She works across the road in that shop."

He pointed to the European Coffee shop.

"She's got a master's degree in sports science, or something similar – and she was a gym instructor in Sydney, Australia. You're Australian, right? You probably even know each other."

"Mate, there are twenty-two million people in Australia, so I'm hardly likely to know every person who's Australian – plus, I left the country when I was thirteen." I shook my head in disbelief at how naive Lars could be at times.

• • •

HOWEVER, LARS MENTIONING Cheyenne Holly to me proved to be a masterstroke.

I quickly discovered that Cheyenne had all the attributes and skills needed to design the exercise program I'd envisioned for the initial launch of my new fitness app. Lars was correct. Cheyenne had a master's degree in sports science, as well as experience being a gym instructor in Sydney.

The next few months were a blur as I met with accountants and lawyers in Bangkok and negotiated contracts with digital media experts, along with a professional video company to record the videos.

Cheyenne had located two male and two female Thai gym instructors to be the faces of the apps we were building.

I suddenly found myself constantly traveling between Koh Samui and Bangkok, now spending more time in Bangkok than Choeng Mon. The thought did cross my mind that perhaps I should have moved to Bangkok with Chimlin back when she'd asked me to – but then reality set in when I reminded myself that she was back living with her German husband.

CHAPTER 29

I WOKE UP to the buzzing of my cellphone. It was Cynthia Fleming of World Focus Publishing, trying to call me.

Shit. I'd told Cynthia I'd have the draft of my book to her in two weeks. There was now only one week to go, and I still hadn't even looked at the book because I'd become so immersed with the finer details of launching my new online exercise program in Thailand.

I'd had two missed calls from Cynthia while I was asleep, along with a short text message that read:

Billy, I've been informed this morning by the Managing Director of World Focus Publishing that if your completed manuscript is not received by our editing department by the 31st of this month, I'm out of a job. The 31st happens to be seven days from now – so please don't let me down. I hope you not returning my phone calls isn't a sign of any problems. Regards, Cynthia

I immediately texted her back:

Hi, Cynthia. Book is going well. Completed seventy thousand words with only twenty pages to go. I reckon I'll have the final manuscript to you by the 29th, two days early. Very unfair response by your Managing Director. Why would he even doubt you, or doubt me for that matter? Tell him from me that he's a dickhead. Once again, thanks for going out on a limb and backing me for this project. Cheers, Billy Houston

Shit, I thought to myself. Five days to write sixty thousand words. Well, I'd better lock myself away for the next five days.

I spent the next five days sitting at my laptop and typing away on my life story and going for walks along the beach – along with the occasional paddle around Choeng Mon Bay. No alcohol, no socializing. Just five days in front of the laptop.

My life's journey, the good times and the bad times, flowed from my fingertips. I was only a two-finger typist, and Cynthia and I would later joke that if I could type with all fingers, I'd have finished the book in a day.

On the July 29 at 11:45pm, two days before the deadline imposed by Cynthia's Managing Director, I hit the send button and emailed 80,125 words of my life story to Cynthia Fleming.

Those words covered almost my entire life – from initially arriving at Santa Monica as a teenager to retirement in Choeng Mon. I left the last few months out, as I didn't want to share my plans for the health and fitness industry in Southeast Asia. I didn't want anyone to read the book and steal my idea.

Over the previous few days, I'd also received several missed calls from Tom Carroll, as well as a few text messages asking me to call him. I refused to answer his calls and simply deleted his voice messages without listening to them, and I ignored his text messages. I then blocked Tom Carroll's phone number from my contacts, so he could never contact me again. I couldn't believe the audacity of the man to try and call me after I'd told him to never make any further contact with me.

• • •

THERE WAS A knock on the door of my bungalow three days after I'd sent my manuscript to Cynthia. Two well-dressed gentlemen in suits stood there. In Choeng Mon, that was not the normal attire.

"How can I help you, gentlemen?" I asked.

"Are you Mr. Billy Houston?" The older of the two spoke with a deep, American accent.

"I am – and who might you be?"

"I'm Fred Jones and this is Shaun Ratcliffe. We're lawyers from the States acting on behalf of Tom Carroll. Mr. Carroll has asked us to meet with you personally, given you don't appear to be taking his phone calls or responding to his text messages."

"What business is it of yours whether or not I return Mr. Carroll's phone calls?" I didn't raise my voice, but I did start to close the front door. "Gentlemen, good day."

Fred Jones suddenly placed his hand on the door to prevent me from fully closing it.

"Mr. Carroll is aware that you're about to publish a book about your life story," he told me. "Mr. Carroll is concerned that you might falsely represent him in your book. Obviously, if that was to happen, you'd face major defamation damages."

Fred Jones spoke with a smirk on his face.

I narrowed my eyes.

"Gentlemen, I'm somewhat surprised you're not aware of the defamation laws, considering you're both lawyers. You can't be sued for defamation if you're telling the truth."

"Correct," Jones nodded, "but Mr. Carroll is concerned that you *won't* be telling the truth."

"Well, gentlemen," I scoffed, "there are enough people who *are* aware of the truth – and they'll verify that whatever I write about Mr. Carroll will be nothing but the truth, and the whole truth."

I further added: "I'm somewhat surprised that Mr. Carroll has the financial means to send both of you turkeys here to pay me a visit. It's a long way from America."

The younger of the two gentlemen murmured: "Mr. Carroll is part of a major consortium negotiating with the government of a large country to be given rights to a casino. If your book were to incorrectly paint an adverse picture of Mr. Carroll, it might jeopardize the awarding of that casino license. If that were to occur, then the defamation damages would be very large."

"Well, you tell Mr. Carroll that he should buy a copy of my book. Better still, I'll organize for a copy to be sent to him before it goes on sale. I'd also suggest he gives a copy to the government of whichever country he's negotiating with, so they're fully aware that Mr. Carroll is very lucky he hasn't spent any time in jail."

I straightened up and looked the two men in the eye.

"Please, gentlemen, hop on your merry way and return to wherever you came from. Otherwise, I'll call the local police and advise them you're trespassing on my property." I had a big grin on my face as I shut the door in front of them.

I thought I'd better inform Cynthia Fleming of my encounter with Carroll's lawyers, who appeared to be less than professional. They resembled "heavies" rather than legal professionals.

• • •

"AH, BILLY, LET'S just *hope* they issue an injunction to stop the publication of the book. That will give us a lot more free press exposure!" Cynthia wasn't as upset as I'd expected her to be. "You can imagine the headlines now: 'Billy Houston's life story put on hold due to telling the truth about Tom Carroll,' or 'Carroll concerned he may lose casino license bid if Billy Houston's book tells the truth about him.'"

308

She continued by saying: "Oh, by the way, Billy – we love the book. Did you really pee on the police officer's foot? We all broke up in laughter when we read that."

"You're lucky I didn't tell you about the rock band I was in."

"A rock band? Tell me more!"

"I was the weakest link in the band, believe me. I'm tone deaf – and perhaps the worst musician ever born – but that conversation can wait for another time. Got to go Cynthia. Talk soon."

CHAPTER 30

"ANOTHER MARGARITA, CYNTHIA?" I asked.

"Why not? It's simply so beautiful, sitting here on the beach, peering out across the bay – the sun going down in the distance. You live in a beautiful part of the world, Billy. I'm very envious of your lifestyle. No stress, no worries, no hustle and bustle."

"In our homeland, Cynthia," I mused, "there are so many rules and regulations. We're so over-governed. Here, there are rules – but nowhere near as many as we have back home. Common sense prevails. It's what I like about living in Koh Samui. The people are beautiful, and they're friendly and welcoming." I sipped on my third margarita.

"I guess that's why they call Thailand The Land of Smiles," Cynthia toasted me. "By the way, I trust those royalty monies have been flowing through the bank account?"

"I believe so. Pat told me he was amazed at just how much money was coming through. As you know, all royalties from the book sales are being given to the Future Wealth Foundation to help homeless people in both America and Thailand." I laughed. "I don't need the money, Cynthia, and I'm at a stage in life where I need to give back, not take."

"If I may ask – did you keep the initial $500,000 upfront payment?"

"No. That went across to Pat at Future Wealth to launch the Foundation. I never imagined in my wildest dreams that my book would sell so many copies."

"I never doubted you, Billy. That's why I went out on a limb for you in the first place – and struck the deal to give you such a big advance. Though, I must admit, there were a few nervous moments when you weren't returning my phone calls. I'd thought that you were taking me for a ride. I'd even worried that perhaps I shouldn't have given you such a large payment upfront."

"Then, of course, your Managing Director gave you that ultimatum – that if my final draft wasn't there within seven days, you were fired."

"A complete asshole," Cynthia laughed. "He got fired. I think the success of your book may have had something to do with it. He bad-mouthed me for months leading up to the publication of your book – telling everyone what a fool I was for ever getting World Focus Publishing involved in a deal with you. Well, Billy – looks like I've had the last laugh there, believe me."

I asked her: "How much did the Tom Carroll injunction help the book sales, do you think?"

"Enormously," she chuckled. "It was the icing on the cake. Tom Carroll had hoodwinked some high-profile people to be part of that consortium bidding for a casino license in Africa. It was all newsworthy, and I pulled in a lot of old favors from contacts in the press to run the story about the injunction on your book. When we finally managed to get the injunction removed and ran the story, half of America was already waiting ready to buy your book. You must have had the karma gods looking out for you that day, because the stars were aligned and ready for publication."

Then, half-jokingly, she asked:

"I don't guess you have another book in you, Billy?"

"Well Cynthia, funny you ask," I sipped my drink, "I'm about to embark on a new business venture here in Southeast Asia, in the health and fitness world. I reckon this business could become even bigger than Future Wealth."

"Tell me more."

"I can't, for now. It's a three to four-year business build. I'll talk to you in a few years. It might be my biggest business success yet – or perhaps, my biggest failure."

I chuckled, calling the waiter over to settle the bill. As I searched for my money, my phone rang. It was Chimlin.

For a split-second I thought I'd answer the phone – but then I decided not to. Chimlin was in the past, not the future.

In four years, though, I would be placing that call to Cynthia Fleming.

The End

ABOUT THE AUTHOR

I WAS BORN and raised in Melbourne, Australia – before moving to Noosa, Queensland, Australia where I've lived for the past twenty-seven years.

In my last year of high school, at the age of seventeen, I was suspended for drinking and wasn't allowed to attend school for many weeks, all while preparing for final year exams. For a brief period, a colleague and I ran a small raffle at our high school, raffling alcohol on a Friday afternoon to our fellow Year 12 students. We were never as successful as Billy Houston and Chook Burns' raffle business, though!

At the age of twenty, I was one of five boys in a car that collided with a telegraph pole after being run off the road by another vehicle. The injuries Billy Houston suffered are the same injuries I sustained in that horrific car accident, which also claimed the life of one of my school friends. After this, I deferred from university, initially for twelve months, while recovering from my injuries.

I was held up by a man wearing a balaclava wielding a sawn-off shot gun in a Melbourne hotel when I was twenty-one. The armed holdup Billy Houston experienced, including being tied up and then untying himself while the gunman returned, is exactly what had happened to me in real life.

After those experiences, I guess you could say I dropped out – dropped out of university, started drinking a lot, spent time on the west coast of Australia and up in North Queensland. Life was one big party. During these so-called lost years, I commenced a lawn mowing business. Never as big or successful as Billy Houston's lawn mowing business, though.

At the age of twenty-seven, I finally returned to university in Melbourne to finish my degree and commence a career in the accounting profession. Much to my mother's delight, I finally cut my long hair short.

When I was thirty-five, I opened an accounting firm in Noosa, Australia. I was the sole employee and started the firm with three clients. Fifteen years later, my accounting firm was listed by Business Review Magazine (BRW) as one of the top 100 accounting firms in Australia by revenue and one of the top 10 fastest-growing accounting firms in Australia.

While running the accounting firm, I also established a surf clothing company with clothing retailers in Australia, New Zealand, Japan, and the United States of America stocking my clothing label. After operating for three years, with the global financial crisis upon us, I closed this business at considerable cost to myself and other investors.

I commenced one of Australia's first franchised insurance businesses for insurance advisors. This business then morphed into becoming an Australian Financial Services Licensee. With a lot of hard work, this business grew substantially over a six-year period to include over three hundred licensed advisors and accountants throughout Australia.

This business won many national awards and was acknowledged as one of Australia's leading independently owned financial services licensees. In growing this business, I spent a fair bit of time living in hotel rooms, Monday to Friday, while traveling across Australia, recruiting new advisors and accountants. In June 2017, as the largest shareholder, the business was sold for twenty million Australian dollars to a company listed on the Australian Stock Exchange.

In October 2017, I officially retired from corporate life and decided to write my first novel. Most of this book was written while I was living in bungalows on the beaches of Koh Samui, Thailand.

I'm known in business circles as an entrepreneur. Most of my business ideas have come to me on my daily walks along Noosa Main Beach. Like Billy Houston, I find that the feel of sand under my feet and the sound of the ocean aids my creative thought process. The storyline for this book came from my daily walks along the beaches of Noosa, Australia and Koh Samui and Phuket in Thailand.

My partner, Deb, and I now spend half our life in Noosa and the other half in Thailand. A relaxed, stress free, idyllic lifestyle. You might find this hard to believe, but Deb and I have ten children between us—five each. Believe me, I've worked extremely hard over the last twenty-four years building from scratch the businesses I've mentioned above. I've never bought clients and never paid for existing goodwill. All my businesses have been start-ups that started with only me and one or two other employees.

Like Billy Houston, I'm a workaholic, and my personal relationships have suffered as a result. I've endured a lot of stress and worry over the years in building all those businesses, but I've also had a lot of fun and laughs, and have met some great people.

I never went to school in America and have never set up any form of business in America.

All characters in this publication are fictitious, and any resemblance to real persons, living or dead is purely coincidental.

I've now commenced writing my second novel, which is being written while I'm living in a house on the beach in an idyllic small Thailand beach community.

I hope you enjoyed reading Billy Houston: Rags to Riches as much as I enjoyed writing it.

Feel free to connect with me at - www.gregholman .com.au/blog.

To subscribe to my mailing list and to receive a free copy of the first chapter of my new book (when complete), please forward your email address at www.gregholman.com.au.

Kind Regards
Greg Holman

P.S. - did I pee on a policeman's foot a la Billy Houston? I'd rather not say, though there are a couple of old school friends who were with me on that eventful evening who know the truth.